Detective Inspector Watson i﹐
Squad in Westhampton, a
Midlands of England. Fightiⁱ　　　　　　　——₅ ₐₙₐ
serious vice, the DI in charge must combine the qualities
of ruthlessness, tenacity and dedication — not only to
beat the vice and drug rackets, but to survive the
internal politics in a force of hardened, overworked men.

DI Watson, however, is a woman. Twenty-nine,
attractive, self-willed and with a terrible temper, she
joined on equal terms with the men and has risen
through the ranks on merit alone. Now under
extraordinary pressure, Molly faces hostility and sexism
from her superintendent and junior officers alike, as she
fights treachery and corruption in the ranks.

The battle involves slippery police informants, raids
on drug dealers, a shebeen, and a teenage brothel. She
also makes a dangerous rendezvous in London's West
End, assisted by Scotland Yard's elite undercover
squad. As the story unfolds, Molly discovers that the
worst threats are not necessarily out on the inner-city
streets, and she throws away the rule book in a desperate
attempt to catch the man who threatens to ruin her
career and destroy the Drug Squad.

* * *

Brian Windmill is a former senior police officer, who
served for thirty three years in the West Midlands.
Fourteen of those years were spent in the CID, including
seven years as a detective inspector in charge of Vice
and Drug Squads. He later rose further through the
ranks to become a commander at Birmingham,
Wolverhampton and Dudley.

Born in Lincolnshire, Mr Windmill, who has a degree
in Social Science, also served in the Royal Navy for eight
years before joining the police service. He is now a full-
time writer, working on his next Molly Watson novel,
contributing to magazines on various subjects, and
writing for local newspapers on police matters.

*This book is dedicated to the
men and women of specialist
police squads.*

DRUG SQUAD

A DI Molly Watson Novel

Brian Windmill

Temple House Books
Sussex, England

The Book Guild Ltd,
25 High Street,
Lewes, Sussex.

First published 1994

Reprinted 1994

© Brian Windmill 1994

Set in Baskerville

Typesetting by Formaprint Limited,
Worthing, Sussex.

Printed in Great Britain by
Antony Rowe Ltd,
Chippenham, Wiltshire.

A catalogue record for this book is
available from the British Library

ISBN 0 86332 907 1

1

The black cat stirred as a gust of wind brushed along the curve of his back and it started to rain. Reluctantly, he raised his head, sniffing the cold night air, before dropping silently off a low garden wall.

Crossing the pavement he sought shelter under a large van with rusting wheel arches, moving instinctively towards the residual warmth of the engine. Crouching, head forward, he tracked a pair of white trainers ghosting along the footpath.

His whiskers twitched an instant before a steaming jet of urine struck the top of his head. Screeching, he bolted back over the wall, stopping on the grass to shake himself. The end of his raised tail thrashed with anger. Looking back at the van, yellow eyes fired with hate, he spat out his fury.

Inside the van, Detective Constable Bannister, zipped up his Wranglers and quickly screwed the top onto a foul-smelling funnel in the corner. He moved round the van walls, searching the empty street through eye level spy-holes, then resumed his observations on an old house across the road. A solitary holly tree stood guard at the end of a short drive leading to the front door. A red hall light glowed dimly behind the door's leaded window.

The light went out and the door opened. The dark figure of a man emerged from the shadows of the holly tree. Sprinting up the drive, he disappeared into the open doorway.

Bannister wrote in the Drug Squad surveillance log: '20.00 hrs. Caucasian youth. Dark bomber jacket, white trainers. Entered target premises.'

A few minutes later the door opened again and the same man darted down the drive. Looking furtively about him, he hurried off toward Westhampton city centre. The hall light came on again.

Bannister pressed the transmit button of his multi-channel radio. '96-96, 6, 10, 9, 73, 51, 620, 6,' he said quietly, alerting the stake-out crew at the north end of Park Street.

There were three sharp taps on the side of the van. Bannister scribbled the last entry of his observation notes, brushed back his hair, then opened the doors for Detective Inspector Molly Watson. Twenty-nine and single, she was known throughout the force for her stunning figure and fiery temper. Intelligent, forceful, and at times ruthless, she was the first woman DI, and she had been commended many times for her skill and courage. Unable to fault her as a thief-taker, her enemies had resorted to rumour and innuendo, claiming she had made it by sleeping with the chief or, at the other end of the spectrum, that she was a raving lesbian. None of these allegations had stuck and, if she knew about them, she had kept her own counsel.

In fact, it was her remoteness and independence that caused most concern and speculation amongst the rank and file of the CID. What motivated this good-looking, vital and seemingly self-assured woman who made other DIs feel insecure? they asked. Why hadn't she married? Why didn't she go to the senior officers' bashes at HQ? What kind of woman was it who said so little about herself, and hid her feelings behind a mask of clinical efficiency?

Bannister didn't know. He stood aside as she climbed into the van, wrinkling her nose at the competing smells of fresh urine and stale tobacco.

'Any action yet?' she asked shortly, looking through a spy-hole at the row of terraced houses across the road.

'Prisoner half an hour ago, ma'am. Five deals of resin. Sergeant Smith and DC Gilbert took him to Central Lock-up.'

'There'd been half a dozen this time last Monday.'

'Perhaps Jackman's run out of gear.'

'He had a delivery on Saturday night . . . How's the new code working out?'

'All right, ma'am. Should fool the press for a while — they'll think it's Radio Bingo or something. I just hope he doesn't pick it up on the box, like the last guy we were watching.'

'Any sign of Jackman?'

'No, sir—ma'am.'

She peered through the spy-hole again. 'Informant says he keeps an eye on the street from an upstairs window.'

'Haven't seen him.'

'How many uniform people did we get from A Division?'

'Seven, ma'am. A sergeant and six PCs. One's a tart —'

'Policewoman!' Molly snapped back.

Bannister concentrated on his observations as if wishing to distance himself from his short-tempered boss.

She added the numbers he had given her to the eight Drug Squad men waiting in unmarked cars at each end of the street.

'It should be enough,' she said quietly, more to herself than the detective.

Something struck the side of the van which reverberated like a drum. They moved in alarm to the ventilation grills behind the driver's seat, and saw the backs of a group of youths who were chasing an empty can along the pavement.

Three weeks is too long for static observations in the street, Molly told herself. The whole neighbourhood must have

7

clocked us by now. She ran a slender finger through rivulets of condensation which streamed down the sides of the vehicle, remembering long hours of other observations in the freezing cold of winter and the dehydrating heat of summer.

How much longer? she wondered, buttoning up her well-worn sheepskin coat. How many more raids on drug dealers, acid parties, casinos, night-clubs, dirty bookshops, shebeens and private homes? After three years she needed a change. No one had previously run the force's vice and drug operations for more than two years. I should be sitting in a comfortable chief inspector's office at headquarters or a busy divisional station, she thought.

The head of CID departments, Superintendent Davids, had blocked her promotion, alleging she had no respect for those above her, led from the front rather than directed her detectives, and regularly bent the rules. He had objected to her appointment as head of the force's Drug Squad, and had never forgiven her for being a success. Apart from a few like him, there wasn't much discrimination against women any more. She was just unlucky to have a boss who should have retired years ago.

She smiled wistfully, recalling her first months in the job. Policewomen were still a novelty on the units in those days and she had soon realised that most of the men were only out for the main chance. They hadn't even dressed it up.

"Come on Molly, let's go and knock a round off," a married PC had said during a quiet spell on the night shift, cursing under his breath when they were called to deal with a road accident.

But the problem didn't end there. It was made clear to her in a number of unsubtle ways that a good performance with a male member of the unit, and preferably more than one, was an essential part of every policewoman's initiation. She hadn't wasted words decrying the system, but when

8

her tutor constable had tried to pin her down on the medical examination couch, she kneed him so hard he had walked bow-legged for a week.

It was different now. There were often as many women as men on the units, some of them marrying their partners so that couples patrolled together. Occasionally, women were promoted ahead of their husbands, becoming desk-bound senior officers while their spouses still dashed about in panda cars.

She sighed, deeply. Her chances of further promotion were non-existent as long as Davids was her boss, but she was damned if she was going to give him the satisfaction of asking for a transfer. Sometimes she wondered why she bothered so much about getting on. It certainly wasn't a thirst for power. It was more the challenge, the need to test herself and to prove to herself that she was as good, and perhaps a little better, than the others. It was also frustration at the inept, laid-back attitudes of some of those above her: those who seemed more interested in golf handicaps than doing the job.

No. Bugger Davids, the only way I'm leaving the Drug Squad is on promotion. All I need is a break — a spectacular case that will hit the headlines.

Now accustomed to the darkness, she found the thermos, poured warm coffee, and handed a cup to Bannister.

'What's he like, ma'am?'

'Who?'

'Jackman.'

'Typical drug dealer. An evil, two-timing toad who'd sell his sister for the price of a pint.'

Bannister looked at the house. The hall light was off again.

'Two men coming out of Jackman's,' he announced.

'Did you see them go in?' Molly asked, suspecting he had missed them.

9

'They're coming this way, ma'am,' he answered quickly.

Keeping perfectly still, the DI and her detective waited until the men had passed, then Bannister spoke briefly into the radio.

'85-85, 602, 63, 27, 34.'

'Who's 85?'

'Sergeant Conrad and DC Williams, ma'am.'

A short time later, Conrad reported from his car at the top of the road that two men had been arrested in possession of cannabis bush.

Molly looked again at the houses opposite the van, wondering who had planted the holly tree.

'Antiques,' she said.

'Where?'

'Those Victorian villas. They're over a hundred years old. Used to be a posh area, the habitat of well-heeled, middle class merchants.'

Heavy rain beat noisily on the thin metal roof and the van rocked, as strong winds gusted between the houses, blowing over dustbins and sending their contents cart-wheeling down the road.

Yes, she thought, it had once been a bustling city, grown rich on its ability to produce the finest motor cycles in the world, and boasting a football team that was the envy of Europe. Now the factories were empty and the football team languished at the bottom of the Third Division. Blocks of concrete flats dwarfed a jumble of faded terraces. Unemployment was a way of life, and crime had escalated as rival gangs fought to defend their graffitied streets.

A car dropped off a prostitute. She paused to light a cigarette, then waltzed along the edge of the pavement, handbag swinging. There had always been prostitution in Westhampton, but now it was big business controlled by a ruthless gang of ponces. Within minutes the woman had gone, driven off in a Toyota saloon that had been prowling around for some time.

Molly glanced at the man beside her. Twenty-three, his long untidy hair was straw-coloured, but in the gloomy van it looked darker. Big and friendly, he had the trusting openness of someone yet to experience the harsh realities and disappointments of life. New on the squad, he could hardly take his eyes off her chest, or her legs for that matter.

He ducked away from the icy wind that whistled through the small aperture and cut painfully into his eyeball.

'It's a filthy night, ma'am. Even the druggies should have enough sense to stay at home in this lot.'

'Probably suits them.'

'You're not going to call it off, are you, ma'am?'

'Not after we've spent half the flaming winter in this tin coffin, I'm not. Jackman's got drugs, and there's prisoners in the traps to prove supplying.'

She rubbed her hands together briskly, as if to hurry along time itself; a habit familiar to every member of the squad. They had learned to gauge her moods by the vigour and frequency of her hand rubbing.

'We'll see if we can catch one more.' she added, bending over a cardboard box and rustling through paper bags. 'Don't tell me you've eaten all the food?'

'I was frozen stiff.'

'Not your mouth, it seems.'

She moved restlessly round the van, occasionally checking the empty street for signs of movement.

'Are the arrest teams back?' Molly asked Bannister an hour later.

'Yes, ma'am. Smith and Gilbert have just resumed.'

'Been for a pie and a pint, if I know young Gilbert — no wonder he's fat.'

Scanning the deserted street she picked up a radio and

ordered the waiting crews to close up.

A car crept past and slid into a parking space ahead of them. More vehicles followed, headlights off, nosing silently into the kerb. The last car to arrive was a new Saab. Recognising it as Detective Sergeant Conrad's, Watson wondered how he could afford to run such classy wheels.

After three years, the men were accustomed to working for a woman, responding to her enthusiasm and giving her their best. She knew that they called her ''Watty'' when she dished out extra overtime, and ''That Bloody Woman'' when they thought she had been driving them too hard. But they always defended her stoutly against outsiders.

Conrad was the exception and she didn't trust him. Several times she had caught him looking at her warily, like a hunter stalking his prey. He was always respectful, but there were many different ways of saying ''ma'am''. Whenever Conrad said it, she felt threatened. During his first few months on the squad, she had tried to win him over, spending more time with him than the other sergeants. That approach had failed because he had seen it as a sign of weakness and boasted that the boss fancied him. She had pulled him up sharply before he started to take liberties, and he had struck back. The walls between the squad offices were made of plasterboard and she had heard him ridiculing her in front of the men, calling her a two-faced bitch.

Eventually, she had seen him formally, and suggested that his talents might be better employed on a division; promising to give him a recommendation that would not adversely affect his career if he put in a request for a transfer. Not only did he reject her advice, he intimated that he had powerful friends at headquarters, and she might be the one going back into uniform.

Molly shook her head. She needed to concentrate on the job in hand. 'Ready?' she asked Bannister.

'Yes, ma'am, all units in position.' He exercised his arms to loosen cramped neck muscles.

Molly paused, feeling a tightness in her chest: the excitement tinged with apprehension that preceded every raid. She slid back the bolts at the top and bottom of the rear doors.

'Let's go,' she said, jumping out into the driving rain and racing across the road to shelter in the open porch of one of the houses. Waiting for Bannister to catch up, she then led the way towards Jackman's house. Other figures closed in, dark shapes skirting large puddles and dodging between parked cars. The house loomed above them, heavy curtains blacking out the windows. A mournful wind howled and rain-water gushed out of downpipes, flooding the gutters.

'We could've marched up the road behind the Salvation Army band,' Bannister muttered, just out of his inspector's hearing.

Passing the old holly tree, they moved cautiously to a recess at the side of the bay window. Sergeant Turner and DC Macdonald joined them and Molly whispered instructions, pointing at the house as she did so.

Macdonald then stepped forward into the glow from the hall light, his wet facing shining red, his hair streaming in the wind. He raised a heavy lump-hammer above his right shoulder, hands trembling as he waited for Molly's order to strike.

2

Satisfied that everyone was in position, Molly nodded. Black steel arced through the air like a cannon-ball, shattering the lock and knocking back the door.

She ran into the house and down the hallway towards Jackman's living room at the far end, hearing heavy bolts being rammed home behind the door ahead of her. The lump-hammer swept past her head and thundered into the woodwork, splitting it. The door held. Macdonald cursed and the hammer rose and fell again, blasting away one of the bolts, but still failing to break open the door. Bannister tore the hammer from Macdonald's grasp, swung it dangerously around his head, then chopped down with all his strength, demolishing the door and sending large chunks of splintered wood flying across the room.

The Drug Squad detectives tumbled inside, stopping abruptly when they saw the fire, fresh flames dancing across the coals. They were too late.

'Bastard,' Bannister spat savagely, leaning against the door frame as he recovered his breath.

A jockey-sized black man with tight, curly grey hair and a wizened, old face stood fearfully beside a table covered with a green velvet cloth. Upstairs the sounds of running feet and the banging of doors echoed through the house as rooms were quickly searched. A woman screamed abuse and a child cried.

'Get the policewoman up there,' Molly ordered as she drew an official-looking document out of her pocket. 'Delroy Jackman, this is a search warrant. Do you want to see it?'

The man beside the table shrugged his puny shoulders. 'You've had that piece of paper for years, missy. You just keep changing the date.'

He looks smaller than ever, Molly thought, noting the long, beer-stained jumper and the craggy toes poking out of worn carpet slippers.

'Who's the woman upstairs?'

'Don't know. — Rents the flat.'

Sergeant Conrad pushed through a ring of detectives. 'I've sorted her, ma'am. She says she's nothing to do with Jackman. Denies even knowing his name.'

'She's probably his sister.'

'Shall I search her room?'

Molly's gaze took in the sergant's sleek black hair, his permanent tan and dark eyes. He was not her type, but she hadn't been surprised when she discovered that he had a fan club amongst the typists and secretaries at headquarters.

'No, leave it,' she said shortly. 'Just make sure the policewoman stays with her.'

The other members of the squad exchanged looks. They knew that the gaffer was gunning for Conrad. The probable reasons had been canteen gossip for weeks.

''Perhaps he tried to get his leg over,'' a detective had suggested.

''Nah, he was saying thc other day that she hadn't got a good fuck in her,'' commented another.

''Yes she bloody well has; she's just particular about who she opens her legs for,'' observed a third. ''He'd stick it in an oil drum if it was the only hole he could find.''

Molly looked around her. 'Where's Sergeant Smith?'

'Here, ma'am,' called her deputy, pushing through the onlookers.

'Organise a search please, Gordon. Use the dog. We'll do this room as soon as I've had a few words with

Jackman.'

Smith gave a brief nod, then led his men into the hall and started to issue instructions.

Molly took off her wet coat and sat at the table opposite Jackman.

'Right!' she began. 'What have you got to tell me?'

The little man's frown turned his face into a walnut.

'You's got no right to smash up my home. I ain't done nothin', I ain't got no gear, and I ain't dealin' no more.'

'That won't do, Delroy. We've arrested several guys with drugs tonight — after they left this house.'

'They didn't score off me, missy. They must've got it from somebody else.'

She looked intently at him. He had always called her missy and she knew that her men found it amusing.

'The Bench will love that.'

A burglar could have told Bannister that the best way to search a set of drawers was to start at the bottom and work upwards, saving time because it is not necessary to shut one drawer to see inside the next. It is also safer, as he found out when the telephone on a hall table beside him started to ring, causing him to jump up in surprise. He hit his head on the corner of the top drawer he had left open.

'Bastard!' he cursed.

Conrad laughed. 'Are you going to do the highland fling or answer the phone?'

Blinking away the pain, Bannister lifted the receiver. The caller's first words immediately focused his attention and he signalled to Conrad for silence.

'Someone wants to score,' Bannister said after finishing a brief conversation. 'Seemed suspicious at first but I managed to convince him that I was helping Jackman. He'll be here shortly.'

16

'Great! Clean up this mess, then get everybody out of sight. We'll give the stupid git a welcoming party he won't forget in a hurry.'

Bannister examined the broken door lock. 'It's a good job I've got my City and Guilds in DIY.'

Conrad passed the news to Molly without mentioning his detective's good work on the telephone.

'Another customer bringing his own drugs?' she asked Jackman.

A long sullen silence was broken by a sharp crack and the hiss of escaping gas from the fire. Molly rose and kicked smouldering pieces of coal off the shabby carpet.

'Battened down the hatches and burnt our dealing gear, did we?' she asked, returning to her seat.

Jackman shook his head.

Molly looked about her. It was more than his living room. It was where he conducted his business; buying drugs cheaply from traffickers and ripping off the local druggies. It was also where he slept at night, preferring his comfortable fireside chair to a cold bedroom and icy sheets.

The only time Jackman left his lair was on Sunday mornings when Precious McKenzie, his sister-in-law, visited to clean the house and restock his fridge. It was the day when he put on his best suit and yellow-spotted bow-tie, then strolled down the street to the Horse and Jockey. After two hours of noisy dominoes and half a bottle of Pusser's Rum, he returned home for his only hot meal of the week, and half an hour on the rug with Precious.

"Just to make sure there's still a bone in my old pecker," he told his cronies.

Molly sighed, then continued the questioning. 'Where have you hidden the rest of the drugs?'

'I ain't got no gear.'

'Half the druggies in town say they've scored off you.'

'They're lying.'

'Where are the drugs?' she repeated, sharpening her voice.

'I don't know nothin' about no gear,' he insisted.

She gestured towards a set of well-used brass scales at the end of the table. 'I suppose they're for cook —'

'Our man's coming,' Conrad interrupted.

In acknowledgement, Molly raised her hand, keeping an eye on Jackman. 'Just sit tight and we'll hear what your visitor's got to say for himself.'

Someone knocked: three quick, three slow, and then three quick taps, like an SOS. Bannister switched off the red light and opened the front door. A slightly built youth slid past him into the dark hall.

'Who're you?' he gasped.

'Stay cool,' Bannister soothed. 'I'm the guy you spoke to earlier. Del's nipped out for some more gear. What do you want? We've got plenty of bush, nine quid a wrap . . .'

'You're the fucking fuzz!' the youth burst out, throwing himself towards the open door. Bannister grabbed the collar of the youth's coat and they fell to the floor as detectives poured out of the back room. Handcuffed, and screaming for his solicitor, the young man who had come to score was led away.

Conrad returned to the living room. 'Bannister blew it, ma'am.'

'He'll never get his Equity card that way. How's the search going?'

'Finished. There's nothing. Smithy's got them digging up the backyard.'

Molly leaned towards Jackman. 'Come on, Delroy. You've got one last chance. Tell me where you've put the rest of the gear or I'll have to turn this little palace of yours into a disaster zone.'

Jackman rolled his eyes. 'Jesus Christ in holy heaven, I keep tellin' you. There's nothin' here, woman. No shit, nothin'. I swear it on my mother's life.'

Unimpressed by the outburst, Molly picked up a pile of unused brown paper bags from a nearby chair. 'What are these for, picnics in City Park?'

Getting no reply, she stood up and walked around the cluttered room, fingering the old settee and tapping wooden panels above the mantlepiece.

Here we go again, she fumed silently. It could be anywhere. But if Jackman thinks I'm leaving this place before I find it, he's wrong. I don't care if it takes all night.

She turned to Conrad. 'You know what you've got to do, Sergeant. I want this room taken apart. Don't forget behind those panels over the fireplace, and under the floorboards.'

Conrad beckoned to the recently arrived Special Patrol Group men. Dressed in blue overalls, they were armed with jemmies, claw hammers and long powerful torches.

Leaping out of his chair, Jackman tried to stop them. He'd seen a house after the SPG had searched it.

'No, man, no!' he cried. 'There's nothin' here. You're wastin' your time. Honest to God. You'll ruin my place for nothin'!'

Molly's voice cracked like a whip. 'Sit down!'

He fell back into his chair and Conrad barked orders at his search team.

'Keep an eye on him,' Molly said to the sergeant. 'I'm going to have a look around with Smithy.' The sounds of moving furniture and squeaking nails followed her out of the room.

When Molly returned, the room had been completely gutted. Above the fireplace, bare bricks and crumbling mortar were criss-crossed with dusty cobwebs.

The rummage crew had been systematic. Starting from the fireplace, they had stripped out half of the room, then moved all of the furniture into that area before continuing

19

the search. A dozen or so floorboards taken from an area adjacent to the door were still propped up against the wall, exposing dark, dank cavities that had not seen the light of day for over a century.

Sweating men with dirty faces stood wherever they could find a foothold, still gripping the tools they had used to such devastating effect.

Jackman, eyes glazed in shock, sat rigidly among the ruins, having been mesmerised by the sight of his home being ripped apart. Nothing had been spared, no corner missed. Two men had ripped the fabric off his old settee and pulled out large wads of stuffing in a frenzy of legalised vandalism.

'No luck, ma'am,' Conrad said. 'That drug dog couldn't find a butcher's bone if you stuck it up his arse.'

'The drugs must be here somewhere,' Molly replied. Using the floor joists as stepping stones, she crossed the room to a battered old chest of drawers.

'How long have you had this?' she asked Jackman. He didn't move a muscle. 'Answer me!' she shouted.

'The old woman who lived here left it . . . She died.'

Molly ran her hands along the oak top and mahogany sides of the chest of drawers, noticing the matching veneers. It had once been a fine piece of furniture. Pulling out the drawers one at a time, she carefully examined the insides; they were of the same quality.

'We've checked that,' Conrad said, clearly annoyed at the implication that he didn't know how to organise a search.

Molly ignored him and continued her inspection. When she had finished, she stood back and slowly rubbed her hands together. 'I've got an idea. Wait here while I make a phone call.'

'I'm going nowhere,' Conrad replied indifferently.

Molly, who was leaving the room, spun round angrily,

eyes like green ice. 'In that case you can search Jackman — you might even find something.'

The buzz of conversation died when Molly swept back into the room a short time later. The shoulders of her coat were once more darkened by rain. The men watched closely as she returned to the old chest of drawers. Sliding a hand underneath the top, she pulled a small lever, causing a concealed lid to spring open and reveal a secret compartment. Seven slabs of cannabis resin lay inside, each piece sealed in clear plastic.

There was a universal sigh of relief from her audience. DC Gilbert clapped, but only once. Someone rammed a knuckle into his back: squad officers were supposed to be blasé about drug finds.

Jackman, sitting at his table next to the fireplace, groaned in despair and dropped forward, burying his face in his arms.

Molly went over to him and shook his shoulder until he looked up. 'What have you got to say for yourself now, Delroy?'

What could he say? He had thought it was the perfect hiding place for his main hoard. Without it, he wouldn't have risked dealing while the Drug Squad van was parked across the road.

'Must be three kilos at least, ma'am,' Conrad exclaimed, removing the slabs of cannabis and lining them up on the table. Picking one up, he bit off a corner of plastic, then held the resin to his nose, taking a deep breath. 'Umm, this is good gear all right, ma'am.'

Molly examined each block, noticing faint traces of blue paint, but keeping her observations to herself.

She pushed them towards Conrad. 'Get this lot bagged and labelled. The sooner it goes to Forensic the better. And clear the room, me and ''No-cannabis Jackman'' are due to for another little chat.'

'Sergeant!' she called as Conrad reached the doorway. 'Did you find anything on him?'

'Three hundred and twenty-two pounds cash. I've put it in as an exhibit, ma'am.' She nodded and waited for him to leave.

Jackman found a way through the pile of furniture and collapsed into his old armchair. He'd known he was in for a bad time from the moment Inspector Watson had stormed into the room. Squealers were the problem; snouts, grasses. No one knew who they could trust any more. All the dealers spent time with Watson. In the night-clubs, mostly, springing her drinks. Not only was she well put together, she was the drugs chief in these parts; high-powered connections impressed. Some of the dealers boasted that they had knocked her off, but he didn't believe them.

'I'm sorry, missy, I've always been a dealer; it's what I do. You can keep locking me up, but it won't make any difference.'

Molly said nothing.

'It's only shit. It'll be legal soon,' Jackman wailed, tears of self-pity gathering in the pouches below his eyes.

Molly pushed a pile of *Sporting Life* papers off a stool so that she could sit next to him.

'Like to have a flutter on the horses then, do you, Delroy?'

Jackman, eyes half-closed, did not respond.

'What'll I get, missy?'

'Difficult to say these days. With your record and a dealing charge, two, maybe three years . . . unless I can tell the Magistrates Clerk how helpful you've been to the police.'

'What d'you mean?'

She slammed her clenched fist on the top of a biscuit

tin, tipping it over and spilling small squares of brown paper. 'Don't start acting daft with me again,' she said angrily.

Her voice fell to a menacing whisper. 'You've been messing me about all night. Where's it got you?' She picked up a handful of paper squares. 'Look at these, there's enough here to make up a hundred wraps of bush.'

She moved closer. 'You know the score, Delroy. It's the big operators, the traffickers, that I'm after. Help me and it's a small fine for possession.'

'I've never been an informer.'

'That's right, Delroy. But people on the scene talk. I found your hoard of gear, didn't I? Come on — just give me a name.'

He knew that no one could have told her about his hiding place: he hadn't mentioned it to anyone. But he needed her help with the magistrate if he was to stay out of prison.

'You've always been straight with me, missy.'

She rested a hand on his shoulder. 'I'm the best friend you've got Delroy. I'll look after you. But you must start naming names. It's the only way I can help you.'

'If it got out that I was grassing, I'd be a dead man.'

'You'll have to trust me, Delroy. It's for your own good.'

Beads of sweat lined the creases of Jackman's forehead but he shivered and turned the pale palms of his hands to what remained of the fire. His words came slowly.

'Catweasel. He's making a delivery . . . tonight. Ten kilos.'

'Of what?'

'Shit.'

Molly had difficulty containing her excitement. Catweasel was one of the biggest traffickers in the country; she had been after him for years.

'When?'

'Don't know.'

'What's he driving?'

'Keeps changing.'

She squeezed Jackman's arm reassuringly. 'You and me have been on different sides for a long time Delroy, but I think we understand each other now. I'll do my best to keep you out of prison this time. In return you've got to pack in the dealing. You don't want this aggro at your age. Get yourself a nice little job. Not too much, just a few hours a day. You'll be drawing your pension soon. I'm not going to bust you for the odd smoke, you know that.'

Misery was etched into the burnt leather of Jackman's face.

Leaning forward, Molly gently picked a small splinter of wood from the curly grey hair. She felt genuine sympathy for the man.

3

The derelict house across the road from Jackman's place was an empty shell, but detectives standing on bare boards littered with broken glass, plaster and other debris, were sheltered from the torrential rain by the floor above and what was left of the roof. They had approached the house from the back, cursing as they stumbled through piles of rubbish in the dark. Street lights bathed the bare walls but Molly, standing in an alcove, was hidden from view. Cold and wet, she could put up with the discomfort; only Catweasel was important.

She remembered her first arrest a week after leaving the training school. Checking the back of a sports shop, she had disturbed a burglar so that for an instant they were face to face, and she had never known who was the more scared. Reacting first, he had tried to escape, but, driven by the fear of not catching him, she had bowled him over with a flying tackle, skinning both her knees and one elbow in the process.

She smiled to herself. That first commendation would always be the one she treasured most. After that it had been all one way: snapped up by the CID, promoted sergeant after four years, and inspector three years later. She didn't regard herself as a brilliant policewoman, but hard work, commitment and determination had combined with the simple expedient of being in the right place at the right time. As her training sergeant had said on passing-out day: "You make your own luck in this world, Molly Watson."

Shortly before midnight a dark-coloured Jaguar emerged through a curtain of rain, cruised silently along the road, then stopped a short distance away. Members of the Drug Squad prepared for action. Some of them moved into the alley at the side of the disused house; others took up positions close to the open doorway.

Inside the Jaguar a match flared and a cigarette glowed behind the double-speed windscreen wipers. Rain swept across the tarmac, bounced off the car and bent back the branches of the holly tree. A passing taxi lit up the Jaguar and in that instant the driver's face was clearly visible. It was Catweasel.

Molly's heart started to pound. At last, she had him. In a few more minutes he would make his move. She watched the dark car, admiring the man inside. He was a professional, always cautious, never taking unnecessary chances. But her men were also professsionals, the foul weather and low visibility giving them the edge she needed.

But it all went horribly wrong. A woman screamed a warning into the night and the powerful car leapt forward like a startled stallion. In a desperate attempt to stop it, Conrad and Williams dashed into the road, only to be met by walls of water thrown up by the Jaguar's front wheels and augmented by the rear. A police car sped past in pursuit, dousing them again.

Detectives rushed into Jackman's house. The woman upstairs who had saved Catweasel screeched hysterically as she kicked and scratched at the policewoman who struggled to pull her away from the open window. Furniture toppled over, crockery smashed, and the child howled in terror.

Molly shouted orders, sending her men racing up the stairs and charging into the bedroom. The fighting stopped and those listening below in the hall could hear the sobbing of the child and the soothing sounds of its mother.

Sergeant Smith slowly descended the stairs. Stopping halfway, he looked down at his boss.

'I don't know how I kept my hands off her, ma'am.'

'What was the policewoman doing?'

Smith mimicked her. ' "Sorry, Sarge. I was absolutely bursting, Sarge. Honestly, Sarge . . . I just had to go, Sarge." ' He glanced over his shoulder at the closed door. 'That crafty cow in there has been filling her up with tea all night.'

Molly was more annoyed at her own shortcomings. She should have had more mobiles, unmarked cars forming a ring of steel that no car could have broken through.

'Is the policewoman hurt?'

'Nothing serious, ma'am. A few scratches and bruises I shouldn't wonder. Teach her a lesson.'

'What about the woman?'

'Once she knew that Catweasel had got away, she started to take the piss.'

Conrad and Williams splashed into the hall, water dripping off their clothes onto the black and white quarry tiles.

'I'm going to fix that woman upstairs,' Conrad growled.

Molly blocked his path. He was broader than she was but they were the same height. 'What are you going to do, drown her?' she challenged.

Conrad, face evil with rage and obviously blaming her for the whole mess, held her gaze for a few moments. Lips quivering, he was on the point of open rebellion. But even now he was sharp enough to hold his tongue. Lowering his eyes, he backed off, satisfying himself with a gesture of contempt as he led his detective out of the house.

Sergeant Turner, dashing in from the street, coat over his head to keep his bifocals dry, almost collided with them.

'Traffic car's lost Catweasel, ma'am. He's no doubt belting up the M6 by now. I've circulated details to

Motorway Control and surrounding forces. We might get lucky.'

Molly was too angry to be optimistic. 'We had our chance and we blew it. You only get one shot at the likes of Catweasel. He's half way to Leeds by now I shouldn't wonder.' She looked at Smith and the disappointed men gathered around her. 'Clear the house, Gordon. We'll debrief in the canteen at one o'clock.'

Sitting in her white Fiesta XR2i parked a short distance from Jackman's house, Molly seethed. She should have made it impossible for Catweasel to have escaped. The last time someone had tried to arrest him he had rammed several police cars, ditched a stolen jeep and swum across the River Severn. He had no roots and kept on the move, rarely sleeping in the same bed or with the same woman.

'A big fish got away tonight, Holmes,' she said sadly, stroking her small spaniel as he snuggled deeper into her lap. 'But I'll get him one day, even if I have to drive over his flaming head to do it.'

Opening her window, she caught a glimpse of the stars. It had finally stopped raining. Waiting a few minutes until she had calmed down, she moved the dog onto the front passenger seat. Starting the engine, she drove through the sleeping city.

The turreted Central Police Station had served Westhampton as a lock-up since the days when felons were lashed with a cat o'nine tails or dispatched to distant colonies. Molly parked in the duty inspector's bay before taking Holmes on a quick circuit of the station yard. Returning him to the car, she then made her way to the old stable block, now a dreary, brown-painted canteen. Entering the building, she saw that the bar shutters were firmly bolted to the counter so that it looked more depressing than usual.

Some of the men made an effort to stand; the majority stayed where they were, slouched against the walls or spread across hard-backed chairs.

'Anyone seen the policewoman?' she asked.

'Sent her to hospital for a check-up, ma'am.' replied the uniformed sergeant.

She nodded her approval then scrutinised the weary faces of her team. They had done their best in the atrocious conditions and, in spite of her own disappointment, she knew she had to lift their morale.

'I won't keep you long. You've done a good job tonight. We found at least three kilos of resin; Jackman's admitted supplying; and three men have been charged with possession. We're still making enquiries about the druggie who tried to buy gear from Bill Bannister. Any questions?'

DC Fletcher asked the question that was on all their lips. 'What about Catweasel?'

'Probably making a delivery somewhere up north. Don't worry about it, there'll be another day.'

No one showed any further interest. They'd plainly had enough.

'OK everyone, that's it. Drug Squad hang on, the rest of you get off home. Thank you, and good night.'

The room was suddenly full of activity as the uniformed contingent rushed towards the door.

Molly's squad of three sergeants and six constables were clearly tired, but she felt fine. Leading the squad into action was a turn-on for her; others could hide behind their nine-to-five desks issuing endless memos.

'Well,' she said, 'apart from Catweasel, it's been a reasonable night's work. Any comments before we pack it in?'

'What do you want me to do with Jackman, ma'am?' Conrad enquired, fresh-faced after his recent drenching, and showing nothing of his earlier resentment.

'Get a statement after caution and bail him. He'll claim to have sacrificed himself to save Catweasel. Knowing him, he'll live off that for months — years even.'

Gilbert, who had joined the squad at the same time as Bannister, raised his hand like a fourth-former, 'Can I ask a question, ma'am?'

'Go on.'

'How did you know about the secret compartment?'

Molly paused, always reticent about her private life. When she had first joined the force she had lived with an elderly spinster, Ishbel Plowright, who was rattling around in a large house on her own and needed a companion. In return for a rent-free room, she had spent as much time as she could with Ishbel, a fastidious lady with a sharp mind, and the graceful elegance of nineteen-twenties high society. Ishbel had taken her to bridge parties, teaching her to play. There had also been trips to fashion shows in London where she met many of Ishbel's friends and relatives. Afterwards, they had gone to smart Eton Square town houses for afternoon tea.

It was a different world, and she had learned not only fashion and bridge but how those with unlimited resources managed their full social calendars. One year she had mingled with the rich and famous at Ascot on Ladies Day; and another she had watched the women's final at Wimbledon's Centre Court.

Ishbel never made a lady out of her, and indeed, she never tried to, but the experience broadened her horizons and gave her more confidence, so that she was no longer in awe of wealth and inherited privilege.

After four years, on her ninety-seventh birthday, Ishbel had died in her sleep. The estate was sold off and Molly had been left one hundred and fifty thousand pounds which she had used to buy a house. She had also taken a few pieces of Goss crested china which no one else wanted. Ishbel had collected them when she was a child. They were miniature ornaments decorated with bright enamel heraldic crests or the coat of arms of different holiday resorts, and bought during day trips to the seaside following the introduction of train travel.

She loved to handle the delicate antiquarian shapes, and had soon become a collector, going to auctions and mooching around sale-rooms, looking for more models. It was an antique-dealer friend who had told her where she might find the catch.

'A good contact,' she replied mysteriously.

'Can I make Jackman an offer for the old chest of drawers?' DC woods asked, always one with an eye for a bargain.

'He wants it to go with his missus,' chipped in his partner.

Bannister caught Molly's eye. 'I've got to see Ezra at the Green Parrot, ma'am. Something about a drugs importation job.'

'Good, I'll join you.' She handed him a bunch of keys. 'Get my holdall out of the boot. I'll need to freshen up and change my clothes before we leave.'

Obviously worried by the prospect of a night out with his new boss, Bannister headed for the car park.

Stepping out of her green wool suit, still damp after her soaking, Molly had a quick wash, pausing to study her reflection in the mirror. The weather had reddened her cheeks and the freckles on her shoulders seemed darker against her goose-pimpled skin.

Unzipping her holdall, she took out the change of clothing she always carried in the car: a small parcel of underwear, and a black skirt and sweater. Plain and simple, it was an outfit that she could get away with in most places.

Quickly dressing, she lightly traced her lips with a fresh colour. Apart from lipstick, she rarely used make-up. It was a chore, and she felt better without it. She then ran a comb through her hair. Wet and windblown a few hours ago, it had soon dried. Fortunately, being naturally wavy, it didn't need much attention.

Conrad, who was writing Jackman's statement, looked up and watched the familiar white XR2i drive out of the station yard. A feeling of nervous exhilaration swept through him so that his hand started to shake.

It's started, he thought. There's no going back now.

4

Even the most dedicated prostitute had given up walking Westhampton's cold, wet streets as Molly and Bannister approached the Green Parrot Club.

The single-storey building, which stood at a corner between two converging roads, reminded Molly of the bows of a ship. Portholes would not have been out of place, but there were no windows, and the black painted walls gave no hint of the brash night-life within.

She pressed the bell button and waited, knowing that they were being given a once-over through a concealed viewer. The door opened and they slipped into the warmth of the red carpeted foyer.

'Evening,' growled the bouncer, a one-man tank in his padded tuxedo.

'All right, Peter?' Molly replied as they walked past the pay kiosk.

Bending over a small table she checked the list of names in the membership book. "Batman" and "Robin Hood" were prominent amongst the Smiths and Browns. Bannister and Peter pretended not to notice as the tight, black skirt climbed up the back of her legs.

'Everything all right?' she asked, straightening up and turning to face the bouncer.

'I'm not complaining,' he said with a smirk.

Molly saw him press a button to warn the owner that they were about to enter the cabaret room. She also noticed the baseball bat which Peter used to eject disorderly drunks. Like many of his kind, he took his job seriously.

Leaving the glare of the mirrored foyer they entered the

darkened cabaret room, stopping inside the door to get their bearings. The final show was in progress and a big brunette on the wrong side of forty was doing her number. G-stringed hips girated like giant boulders and oversized breasts flopped about furiously, spinning brightly coloured tassels stuck to the end of her nipples. As the taped music rose to a crescendo at the climax of the act the artiste deftly jerked her left tit, then her right, sending the tassels spinning in opposite directions.

'Perhaps she'll lift off?' Bannister ventured.

Molly looked disdainfully at the dimple-fat thighs. 'I wouldn't put money on it.'

Peering through a haze of blue smoke, she saw a scattering of middle-aged men sitting in the front seats, staring fixedly at the sweating performer who turned her back on them and slowly bent forward to pick up the clothing she had discarded during her act.

'Kept her best feature till last,' Bannister grinned.

Turning towards the bar, Molly spoke briefly to several cigar-smoking members, then ordered drinks.

'I'll get those,' said a small man of about fifty who looked as though he could do with a good night's sleep.

'Thank you,' Molly said, nodding distantly at the heavily made-up woman who clung to his arm.

He was a frequent advertiser in the personal column of the local rag, and was always turning up with a new woman. The wording never changed. "Rich, lonely widower wishes to meet interesting lady for holidays and lasting companionship. Please send photograph."

'How's the garage going, Ginger?'

'Great!' He gave his latest interesting lady an expansive smile. 'I've had to double the mechanics.'

Molly played her part and looked impressed. He only employed a pensioner at weekends but they sometimes borrowed his cars for stake-outs and he often came up with

34

useful snippets of information. In return, she squared up the odd traffic offence and tapped registration numbers into the Police National Computer to trace car owners who hadn't paid their bills.

She finished her drink, then led Bannister into a small room with brass chandeliers and gold flock wallpaper. A television was showing the regular midnight horror film which no one bothered to watch. Perched on high stools, a pair of miniskirted blondes sipped cherried drinks and looked on as their shirt-sleeved boy-friends played three card brag.

Steve Foster, immaculate in a white dinner-jacket, stood at a small corner bar watching fistfuls of money change hands across the green baize. Seeing the squad detectives, he ordered large whiskies, then stepped forward and shook hands with his visitors. Molly enjoyed the owner's company but knew that the special attention she received was in deference to her position. His smile was as broad as it was false.

'Pleased you could drop in, Molly.'

She smiled back, appraising his lean face and carefully waved hair. Somewhere in his fifties, he thought himself irresistible to women.

'Not likely to be raided are we?' he asked anxiously.

'You're OK tonight, Steve, but you'll have to be careful. It's being put around in certain quarters that you're getting special treatment.'

'Thanks for the tip.' He glanced at the card players. 'They'll be leaving soon. Bookies from out of town: cleaned up at the races.'

The barmaid served their drinks. Pru had once been the runner-up in Westhampton's May Day beauty contest and many a man visited the club to chat her up and try his luck. She pouted at Bannister.

'Hello, darling, where've you been?'

Managing a sickly grin, he turned away from the bar and stared fixedly at the horror film.

'What brings you here on a Monday night, Molly?' Foster asked.

'A quiet drink and the need to wind down after a seventeen-hour day.'

'You should buy a night-club: we work the same shift. Is it anything I should know about?'

'Not really. A raid at Delroy Jackman's drug emporium, that's all.' She knew that Foster had a loose tongue but she saw no harm in giving him the occasional titbit in return for hard information. 'Have you seen Catweasel lately?'

'In here last night. Absolutely loaded. Doubles and trebles all round. Said he's going to retire and buy a mansion in the Bahamas.'

Molly shook her head, soft lights catching the hints of gold in her hair. 'If you see him again, Steve, give me a bell.'

The club owner looked doubtful and she realised she'd been wasting her breath. Catweasel was a big spender who had his own ways of dealing with squealers.

'Can I get you something to eat, Molly?' Foster asked.

'A plate of chips and a ham sandwich wouldn't go amiss, thanks. How about you?' she asked Bannister.

'Good idea,' replied the detective, who never refused food.

Foster went to see the chef and Bannister wandered back into the cabaret room to find Ezra.

Sitting on a stool at the bar, Molly ate her food. The bookies and their girl-friends had left; spirited away through a back door known only to a select few. She liked the shady, secretive atmosphere of nightclubs. When she had first joined the Drug Squad she thought they were unpleasant, threatening places, but as she got to know the owners and the regular members, her feelings had changed and she looked forward to her weekly visits. The metal dealers were the best crowd. Likeable rogues with big wallets and bigger hearts, they laughed a lot and told her the latest jokes. She also knew that if there was any trouble, they would be the first to help her.

Foster made a fuss of her, and kept her glass topped up with his best malt, but that was for his own ends. He knew she organised the club raids and could close him down at any time. Like every club owner, he was obliged to break the law simply to stay in business. The ''Members only'' rule stated that no one could enter a club until they had been a registered member for at least twenty-four hours. Clubs relied on passing trade from late night drinkers and that rule alone, if strictly adhered to, was enough to bankrupt them.

Bannister returned, tripping over his size eleven Hush Puppies as he hurried across the room. 'Ma'am! It's fantastic. Ezra's got onto these guys who want to knock out tons of ge—.'

'Good news?' interrupted Foster as he sidled up to them.

'Maybe,' Molly replied shortly.

'Sweetheart!' called a large, red-faced man, surrounded by three other large, red-faced men, all bearing down on Molly like a rugby pack. 'You're just what we need: a bit o' talent to liven up the party. Jack's traded in all his non-ferrous today. Made a bleeding bomb he has, and we're going to help him spend it.'

Bannister fumbled for the lock, opened the door of his neat semi, then staggered into the hall. He quietly closed the door, then stepped forward and immediately tripped over a child's tricycle, demolishing a Lego model of Conway

Castle.

Cursing under his breath, he struggled up the stairs to the bathroom. Sighing with relief, he was careful to aim the strong flow against the side of the bowl so as not to disturb Liz.

He stripped down to his underpants, and crept into the bedroom. Eyes focussed on the knot of black hair on the right-hand pillow, he tiptoed around the bottom of the bed to the other side. Lowering himself between the sheets, he prayed that he had made it without waking her. He lay perfectly still for a few moments, then, feeling safe, snuggled up to the soft, warm night-dress.

'Where the bloody hell have you been?' Liz shouted into his ear. 'It's bloody morning!'

Bannister cringed, forcing his tired mind to think. 'Sorry, luv. I thought you were asleep.'

'Asleep? Asleep? I should think you've woken up the whole bloody street.' She jumped out of bed. 'And the first thing you can do when you recover from your drunken stupor is to rebuild Robert's bloody castle.'

The door slammed, the light shade danced, and dust motes glistened in the pale morning sunlight, settling on the soundly sleeping detective.

5

It was eight o'clock the same morning when Molly drove into Dinsall, a small industrial town swallowed up in Westhampton's boom-time expansion. She parked her car at the side of the blue-brick police station which had been opened by the mayor at the beginning of the Second World War. It was well away from the city's mainstream policing and an ideal base for the Drug Squad which occupied the first floor, sharing the kitchen with local officers. A reporting station only, the old cells were used as store-rooms. Prisoners had to be taken to the Central lock-up.

She headed for the kitchen door at the back of the building, pausing on the way while Holmes cocked his leg at the side of the dog pound. It had always been his favourite spot, ever since she had rescued him one Sunday morning two years ago. The wobbly-legged puppy, shivering in a corner, had whined pitifully as she was passing and she had stopped to gather him in her arms. Taking him to her office, she had shared her lunch with him.

When no one claimed the dog and he was due to be put down, Molly had found herself saddled with a responsibility she didn't want. Now they doted on each other. At first she had called him "No Home" but it had soon become Holmes.

Because of her hectic life-style they both had to make compromises. But he was a cheerful little dog and always pleased to see her, no matter how long he had been left alone at home, in the car, or at the office. On her part, there were the problems of finding time for him and making sure he was properly cared for when she was away on a job or at a conference.

The kitchen was alive with the sounds of cooking and the mouth-watering smell of bacon. The dog licked his lips and Molly peered under the grill at the curling rashers.

'Keep your hands off and sit down if you want your breakfast,' scolded the cook.

'Feeling better today, Vera?'

'I'm all right, thank you, Molly.' She eased her back, wincing. 'I just wish it'd stop raining. It gets into me old bones you know.' She glanced across the kitchen at the younger woman. 'If you don't mind me saying so, you're working too hard.'

Molly smiled to herself. The cook treated her like a headstrong daughter. ''What you need, m'girl, is a good man,'' she had said every month since Molly had taken over the Drug Squad.

'Bit of a party last night, Vera.'

'A proper night's sleep is what you need, m'girl.' She put some fried eggs into the oven and dropped a piece of bread into the pan. 'One round or two?'

'One . . . The navy taught me how to survive on a few hours sleep.'

'And how to drink the sea dry. It's a pity you didn't marry one of them nice officers with their fancy gold braid.' She pushed aside the *Daily Telegraph* and placed Molly's breakfast on the white-scrubbed table.

When Molly had finished eating, she went over to the sink and slid the empty plate into the soapy water, putting her arm around the cook's shoulders as she did so.

'Thanks, Vera. I don't need a husband as long as I've got you to look after me.'

'Oh yes you do — I can't give you babies.'

Leaving Holmes in the kitchen, head on one side as he waited for Vera's titbits, Molly climbed the stairs to the

40

general office.

She was met by Joan Fellows, the squad secretary. Short and fine boned, with delicate features and pale skin, she looked more like a school girl than a woman who had been married for two years. Her face was plain but she had large luminous brown eyes which enhanced the aura of vulnerability.

'Good morning, ma'am,' she welcomed.

Catching a whiff of fresh polish, Molly looked around her with approval. Everything had its place and the furniture shone. Most CID offices were tips, detectives believing that heaps of dog-eared files, overflowing ashtrays, and blotters of a thousand telephone numbers were proof of hard work.

'Good morning, Joan. Any calls?'

'I've only been in a few minutes, ma'am. How did last night's job go?'

'Up and down. The lads will tell you all about it when they arrive.'

Walking through the sergeants' office, Molly saw that Roger Turner's desk was empty as usual. I must sort out that man's Gaming Team before they lose control of the clubs and the bingo halls. If I don't, the sharks will take over, she thought briefly.

Her small, square office was at the end of a short corridor and next to the bathroom. No framed certificates or annual arrest charts lined the walls. Instead there were water-colours of country scenes and a Turner print of a stormy sea. A hand-crafted model of a kingfisher stood on the filing cabinet. Beside it, hanging from a nail in the wall, was a brass horse-shoe, a farewell present from her driver when she was a detective sergeant in the Crime Squad. On her desk, next to the telephone, stood the photograph of her parents. It was fading now, but it was all she had to remember them by.

She had been five years old when masked gunmen burst into their off-licence in London's East End and demanded money, blasting away at her parents when they refused to open the safe. The memory of the acrid smell of the guns and the warm sticky feeling of her father's blood was not so vivid now, but she knew it would never go away. Nor would she forget the coldness of the children's home, where loneliness and despair had replaced love and tenderness.

A scrawny, poorly dressed kid, she had been bullied and ridiculed at school, often returning to the home with bleeding knees and torn clothes so that she was sent straight to bed without any tea. It was her violent temper that got her into trouble. When the insults became unbearable, she lashed out at whoever was nearest, irrespective of their size or sex.

When she moved to the senior school she had a reputation for being a scrapper. Even so, the hurtful taunts had continued. Already hardened and better able to control her feelings, she had taken refuge in her studies, gaining top marks in most subjects, and further alienation from her peers.

Enlisting in the WRNS when she left school, primarily to escape living in care, had been a mistake. She had simply moved from one regimented institution to another. Masses of noisy, similarly dressed bodies, marching from place to place; living without peace or privacy, and in accordance with pointless rules and regulations. Freedom of expression and originality of thought were the enemies of good order.

She made a sound in her throat, a pugnacious "Hum!" A rebel by nature, it was small wonder that she detested bureaucrats and mindless management.

Leaving the Navy, she had joined the police at nineteen. After ten years at the orphanage and three in uniform, knuckling down to police discipline had been a doddle, and she had a head start on the other recruits, most having joined straight from college.

She had excelled in the job and moved quickly through the ranks, but there had been a down side. Toughened by the experiences of her early life and ten years at the sharp end, mostly in the CID — the rough edges having been smoothed off by Ishbel Plowright — she was, on the surface, the high-flying professional woman: good-looking, smartly dressed and extremely competent. But inside the polished shell she was lonely, craving love and affection, and for all her worldliness, she had no idea how to sustain a meaningful relationship.

Joan followed her into the office. 'Anything special for me today?' she asked.

Molly held up a bundle of paper. 'Redo this ecstasy file will you, please? It's time Gilbert understood the rules of evidence.'

Turning to leave, Joan caught her elbow on the door handle, dropping the file and scattering the papers. Helping Joan to pick them up, Molly asked her if she was feeling all right.

Joan brushed a hand across her cheek. 'Got to be, haven't I, ma'am.'

'How long's your soldier husband been away this time?'

'Over a year. We had just eleven months together.'

Joan left the office and Molly returned to her desk, thinking that it was wrong for a young couple to be separated so soon.

She glanced at the in-tray. Every time Headquarters Administration said they had reduced bureaucracy, it got worse. After signing some overdue files, she examined the arrest reports. They weren't good enough. The squad was spluttering along on two cylinders, and she'd have to make changes.

Gordon Smith's Vice Team, Macdonald and Gilbert, were doing well. The sergeant knew all the tricks and kept them in line.

Conrad's Drug Team, Williams and Bannister, had increased the number of arrests, but the sergeant was pushing them too hard. He wasn't interested in his men, only in furthering his own career.

Roger Turner's Gaming Team was a different problem. Her two experienced gaming detectives had recently been moved because of a Complaints Department investigation, and she had transferred Woods and Fletcher across from the other teams, replacing them by the latest arrivals, Bannister and Gilbert. It had soon become apparent that Woods and Fletcher were not suited for gaming enquiries and she had asked for two women detectives who had worked in casinos before they joined the job. Davids, as expected, had refused to have them on the squad.

Time I got rid of gaming altogether, she thought. And vice. We've got enough work to do with drugs. It's the biggest growth industry in the country.

'More work,' Joan announced walking into the office and placing a bundle of forms on the desk.

Molly yawned. 'Excuse me. Late night, I'm afraid.'

'Too many late nights, ma'am.'

'You sound like the cook . . . Not more expenses!' Molly groaned as Joan walked towards the door. 'No wonder they don't want to go back into uniform.'

Bannister's "Detective Expense Claim" was on the top of the pile.

£15   Spent in the White Dog with informant.

£100   Paid to informant re. execution of warrants at Edinburgh Road.

£10   Spent during observations at the Blue Follies Night Club re. illegal gaming offences.

£100   Paid to informant re. arrests for supplying amphetamine sulphate.

£40   Test purchase, Swedish Porn.

£25   Spent in The Green Parrot with informant.
        Total: £290

She checked the figures. Detectives were atrocious at counting, even in their own interest. At least Bannister had got it right. She signed the form, then banged down her date stamp.

Finishing the expenses, she turned to Conrad's personal file. Born in Chelsea, 1966, he was the son of a Deputy Assistant Commissioner in the Metropolitan Police. His school report was only average and he had not obtained a single qualification. A teacher had written: "A likeable, if cocky individual, who has ability but lacks motivation — except when kicking leather or feeling girls' bottoms."

Conrad had followed his father into the police service, joining the cadets at sixteen and transferring to the regulars three years later. He had been a slow starter, only just scraping through his probation. After four years, however, there was a marked change and his staff appraisal reports noted a sudden and surprising determination to succeed. Some reverently mentioned his father, using the hackneyed phrase "a chip off the old block". More astute assessors had commented that he tried too hard and distanced himself from his colleagues.

When he had been promoted sergeant after five years' service, the Chief Constable, using his distinctive green ink, had written: "This dedicated young man has the ability to attain the highest ranks in the service."

She put down the papers with a sigh. The staff appraisal system had been useful when the reports were confidential, but now that officers were entitled to see everything that was written about them, it had lost its value. Most senior officers were not prepared to tell their men and women that they were incompetent or had an attitude problem, and therefore everybody had a good report. She suspected that whatever reservations past supervisors had about Conrad,

45

they would not have included them in his personal file.

Returning to the papers, however, she noticed a plain, brown envelope which was sealed but bore no marks. Frowning, she held the envelope up to the light, then opened it. Taking out a small slip of paper, she read two lines of standard type. "This man has serious personality problems — be careful." Someone had bucked the system, but whoever that person was, he or she wouldn't have taken such a risk unless they thought it imperative to give Conrad's future boss a timely warning.

What personality problems? Molly wondered, wishing the assessor had been more specific and resolving to find out before it was too late. She had objected strongly to Conrad's transfer to the Drug Squad, having learned on the grape-vine that he was too aggressive and selfish to be a useful member of a small cohesive unit that had to work together merely to survive. But it was no surprise when Davids had overruled her, claiming that Conrad needed an attachment to a front-line unit as part of his career development.

The subject of her thoughts entered the office and she hurriedly turned over the file, concealing the brown envelope and the typed note.

'Tell Bannister that if he doesn't stop trying to double his wages by making inflated expense claims, he'll be back on the beat.'

'Yes, ma'am.'

She searched through her papers and took out a brown folder.

'Pity about Catweasel, ma'am.' His voice was soft and syrupy.

'Yes,' she replied, convinced he was trying to wind her up. 'I want to discuss your team.'

'My team! You needn't worry about my lot, ma'am. We're well into the scene. Bannister's coming along nicely.

He's as strong as an ox, and frightened of nothing. And he's getting well into Ezra who's turning in some good info. The lad's still green, mind you, but he's willing enough. All I've got to do is point him in the right direction and say "fetch, boy". I'll teach him how to nail druggies, and how to make it stick.'

'I thought you ran Ezra.'

'I did, but I like to give my young D's a chance.'

She fingered her Biro. What was he up to? He never gave anything away. No detective gave up his informant without a very good reason. Informants, used properly, were for life, and they rarely worked for more than one person.

She cleared her throat, breaking an awkward silence. 'Gaming Team's the problem. The chief was wrong to suspend two of my best men because somebody said they'd been getting backhanders from the club owners. There's not a shred of evidence against either of them.'

'Roger Turner's had enough trouble looking after the kids since his missus left him, ma'am. He's got no time to chase up Woods and Fletcher.'

'It hasn't helped,' she agreed. 'He's got no support. Those two are wrong for gaming. It's a specialist job that can't be learned in a few weeks. I'm wondering whether to swap one of them with your DC Williams.'

Conrad sat up as if someone had hit him in the back. 'Spare me that, please, ma'am. For all Woods' smart chat, he hasn't come up with a single snout in two years. I think we should kick him out.'

'Fletcher?'

'You know what I think about him, ma'am: he's only interested in one thing. Being on the job to him means exactly that, having it away with some bird in the back of a CID car.' He leaned forward. 'One of the lads was telling me the other night that he was knocking off an

ACC's daughter.'

'Shall we return to gaming, Sergeant? Where am I going to get replacements?'

Conrad shrugged and she guessed that he was satisfied with putting the knife into Woods and Fletcher. Woods had always been a problem, and she could accept some of the things the sergeant said about him, but he had his good points and was a live wire who somehow seemed to fit in well with the rest of the squad. They couldn't all be super-cops. Fletcher, her only black detective, was very popular and, although he was taking time to settle down, she felt sure that he would do well.

'It's never been done before,' she said thoughtfully, 'but I'm going to try and get an experienced gaming man back for a second attachment. Ask Joan to let me have the list when you leave.'

He ignored the implied dismissal. 'Bannister said you didn't give him a chance to fill you in about Ezra's info last night, ma'am.'

'Last night was four o'clock this morning, Sergeant.'

'He's really bubbling about this one,' Conrad went on. 'He said it's a mega job . . . His words, not mine.'

'What's the catch?'

'The same question I asked, ma'am. They want an outsider because they don't trust the regular dealers. They're after a buyer with big bread. Someone who has the contacts to move it through third parties. They don't want the gear traced back to them.'

She scanned her desk diary. 'Where's Bannister now?'

'City centre.'

'Get him. I'll see him here at seven.'

Conrad smiled. 'He'll love that. He's got visitors tonight.'

'That can't be helped, I'm afraid. I want you here as well, and don't forget that list.'

After he had left, Molly went to the bathroom and checked her appearance. She was pleased with the new biscuit-coloured cardigan jacket and the matching loose trousers. Dressing for CID work was difficult for women, and the Drug Squad made it doubly so. Designers didn't have in mind detective inspectors who divided their time between office work, enquiries, observations, meeting ponces, briefings and raiding premises, which ranged from dusty warehouses full of pornography to inner-city squats teaming with weirdo junkies. She was feminist, but she believed that women who aped men by wearing pin-striped business suits somehow betrayed their sex.

When she walked into the general office, the day shift were busy doing their reports. Tuesday morning was a good time for catching up on the previous week's paperwork.

'I'm going to court, Joan. Our chemist friend is up for supplying diamorphine to the young girl who died. With any luck they'll give him twenty years.'

'Probation more likely,' Macdonald said from across the room. 'In line with the government's tough new sentencing policy.'

Woods looked up from his CID diary which should have been completed at the end of every working day. He was three weeks behind and couldn't remember what he had done three days ago. 'If his brief tells them he was only trying to make her happy, they'll throw the case out.'

Molly smiled, then spoke to Joan. 'After court it's a liquid lunch with Clifford Rainsford Spence. I should be back later this afternoon.'

'I'll make sure your coffee's ready, ma'am.'

Nodding briefly in the general direction of her detectives Molly left the office.

The men sat back and Joan cleared her screen.

'It ain't coffee that she needs, it's a length of hot cock,' Woods said, stretching his aching fingers. 'And I'm in the

49

mood to give it to her.'

'You're horrible, you are,' Joan retorted. 'She's a nice person. You just don't like taking orders from a woman.'

Woods shut his diary and threw it into a drawer. 'She's a dyke. I should keep your muff-box stuck to that seat if I were you.'

'No she isn't, she's had lots of boy-friends. They're always on the phone, begging her to go out with them again.'

'That's her fucking trouble, she's too bloody particular. I bet they get a short-arm inspection before she allows them to do the business.'

'Sex — that's all you think about.' Joan's disgust was plain as she watched Woods sort out his testicles so that they hung down the right side of his tight jeans. He was always messing with his crotch and she suspected that he did it solely to embarrass her.

Woods chuckled. 'What else is there? She should take care of my bodily needs, not waste herself on that mangy flea-bag of hers.'

Stubbing out his half-finished cigarette, Fletcher stood up. 'Leave it off, mate. Let's go and check out the latest fiddle at Billy's Bingo.'

'Letch! You only want to have a gander at the caller's big tits.'

'The Black and White Minstrel Show,' Macdonald said as he watched the two detectives drive out of the station yard.

'Fletch's all right,' mused Joan. 'And I'm not saying that just because he's black. He's considerate and he's not uncouth like the rest of them.'

Macdonald raised an eyebrow.

'I don't mean you,' she said quickly.

'That's a relief. I'll go and put the kettle on. You look as though you could do with a good dose of caffeine.'

'Thanks.'

6

Later that evening Conrad led Bannister into the inspector's office.

'What've you got?' Molly asked Bannister without preamble.

The detective glanced at his feet as if summoning up his courage, then looked her in the eye. 'It's like I told the sergeant, ma'am. Ezra's met these two white guys from Manchester who want to knock out loads of gear.'

'Where's it coming from?'

'An Arab gets regular boatloads from Morocco.'

'What's the asking price?'

'I didn't get down to that.'

'You should have. It's important. If they're real traffickers, and not somebody like the Complaints Department trying to set us up, they'll be very suspicious if you don't.'

Conrad struck a match on the side of his chair and lit a cigarette. Inhaling deeply, he dropped his head back and aimed smoke at the ceiling. 'If we ask too many questions they might get nervous and do a bunk.'

Molly, a non-smoker, rounded on him. 'I'd be grateful if you didn't interrupt, Sergeant!'

Conrad opened his mouth as if about to argue, then thought better of it and studied the worn carpet.

'Go on,' Molly urged Bannister. 'What else did he have to say?'

'They think that most traffickers are police or customs snouts. They think it's the only way traffickers can stay in business.'

She nodded. 'I can't argue with that. What's Ezra's cut?'

'Nothing, ma'am, he's doing all right with his women. Just needs to know he's not going to be lifted.'

'Come off it, he's been poncing for years. There must be more to it than that.' Bannister seemed tongue-tied and Molly tried another tack.

'What does he know about the men from Manchester?'

'Not much, ma'am. He only met them last week.'

'Christ!' exclaimed Molly. 'Do you really believe that they're going to trust someone they've only known a few days with deals of this size? The next time you see him, find out all you can. It's vital. Tell Ezra from me that if he expects us to do business with the Manchester duo and their Arab friend, then we need to know a lot more about them. And tell him there's a buyer, subject to prices and the arrangements for the switch being right. Any funny business and it's no deal.'

'Yes, ma'am.'

'When's your next meeting with Ezra?'

'Tomorrow, midday.'

'OK. I've got a meeting in the afternoon. Report back here at seven and let me know how you get on.'

'Yes, ma'am.'

Molly stared out of the window at the suburban lights. Something was troubling her but she couldn't put her finger on it. Conrad and Bannister exchanged looks as they waited.

She turned back to Bannister. 'I'm not sure we can trust Ezra.'

'He seems keen enough, ma'am.'

Yes, she thought, that's what worries me. And why has Conrad handed Ezra over to you? She felt she was missing something, something important. Giving the sergeant a questioning look, she sat back as the spiral of cigarette smoke drifted past her. She spoke to Bannister. 'All right, that'll do for now. If you've missed your guests, give Liz my apologies.'

'A big guy like that, and he's scared of his missus,' Conrad mumbled after Bannister had left.

Molly looked briefly at the window as rain thrashed against the glass. She had met Bannister's wife and she had been impressed, envious even. Liz knew what she wanted; a good husband and two kids she could wrap her life around. She would do anything to defend her family, and Bill Bannister was the most important person in her life.

'She worries about him, that's all. More importantly, can he handle Ezra?'

Conrad smiled but his cold eyes betrayed him. 'He can with my help,' he said unconvincingly.

Molly thought for a moment. 'I hope so. Some of these youngsters don't know the first thing about running informants. They're far too gullible. A few quick halves and they give away more information than they receive. The druggies know our duties, our annual leave, our car numbers and goodness knows what else. It wouldn't surprise me if our duty rota isn't pinned up next to the dartboard in the Pickwick Arms.' She fanned away the cigarette smoke. 'If this comes off it could be the biggest job we've ever had. He must get it right.'

The sergeant loosened his tie. 'D'you think it'll be that good, ma'am?'

Again, she paused. 'I don't know why, but I've got a strange feeling about this one.'

'It'll make those idle pratts at the big house sit up.'

'Yes, we'll have to be careful how we handle it, or headquarters CID will poke their noses in.'

'They'd definitely balls it up, ma'am.'

Deep in thought, Molly slowly rubbed her hands together. An international operation followed by a presentation at the United Nations Commission on Narcotic Drugs. Their last conference had been in Moscow, but she had no idea where the next one was to be held. The chief would certainly sit up and take notice. Knowing his love for junketing, he would probably insist on going with her.

'What are we going to call it, ma'am?' Conrad asked.

'What?'

'The job.'

'Operation Moscow.'

Conrad was obviously unable to make the connection. 'No, ma'am. I don't get it. What has Russia got to do with this lot?'

She stood up and reached for her coat. 'Don't worry about it. I've got some serious dog-walking to do.'

Conrad followed her into the general office, but she bid him goodnight and clattered down the stairs. As she entered the kitchen, a tail-wagging Holmes jumped into her arms. 'Nuisance!' she yelled. 'You've got smelly dog hairs all over my new outfit!'

Driving too fast, Bannister worried about Liz. My old man was right, he thought, I should've stayed in the family transport business. Would've been a director by now with a golf club apartment on the Costa del Sol, an Audi Quattro, and a bit of spare at the office.

Arriving home, he hung his jacket under the stairs then pulled on his slippers. The house seemed unusually quiet.

'Hello, luv,' he said to Liz as he walked into the lounge. 'Where're the kids?'

'In bed.'

'This early?'

'It's nine o'clock.'

'I thought we'd got visitors.'

'We had. I cancelled.'

He sat down. 'Nothing on the box?'

'Where've you been until now?' she demanded, giving him a quick, miss-nothing inspection.

'Work.'

'What else is there?'

'It's Watty. She's a workaholic and she expects everybody else to be the same. I've had some cracking info about a big drug job. She wanted to know all about it. You know how she is; she gave me the third degree. Said she needed to know everything about the traffickers. She's getting on my left tit. You don't shout at informants like she shouts at detectives. You chat them up; tease out the info a bit at a time.'

'You were saying yesterday that she was magic.'

'I know, but she's a bit much.' He leaned forward, suddenly feeling hungry. 'She did thank me. And said she was sorry for keeping me back when we'd got visitors.'

'Hooray for her. If you ask me, she's yampy. All she cares about is that long-eared rat she rides around with.'

'It's a Cavalier King Charles spaniel. Eighty per cent pure bred. She told me so herself.'

'There's no such thing. It's a bloody mongrel. That woman should be looking after a husband and kids, not keeping you away from your home and family every night.'

'You said.'

'Why don't you ask for a transfer then?'

He tutted. 'Don't be stupid!'

'I'm not being stupid, and don't you tut me, Bill Bannister. It's not right for a detective to work for a woman — it's obscene.'

'You don't know what you're talking about. Where's my dinner?'

She threw down her knitting and jumped up. 'If you talk to me like that, I'll chuck it in the bloody bin. It's time you got out of that bloody silly Drug Squad. Twelve, fifteen hours a day, and most of them at night. You're all round the bloody twist if you ask me.'

'Oh, piss off! I've had enough for one day.'

Holding back the tears, she bit her lip, then fled into the kitchen.

Returning a few minutes later, she put his dinner on the coffee table beside him. 'I suppose you've had so much booze you won't even taste it.'

He stared at the food with unseeing eyes. It was nothing but pressure, pressure, and more pressure. Whatever they did, the gaffer wasn't satisfied. She was obsessed with her work, as if every druggie left on the streets was a personal affront to her efficiency.

Smelling his favourite Indian curry, he started to eat. He was sorry he'd taken it out on Liz and wondered how he could make it up to her.

7

On dry mornings, Molly liked to wander around her garden before setting out for the office. She examined the new growth on her roses, the result of a mild January. When she had first moved into the house every weekend had been spent working in the garden, but there had been no days off lately and the weeds were taking over.

St Peter's clock struck seven and she glanced up at the church perched on a sandstone outcrop overlooking the village. She was a more relaxed person in Coovers Wood, a small South Staffordshire village which she called "Real England". It was her refuge from the noise, congestion and crime of the polluted city where she earned her living.

Nosing her Fiesta out of the drive, she waved to a neighbour who was busily cramming squabbling kids into the back of a Volvo estate. The scene stuck in her mind during the forty-minute trip to work and she tried to see herself in the woman's place.

'Could I be like that?' she asked Holmes, who was more interested in a dog fight outside a butcher's shop. 'Will I ever have the opportunity, more like?'

She had never been short of men friends but they were mostly brief, casual affairs. Those that had lasted more than a few weeks usually ended in a mess, partly because of her job, but mostly as a result of her inability to give herself completely to any man. Life had made her better at concealing her emotions than expressing them. Perhaps she was looking for perfection when, in truth, she knew it did not, and could not, exist. She had started to believe that she would always be single: successsful in her professional life, but having no one with whom she could share the rewards.

She was still mulling it over as she drove into the station yard. 'It's time you did something useful, Holmes. I need counselling. If you're not careful, your pampered blissful life might one day be shattered by domestic turmoil.' The dog wagged his tail.

'What's up with the gaffer?' Joan asked Conrad some time later in the morning. 'I've just been into her office and she's in a foul mood. Something's upset her.'

'If you promise to be nice to me, I'll find out for you,' he whispered into Joan's ear.

She pulled away. 'I'd rather not know, thank you.'

'Good morning, ma'am,' Conrad said a few minutes later, as he breezed into Molly's office.

'What's good about it?' she replied heavily. 'Complaints have been on. I'm being investigated for burglary, assault and malicious damage at Jackman's place. I tell you, Sergeant, one half of this force does its best to get the job done, while the other half persecutes the half that's doing the flaming work. It's a nonsense. If they had any backbone, they'd have charged the owner of Jackman's house and that daft woman upstairs with aiding and abetting the sale of dangerous drugs. But not them. Oh no! They creep and crawl around a bunch of half-baked political has-beens and civil service drop-outs who've wangled themselves nice little earners on the Police Complaints Authority.' She leaned back in her chair. 'Sometimes, I wonder why we bother. It's the stupidity of it all that I can't stand. As my old inspector used to say ''Those buggers up there don't know what goes on down here''.'

She caught a flash of amusement in Conrad's eyes. Yes,

my boy, she thought, you're delighted I'm in the shit, aren't you?

Aloud she said: 'What do you think of the Manchester pair, Sergeant?'

'I'm not sure, ma'am. We'll have to wait and see what Bannister comes up with.'

'I saw Cliff Spence yesterday,' Molly said. 'He's got plenty of contacts in Manchester, but they've not heard a squeak about two white men trying to move large amounts of gear.'

Bannister dashed out of the rain into the Red Cow. The only people in the bar were three young prostitutes drying out in front of a battered gas fire.

Gladys, fortyish, with green highlights in her red hair and a gold nose ring, pulled his usual half pint of mild. She knew everything there was to know about the vice scene. Most of the squad detectives had tried to get her to come across, but none had succeeded.

She pushed his glass towards him. 'Bit early for you, isn't it?'

'Dropped in specially to see my favourite woman.'

'Balls! A free half, you mean.'

He sipped his drink and looked about him. After the previous night's binge, his stomach wasn't ready for more alcohol. It was a large, drab room without warmth or atmosphere. Gladys was right, he rarely visited during the day. At night it would be alive enough with the crush and chatter of customers fighting their way to the bar. The Red Cow was useful to the squad because it was a watering hole for every prostitute, ponce, petty thief, pervert and druggie in the city.

Bannister stood at the end of the bar and glanced at the toms. They're not a bad crowd, he thought. Apart from the odd squabble over territory, most of the girls supported each other: helping the very young who were still learning the business, or the older ones who should have been baby-sitting their grandchildren.

The three toms looked in his direction, then their heads came together in a conspiratorial huddle. He was not surprised that they ignored his friendly wave. All of them had given him information when he had worked vice at South Road, but they would never admit it to the others.

He turned back to Gladys, who was polishing glasses. 'Not many about.'

'What d'you expect when you lot keep locking 'em up? We should sue you for loss of trade.'

'C Division is having a purge. The big man wants another pip on his shoulder.'

'I'd like to pin it on his fucking head. This place used to be full of girls at this time of the day.'

Cold air blasted in from the street and Conrad's Ezra filled the doorway. Seeing Bannister, the Jamaican stepped inside and shook the rain off his Derby hat, then put it back on his polished ebony head.

Gladys pulled him a pint of bitter.

Who are you? Bannister wondered, watching Ezra peel a fifty-pound note from the thick wad he always carried. He had moved into town three years ago and had been a regular in the city-centre night-clubs ever since. Although a good mixer, he never talked about himself, and no one knew anything about him, not even his real name. Watson had taken away one of his pint glasses and had the fingerprints checked, but the Criminal Record Office had returned the forms marked ''No Trace''.

Bannister had been surprised when Conrad had suddenly handed Ezra over to him. ''He'll do you a lot of good, laddie. Just let me know what's going on, that's all I ask.''

'Keep your eye on the bar a minute,' Gladys asked Bannister as she disappeared into the back.

Ezra finished his pint and surreptitiously slid a small

piece of folded paper along the bar. 'Ring that number at two-thirty,' he whispered before leaving the pub.

'Where's he gone?, Gladys asked when she returned, carrying several packets of crisps.

Bannister shrugged, 'No idea.'

She loaded the crisps into a box behind the bar. 'I don't know how his girls put up with him. He gives me the fucking creeps.' She double-jerked a large gin for herself then reached for his empty glass.

He stopped her. 'Thanks Glad, but I must be off.'

Bolting the door behind him, she spoke to the toms. 'Fucking good riddance to nothing.'

'He ain't that bad,' said skinny chain-smoking Mavis, well turned out in a red leather suit she had stolen when she was in Birmingham. 'At least he gives you a chance, not like some of the cock-sucking bastards.'

Celia, a tall black woman, wearing a shocking-pink bolero jacket, tight jeans and red high heels, pursed her lips. 'Did you dig that whopping great lump in his trousers? I reckon he's a good grind.'

The third girl was Pat, small and round with a spotty face. She sported a white plastic raincoat that reached down to her ankles. 'Calls 'imself a detective. He couldn't detect a bad smell,' she said.

'That lets you out then,' Celia grinned.

'Bannister would be gob-smacked if he knew who'd picked me up this week,' Mavis said, glancing furtively over her shoulder.

'Who?' Celia asked.

'His sergeant. You know, that guy who's always hanging about the patch. Dark hair and terrific eyes.'

'What's he like?'

'Same as all the rest.'

'My wife doesn't understand me!' they chorused as Gladys arrived with three halves of mild.

61

'Is he any good?' Pat asked.

'Shit scared of catching something,' Mavis replied. 'Blow jobs, that's all they want these days. I'm getting like a fucking goldfish,' she added, doing her best imitation as her pals burst into laughter.

'Did you give him one?' Pat asked.

'Not fucking likely. Told him it'd cost him fifty quid. He'd only got a tenner so I gave him a hand job instead.'

'Shall we tell Molly smart-arse?' Celia asked.

'No, let it run,' Gladys replied. 'Might be useful if she starts getting awkward.'

'She'd be good on the game. They'd soon be forming a queue,' Pat said.

Celia laughed, 'You're round the fucking bend, you are, kid. The lads on the squad say it's probably healed up.'

Mavis pinched the end of her half-finished cigarette. 'Well, I can't afford to sit around on mine all day. It's got to pay the rent.'

'What was Ezra doing in here?' Pat asked, lingering by the fire.

'Search me. He's got his girls working the big stores today.'

'They won't find any punters there.'

'Shoplifting, you silly cunt,' Celia laughed as she hoisted herself into the air like a dockyard crane, then stooped to adjust her wig in the cracked mirror above the fireplace. 'Come on girls, my regulars will be panting for it by now.'

Absent-mindedly picking her left nostril with a bright red fingernail, Pat flicked a soft scab onto the floor. 'I wish I'd got a few regulars.'

Leaving a telephone kiosk, Ezra crossed the pavement and climbed into the back of a red Saab. Taking off his hat, he slid down the seat. 'That's it, your boy's given me the go-ahead to fix up the meet.'

Conrad laughed. 'Good. How are you and Bannister making out?'

'He's all right. Too nice for a cop. I'm starting to feel sorry for the guy.'

'You, you old bugger, you'd step on a baby's head because you'd be too lazy to walk round it. D'you think he suspects anything?'

'Not him. Keen type. Eager to please his lady boss.'

'She's too easy on him. You wait until I take over. He'll soon learn what discipline's all about.'

'We'll have to watch her, she's cool.'

'She's not that good,' Conrad murmured. 'But you're right, I suppose. She's already asked Cliff Spence to check out the Manchester scene.'

'You should've jumped Spence when I told you, man. He'd got five weights stashed under the washer in his outhouse.'

Driving into a side road, Conrad made sure that there was no one about before he cut the ignition and turned to face Ezra. He knew there was bitter rivalry between the two black men as they both sought to take control of the streets and double their vice empires.

'Can't stand the opposition, that's your trouble.'

'Ezra scowled. 'Spence's evil. He should be put down like a mad dog.'

Conrad checked his rear-view mirror. 'I might be able to help, but it'll cost you.'

'Why don't you do Spence's shebeen?'

'No chance. Watson's not going to raid her snout's blues party.' Conrad gave himself a sly grin in the side mirror. 'Especially when she thinks she's about to crack a gang of international drug traffickers.'

'There's still time,' Ezra persisted. 'She's good at shebeens.'

'We are, you mean. She just gets the warrants and watches us do all the work.'

Ezra stroked the brim of his hat. 'You get rid of Watson . . . I get rid of Spence. That way we take over the whole town.'

Conrad thought for a moment. He needed money, and he needed it soon. The banks were being bloody-minded.

'It'll be expensive.'

'How much expensive?'

'Thousand.'

'You're joking.'

'I'll have to see a local councillor I know. He needs the readies to keep his latest poke happy. She's a real beaut. In fact, I wouldn't mind a bit of the action myself. She might be very amenable if I promise not to tell her old man what she's been up to.'

'What if your councillor friend doesn't want to play?'

'Simple. I'll threaten him with the tabloids.'

'That would save us some bread.'

'Ezra! You'll never make a conman. We've got to keep them sweet. Leave the hard stuff for emergencies. That way everybody's happy.'

'What can this councillor do for us?'

'Gripe at the local super. Threaten to report him to the chief constable if he doesn't put a stop to Spence's all-night, all-weekend reggae.'

'You've got to find some gear, so Spence goes to jail for a long time.'

Conrad winked. 'Don't I always find gear?' He pulled away from the kerb and drove towards City Road. 'If you're moving in on Spence's girls I should charge you double.'

'Thousand,' Ezra sighed, taking out his roll of notes.

It was five-thirty when Bannister's old Escort shot up the ramp of a multi-storey car-park. He corkscrewed through a series of bends and stopped in the centre of the empty fourth floor.

Listening to the muted sounds of traffic in the busy street below, his eyes slowly grew accustomed to the gloom around him. There were no lights in the car-park, only different shades of darkness with concrete pillars casting shadows across deserted bays. He did not see Ezra until the passenger door opened and the fat Jamaican squeezed in, hat resting on his ample stomach.

'Man, you should spend some of those backhanders and get yourself some sharp wheels.'

Bannister hadn't got time for small talk. 'What did they say?'

'They'll meet the buyer at six on Friday night. Outside the Railway Hotel. But he must be alone. They'll have shooters, and if there's any trouble they'll use them.'

'Why the Railway?'

'Everybody digs trains, man. You can get drunk on a train and nobody asks you to breathe in the bag.'

'Traffickers don't use trains.'

'Maybe there's a cheap-day drugs amnesty on the Manchester to Westhampton Line.'

'The Dope Special,' Bannister sighed.

'You got it, man.'

Bannister gritted his teeth. 'Stop buggering about. I've got to be back at the office by seven.'

'Cool it, man. You's all strung up like a Christmas turkey.'

'It's all right for you, but if I miss anything, I'll get it in the neck from the gaffer.'

'You should get yourself a proper job.'

'Like a fat, rich, couldn't-care-less ponce, you mean.'

'That's it, man. And I'll be the drugs chief who'll look

after you.'

Gripping the wheel, Bannister sighed. Ezra was impossible in his present mood. 'Right!' he said. 'No more pissing about. When are you seeing them again?'

'They'll call me. I tried to get a number but they're too sharp. I could hear metal banging and a lot of shouting though. Can't be sure, but it sounded like a garage. Where they do repairs.'

'Ring nicked cars, more like.'

'Yeah, that's it, man.'

'Watty thinks you're making a packet out of this deal.'

Ezra humped his shoulders and showed the palms of his hands in a gesture of hurt innocence. 'I don't like that woman. She don't trust nobody.'

'You must know something about them.'

'Ah, come on, man, she's got you rattled. We should lose her. D'you want me to drop some dope in her car and tell Complaints?'

Bannister held his head in his hands. 'You know, Ezra, sometimes I have nightmares, but I can only remember the last bit. You and me sitting in a cell, sewing bloody mail-bags.'

'You drink too much beer, man. Addles your brain so you don't know who your real buddies are.'

'Look, I'll ask you once more. Is there anything else you can tell me?'

'You've got it all. I only met them once.'

Bannister felt under the seat for his notebook and instead picked up a rotten apple which came apart in his hand. 'My bloody kids!'

Ezra's Derby rocked with his laughter.

Bannister wiped his hand with an oily rag that left black streaks on his wrist. He then gingerly resumed his search under the seat and found what he had been looking for.

'Right, fatso, fun time's over. It's your choice. Talk to

me or I'll make sure you and your bloody women are put away for ever. I want to know what the traffickers look like. I want to know if they're loaded or broke. What they talk about. What kind of motors they use and whether they smoke, drink, gamble or play with their pricks. In other words, I want the lot.'

'Ah, come on, man, you'll see them yourself on Friday.'

'That's too late. We might get shot. Talk!'

Ezra shifted uneasily, peering out of the windows. 'We should be moving man. Some of the girls bring their clients up here about now.'

'Bit early isn't it?'

'Don't you know nothing? Bosses need relief before facing their womenfolk at home.'

'Makes a change from gin and tonic, I suppose.'

8

Bannister dived into the inspector's office, out of breath from running up the stairs. His face looked pained, partly from exertion but mostly from worry because he was ten minutes late. Sergeant Conrad, slouched in a chair, chuckled at his detective's distress.

'Sorry, ma'am,' Bannister panted, closing the door. 'Informant was late.'

Molly noticed the rise and fall of his huge chest, half expecting the buttons of his shirt to give way under the strain. She motioned towards the empty chair. 'Sit down before you do yourself an injury. What's super-snout got to say for himself?'

The chair creaked under Bannister's weight. 'They've agreed to a meet,' he replied as his breathing eased. 'Six o'clock on Friday at the Railway Hotel.'

'Whereabouts?'

'Outside.'

'Is that it?'

Starting to sweat in the warm office, Bannister leaned forward and struggled out of his denim jacket. 'They want to see the buyer alone.'

'Anything else?'.

'No, ma'am. I tried to get descriptions but Ezra can't remember what they looked like.'

'Doesn't want to, you mean.'

'I did my best ma'am.'

Molly looked thoughtfully at her detective. 'Well, it's not much, but I suspect it's all we're going to get.'

'Ezra said they were very suspicious, ma'am. Kept

asking him about the buyer. They want to know what he looks like when they ring tomorrow. Threatened to bury Ezra in concrete if anything goes wrong.'

'The joys of snouting.'

'Oh, there is one thing. He said they'd be carrying pieces, and if there's any trouble they'd use them. Sorry, ma'am, I nearly forgot.'

Molly waved away the smoke from Conrad's cigarette, then got up to open the office door. 'That's crucial information, Bannister, you're not supposed to forget. If they're going to be armed we have to be ready for a shoot out, understand?'

He nodded, wiping a hand across his brow.

She returned to her desk and sat down, eyes fixed on the detective. 'Make some coffee, please.'

'Kids!' Conrad said after Bannister had left.

Molly was thinking about her next move. 'He'll learn. We will need firearms back-up . . . and the SPG.'

'And all the crew, ma'am.'

'Yes, we're going blind into this one, but we've got no choice until we find out who they are and what they're up to. Gordon and Roger are in court with the heroin case. You'll have to go to the meet with Bannister.'

'It's my law finals on Friday, ma'am.'

She had forgotten. Probably because she didn't see him as a future member of the legal profession.

'Who else is available?'

'There's Macdonald. He knows the score.'

'No, I need someone with rank.' She stared at the ring on her finger. Her father's signet-ring with her mother's name engraved on the inside. 'We could borrow a sergeant from the Crime Squad I suppose . . .'

'I think you should go, ma'am'.

'What! Me and Bannister? He's only just started to tie his own shoe-laces, for Christ's sake!'

69

'That's why he needs someone like you, ma'am. He's got to learn.'

Creep! she thought. But despite herself she started to warm to the idea. It was too good a chance to miss, an opportunity to do some hands-on CID work. She had been so bogged down with headquarters conferences and paperwork lately, she might be losing her edge. She twisted the ring around her finger. The soft gold had worn thin and it was scratched in places.

Looking up at the sergeant, she had a sudden premonition. There was nothing showing in his face but something inside her was sending out warning signals.

'Yes . . . OK,' she said, unusually hesitant. 'I'll go with Bannister. The briefing will be at two on Friday afternoon. Roger Turner can take charge of the stake-out. He's only the exhibits officer; the court should release him at the lunch-time adjournment.' She opened her desk diary. 'We'll go to headquarters first thing tomorrow and fix up firearms.'

'I'm doing the monthly drug disposal at eleven, ma'am.'

'Bring it forward. We'll leave when you've finished.'

Bannister pushed his way through the door with a tray of drinks.

'Have you done a drugs destruction?'

'No, ma'am.'

'In that case it's time you did. Help the sergeant tomorrow.'

She stood up and shrugged on her coat. 'Must dash. I've got a difficult county teams match against last year's winners tonight.'

Bannister waited until he heard the downstairs door shut. 'Never bloody satisfied, is she, Sarge?'

'What've you got to worry about? You're her ace crime cracker. If you're really good at the meet she might even let you have a little bit.'

70

Bannister flushed. 'Cream cracker, more like. What's so special about destroying the drugs?'

'Used to burn it ourselves once. Until some berk at headquarters accused us of being a crowd of junkies. Reckoned that what we didn't use was sold for the tea fund. He had this brilliant idea that everything would be hunky-dory if a gaffer from the "big house" took charge of things. They take it in turns and we have to hold their hands while they throw it into the council incinerator.'

Bannister grinned. 'Do we get to make a wish?'

Conrad made himself comfortable behind the inspector's desk. This will be mine soon, he thought, running his hand along the edge as he contemplated Watson's demise.

'Did Watty say she was playing darts, Sarge?'

'Bridge.'

'Eh?'

'Cards. Sort of pairs whist.'

'I wouldn't want to be her partner.'

'You'll know all about that soon enough. You're going to the meet with her. She's going as the buyer.'

'She's nothing like a bloody drug dealer!'

Conrad laughed, turning over the photograph of Watson's parents and moving her ornaments about the desk as if he had already taken over.

'I'm not joking, Sarge. This is deadly serious. She'll get us both killed.'

'Not her, she's a tough nut. When she was a probationer, she laid out Big Tonky and his missus. They'd wrecked the Brassington Arms — their usual Sunday afternoon trick — and were starting on the other customers when Watson arrived. According to the landlord it was like a bloody film: a couple of quick head butts, a knee in the balls and it was all over. When the troops arrived the Tonkys were laid out like a couple of corpses.'

'That wouldn't be much good against shooters, Sarge.

71

She lives and breathes the bloody job, and she's got fuzz written all over her. She might as well wear a blue lamp on her head.'

'Never mind, when you turn up in your hippy gear, they'll never believe a self-respecting copper would be seen within smelling distance of you.'

Bannister stamped up and down the small office then kicked the wall. 'Didn't think I'd be teaming up with the gaffer.'

Conrad stood up and made for the door. 'Come on, lover boy. A poetic pint in the Bard's brewhouse is what you need.'

They crossed the cobbled square to the Shakespeare Inn, Bannister still worrying about the meet. He was in the mire now, and there wasn't a thing he could do about it. Watson's word was law.

'Here he is, the man every woman lusts for,' called Woods as Bannister led his sergeant into the small lounge at the back of the premises. It was a dark, drab room; green walls lined with brown pictures of Dinsall's High Street at the turn of the century.

Conrad and Bannister collected drinks from the bar then joined the rest of the squad at a long wooden table they had made their own. Every drinker in Dinsall knew that the Shakespeare was the Drug Squad's local, and those who used the place kept out of the back room at lunch-time and in the early evening.

Stuart Williams moved over to make room for his partner. 'Smile, Bill, it might never happen.'

'Yes, it will. I'm on an undercover job with the gaffer.'

'Hark at him,' Woods chimed in. 'Specially selected! We'll have to watch you, lad.'

'It's like going to a brothel with your mother,' Bannister muttered into his beer.

'Some mother,' Woods laughed. 'She can rub baby oil

over my parts any time.'

'Where's she come from?' Gilbert asked seriously. 'She's not from around here.'

'She's a bloody gyppo,' Woods said.

'No she's not,' Turner contradicted. 'I've seen her personal file; she was born in London.'

'What happened to her folks?' Gilbert persisted.

'Well, you see, it was like this,' Woods began earnestly. 'Watty didn't have a mum and dad like you and me. They put her together at an android factory. Fitted her with everlasting batteries, so that she just keeps on going when mere humans, like you and me, have to take a breather now and then.' Some of the men around the table smiled, the others shook their heads. Woods went on. 'And if you look carefully at those hard green things under her false eye lashes, you'll see that they're marbles.'

Bannister took his empty glass to the bar. 'Top it up please, Jim,' he said to the landlord. 'And you'd better put one in for the comedians.'

After they had been tipped out of the Shakespeare and had gone their separate ways, Bannister headed for the city centre. He needed to speak to Monica, one of Ezra's girls. She owed him a few favours. When he was on vice at South Road, he had often helped her out after she had been picked up for soliciting, or when Ezra had beaten her up. An extremely jealous man, Ezra always assumed that if her takings dropped, she must have been making it with another ponce.

He recalled the evening when he had told Monica to go home because the South Road Pro' Patrol were about to swamp the area. Half an hour after the warning he had walked into the station and seen her standing behind the Custody Office desk.

"I'm sorry," she had whispered in her broad scouse accent, as soon as she was able. "But I was going home like you said, when this old geezer in a big white Daimler offered me a hundred quid just to look at it.''

Fortunately, he was able to persuade the sergeant, a former drinking pal, to let her off with a caution, even though her list of convictions for soliciting spilled out of the printer until the paper touched the floor.

When he reached the red-light district, a council street-cleaning vehicle was trundling along the gutter holding up a line of cars, company Sierras and Cavaliers mostly, headlights piercing the fine rain. There were a lot of girls standing about, some of whom Bannister hadn't seen before. Toms from out of town, he decided, wondering which area was having a purge. Sometimes they came from as far away as Bristol and Liverpool, using Intercity or getting lifts on the motorway.

It was easy to find a particular prostitute in Westhampton. The ponces had carved up the vice area into beats which they controlled and occasionally fought wars over. Monica's beat was in Saddle place. She was not there, so Bannister parked up behind the District Hospital and waited.

A short time later, seeing Monica being dropped off in front of the corner shop, Bannister drove forward, but almost immediately another car stopped alongside her. Thumping his horn, Bannister revved up his engine and aimed at the would-be client, who accelerated away. A furious Monica was left standing on the pavement.

'That'll cost you fifty quid,' she complained, as she climbed into Bannister's car and slammed the door behind her.

'I thought we were buddies?'

'Not when you're costing me money, we're not.'

'Ezra's money, you mean. Where is he?'

'Shebeen, Handsworth.'

He parked on waste ground behind a school. 'Here you

are,' he said, holding out fifty pounds.

'Don't be barmy,' she laughed. 'I was only playing my face. You don't owe me a thing, whacker.'

She twisted his rear-view mirror and flicked up a fringe of blonde hair. He knew she was only just seventeen. An absconder from a Liverpool Young Offender Institution, she had told him that she would kill herself rather than go back.

'Take it,' he said in a sudden rush of generosity. 'It's called "Spent with Informant."'

'Blood money,' she said, stuffing it down a knee-length boot. 'What d'you want to know?'

'Ezra's setting up a drug job with two guys from Manchester, and I'm trying to find out who they are.'

'News to me, but he's been easy on us lately which usually means there's something big on.'

'I need to know anything you can get. My job's on the line. Ring me at home if you hear anything, OK?'

'I'll do my best, but you've got to stop that missus of yours talking to me like I was a scouse turd floating down the Mersey.'

9

It was nine-thirty on Thursday morning when Bannister followed Conrad down the cellar steps to the drug store.

'I've got my law finals tomorrow,' Conrad muttered.

Bannister kept his thoughts to himself. They were sick of hearing about the sergeant's degree course at the university. His head was big enough already, with letters after his name he would be unbearable.

Conrad unlocked the store-room and then switched on the cobweb-covered light that hung from the centre of an arched brick ceiling. 'I hope Higginbotham isn't late. I've got to take that bloody woman upstairs to headquarters when we've finished this job.'

Bannister followed him into the former cell. It had once been painted white, but was now a dull, dusty grey. He sniffed at the cocktail of drugs which reminded him of an old pharmacy he had searched during his first week on the squad.

'There you are,' Conrad declared with a sweeping gesture. 'As easy as ABC.'

Rows of wooden shelves, sectioned off in alphabetical order, were piled high with clear polythene bags containing pills, capsules, ampules, amphetamines, barbiturates, cocaine, crack, opium, heroin, LSD, ecstasy, cannabis, reefers, scales, hooka pipes, knives, razor blades and a variety of other items taken from illegal drug users. Yellow exhibit labels were stuck up at different angles or lying flat, like daffodils after a storm. Conrad went to a high table at the far end of the narrow room and opened a red ledger marked Drugs Register.

'And this, Billy boy, is a record of all the drugs and other bits and pieces our busy squad has seized during the last few months.' He looked at the last entry and worked back until he saw a date in the Case Finalised column. Noting the name of the accused, he reached up to one of the shelves and removed the bag he wanted.

'Let's see what we've got in here,' he said, reading the back of the label. 'Nine hundred Drinamyl. Christ! These were banned yonks ago. D'you know what they were prescribed for — by the bucketful?'

Bannister shook his head and waited to be told.

'Anxiety and depression. They're time bombs loaded with stimulants and sedatives — speed and downers to an ignoramus like you. Half a dozen of these little beauties and a couple of drams, and you can shag all night. The druggies loved 'em.'

Conrad broke open the security seal on the polythene bag and took out a brown coffee jar. He then unscrewed the top and shook a pile of round blue tablets onto the table.

'Put 180 of these back into the jar while I sort out the other exhibits,' he said.

Mystified, Bannister did as he was told without comment.

Conrad sorted out more polythene bags, checking each one with the register before dropping the bag and its contents into a cardboard box that had once held a television set.

'I've done that, Sarge,' Bannister called after he had finished counting the tablets.

Conrad screwed the top back on the jar before studying the exhibit label. He then carefully altered the number nine to a two by putting a slight curve in the downward stroke and adding a dash at the bottom. When he had finished he forged the corresponding entry in the register.

Bannister watched the sergeant place the coffee jar and

exhibit label into the polythene bag, loosely fold the top, then drop it into the television box with the other exhibits he had checked. Seeing his pale face, Conrad laughed and shovelled the remaining seven hundred and twenty pills into a paper bag which he put on a shelf near the door.

'Don't look so worried,' he said. 'The money HQ gives us to pay informants is a joke. Gear is what they want.'

'To sell again,' Bannister said quietly. 'We're keeping the drug scene going.'

'You've got it in one, Bill. How else am I going to keep you in a steady job? The druggies are happy, the snouts are happy, and we get plenty of collars. And what's more, it also keeps that bloody woman off our backs. In other words, everybody's having a ball!'

Except the poor sods we keep nicking, Bannister thought.

'The super might notice,' he suggested tentatively. 'You've changed the label to 200 but there's still twenty missing out of the jar.'

'What? Higginbotham, Traffic Department? All he'll do is plonk his fat arse down and fill his face. That's what Traffic are trained for, sitting in big comfortable cars watching other people work. He'll never notice the shortage, or my expert amendments. But if by some miracle he does, I'll tell him the lab used some for analysis, and that they kept a few back for demo purposes. They do sometimes. Mind you, I've always had my doubts about those long-haired weirdos. Last time I went to the lab one of them was wearing a T-shirt with ''Eat Grass in Chernobyl'' stamped across the chest.'

Bannister sighed inwardly and started to check more polythene bags. The sergeant must be mad, risking his job for a few pills.

When the television box was almost full, Conrad pulled on a brown storeman's coat and tucked the register under his arm. He then picked up a smaller cardboard box which was empty.

'That's enough for today. Let's go and play games with old Higgy.'

Bannister, carrying the big box in both arms, trod heavily up the stone steps as he followed Conrad. He was now implicated with the sergeant and there was nothing he could do about it. He couldn't report the incident because he had aided and abetted theft and forgery.

Drinking mugs of coffee, they waited in the kitchen for the superintendent from headquarters.

'Don't forget to give our visitor a couple of your buttered sausage sarnies,' Conrad called across to Vera.

As if on cue, a large man with a friendly face and silver-grey hair blustered into the kitchen. The baggy knees and elbows of his uniform, and the shiny seat of his trousers when he turned to hang up his coat, announced that he was a traffic man.

'Higginbotham's the name, drug destruction's the game,' he boomed, sitting himself down at the kitchen table, eyes locked onto the frying pan. Vera gave him a cup of tea and a plate of sandwiches.

'All right, Sarge,' he grunted through a mouthful of bread and sausage. 'Let's start sorting. You'll have to tell me what I've got to sign. I can't tell a pep pill from a Polo mint.'

Eager to accommodate him, Conrad pulled a polythene bag out of the television box, removed the yellow label and read the number out to Bannister who checked the register before ticking off the appropriate entry. Conrad then took ten deals of cannabis resin out of the polythene bag and dropped them into the smaller box. The polythene bag and the remainder of the stored evidence — an old tobacco tin and a burnt spoon — he threw into the kitchen rubbish bin. Chatting to Vera about his caravan holidays in the South of France, Superintendent Higginbotham took no further interest in the proceedings.

After half an hour the television box was empty. Conrad took the register and the small box, which was now full of drugs, over to the superintendent.

'Sign next to the entries as I point them out please, sir,' he asked with an ingratiating smile.

Higginbotham wiped greasy fingers down his uniform trousers, then signed alongside forty-three exhibits, certifying that he had taken possession of the drugs and destroyed them in the council incinerator.

'Any big stuff this month, Sarge?' he asked.

'No, sir.'

'Good. If we can seal up this box of goodies I'll be off then.' He grinned at Vera. 'Thanks, luv. They don't make sarnies like that at headquarters.'

Bannister followed Conrad into the cellar store and watched in silent disgust as the sergeant patted the coat pockets that were full of drugs he had palmed while Higginbotham was talking to Vera.

'Cheer up,' Conrad said, looking very pleased with himself. 'We'll do bloody wonders with this lot.' Taking a roll of Sellotape out of a cupboard, he passed it to Bannister. 'Here, give this to Higgy so that he can seal his box of tricks. It'll make him feel good. Then go with him and witness the destruction. He'll send you back in one of his jam-rags.'

An hour later, a white Fiesta stopped beside a scruffy, overweight security guard at the entrance of Westhampton City Police Headquarters' car park.

'Detective Inspector Watson and Detective Sergeant Conrad, Drug Squad, to see Superintendent Davids, CID Departments,' Molly announced.

'You'll have to find somewhere at the far end, miss. The

covered area is reserved for the Police Committee.'

Molly bridled as the guard turned his back on her and raised the barrier.

'I'll give him "miss". Don't they teach them to salute around here?'

Conrad smiled happily. 'Only the big chiefs ma'am.'

Making their way around the concrete and glass six-storey office block which operational officers did their utmost to avoid, they entered the shabby green and grey reception area and boarded a lift. Watching the passing floor numbers as it laboured upwards, Molly was uncomfortably reminded of earlier visits. Awkward interviews with laid-back chief constables who thought they were God almighty. Vague, unexpected promotion-board questions from men who had never felt a collar in their lives. Unjustified reprimands from boyish ACC's with silver braid and Henry Cooper aftershave. A disciplinary hearing for the mind-boggling offence of "Smiling at a motorist while issuing a parking ticket".

They stepped out of the lift, turned right and looked down a long corridor of identical offices. A police whistle sounded and doors flew open as many of the occupants rushed for the tea trolley.

'That's a bit tasty,' Conrad said, watching rounded buttocks wrestling inside a tight skirt.

'Only time there's any activity in this place,' Molly said, stepping aside for a spotty-faced youth clutching smokey-bacon crisps and sugar-coated doughnuts.

'Hello, ma'am.'

Molly turned, 'Sergeant Longfellow! Still running the Training Department single-handed?'

'Can't do without me, ma'am. When are you coming to join us?'

'Don't think I could stand the pace,' she replied with a nod towards the queue at the end of the corridor.

'Where's Davids hiding himself these days?'

'Third on the left, ma'am. Somebody's stuck a "No Entry" sign on the door.'

Without bothering to knock, she led Conrad into the superintendent's office and caught him doing his crossword.

'Finished mine before breakfast if you need any help,' she offered.

Unimpressed by the sudden interruption, the sour-faced man scowled as he put down his newspaper.

He was like a bullfrog, she thought. Fat belly, sloping shoulders, protruding red eyes, and a low concertinaed brow under a polished pink dome. His once red hair was now a broken halo of grey; only his bushy eyebrows adding colour to an otherwise plain and podgy face.

'Next time you want to see me, Woman Inspector, make an appointment through my secretary. What do you want?' he demanded in his adenoidal Birmingham accent.

'Permission to deploy a Firearms Team.'

He sat back in his chair and glared at Watson with open hostility. He didn't like the Drug Squad. They were always raiding premises, making mass arrests and getting complaints of assault and damage to property. He had tried several times to have the squad switched from CID Departments to CID Operations.

'When?' he asked.

'Friday evening.'

'You'd better tell me why,' he growled, deliberately leaving his visitors standing in front of his huge desk.

Molly outlined the events of the past three days, starting with Ezra's first contact and finishing with the latest information about the trafficker's threat to use guns.

Davids glanced at the wall clock. He would be late for his lunch with the chief. 'Listen carefully, Woman Inspector.' He spoke slowly, emphasising each word. 'I don't expect any argument because I am not, repeat not, going to let you, and that undisciplined rabble you call a Drug Squad, loose with a Firearms Team in the middle of this city on the say so of some snivelling ponce.'

Molly's chin jutted forward. 'This is a dangerous operation. My men are entitled to protection.'

'So are the people of Westhampton,' Davids snapped back.

Glaring fiercely across the leather-topped desk Molly clenched her small fists. 'It's wrong to expect unarmed men to take on tooled-up villains, and what's more it's stupid!'

'Then call it off!' Davids shouted, face reddening. 'Who cares about a few kilos of cannabis anyway?'

He stood up. 'I'm not going to waste any more time talking to you, Miss Watson. I've got a meeting to attend.'

She jabbed a finger at the vertical blinds behind him, and the city beyond. 'You haven't got a clue what my men have to contend with out there on the streets. You've been hiding away in this office for so long you still think a panda's a frigging cuddly toy.'

Davids snatched his Crombie off the coat rack. 'I should report you for that, but I've got better ways of dealing with loud-mouthed, jumped-up females.' He stopped at the door and turned. 'You're finished, Watson.'

She watched him strut down the corridor. 'With people like him running things, it's no wonder this force is in such a mess,' she said in a quiet, barely controlled voice.

Conrad, who had stood a step behind her throughout the exchange, said nothing.

When they arrived back at Dinsall, Molly ran up the stairs and swept past Joan on the way to her office. Once inside, she dropped the door catch, knocked the handset off the telephone, and collapsed into her chair.

'Oh, God, help me!' she called out. A tear rolled down

her cheek and she started to cry, part in anger, part self-pity, but mostly due to frustration. 'What can I do to get that cretinous creature off my back,' she groaned. 'I'm working in a frigging vacuum.' She ground her teeth, a habit from early childhood, now a sure sign of her wretchedness.

After a few minutes she sat up and wiped her face. She mustn't let a pratt like Davids wear her down. He couldn't hang on forever.

'What's going on?' Joan asked Conrad when he walked into the office shortly after Watson.

'Gaffer's been blackballed by Davids.'

'Shall I take her a cup of tea?'

'Leave her. Where's Bannister?'

'He had to go home. The hot water tank's blown up and Liz's got a birthday party. She sounded frantic.'

Conrad moved behind the desk and placed his hands on Joan's shoulders, leaning forward so that his lips touched the nape of her neck. 'How is it you're so keen to look after the gaffer's needs but don't give a toss about the best looking fellow on the squad?'

'She's the boss, you're just a grubby sergeant,' Joan teased, ducking away to avoid a kiss as she went to put the kettle on.

He followed her into the alcove where she was sorting out the cups, and he wound his arms around her slim waist. 'I'm big enough for you,' he boasted, pressing himself against her.

Excited by the feel of his hard body, she did not resist. 'No you're not, and I'm a married woman.'

'You're a lonely grass widow,' he breathed into her ear, hands rising to caress her. The telephone rang.

'Duty calls,' she laughed, pushing him away with her bottom and going to answer it. Was she pleased, or disappointed by the interruption? She wasn't sure. Her husband had been gone for such a long time any man seemed welcome, even a creep like Conrad.

'Roger Turner's on the line. Anything for him?'

'Yes. I want the whole bloody squad here at three thirty for a meeting about Bannister's job, and that goes for anybody else who rings in.'

Moving into the sergeants' office, Conrad unlocked the top drawer of his desk and took out a small book of ex-directory telephone numbers. Watson's bust-up with Davids would be welcome news to some people at headquarters.

'Ring Bannister,' Conrad ordered, as Joan put his tea on the desk. 'Tell him to be here at three with the latest news from Ezra, and I don't care if his house is about to float away.'

'Listen to the big man,' she said, dodging away as she felt his hand on her leg.

'I'll have you one day,' he said softly at her retreating back.

Joan's chest tightened and the hairs on her arms stood up. Coming from any of the others she wouldn't have taken much notice, but Conrad was different. She knew that he meant it.

10

Bannister had found Ezra sitting on a park bench surrounded by noisy ducks.

'One of those bloody ducks bit me,' Ezra complained, rubbing his leg.

'Serves you right. It's dinner time. You should've brought them some bread.'

Ezra noticed the detective's grazed knuckles. 'Beating up defenceless junkies again?'

'If you must know, I was trying to fix the hot water tank. Missus played hell when I had to leave. Mucky water and greasy tools all over the place.'

Sunlight sparked off the Great Pool and Ezra tipped his hat forward to shade his eyes. 'Why don't you pay a plumber?'

'I'm here. Leave it at that, shall we? What's the panic?'

'They called me early this morning.'

'Early?'

'Tennish.'

'Yeah, crack of dawn for some.'

'They want the meet moved back to seven.'

'Realised British Rail clocks are different from everybody else's, have they?'

'They're still going on about the buyer. Same questions you asked me about them. Unless they know more, the deal's off.'

'They're getting nothing else. You can tell them that from me. There'll be two of us. And if they change the arrangements again, they can stuff their bloody gear.'

'Who's going to the meet?'

'I am.'

'Who else?'

Bannister watched the ducks as they made for the water. 'You're not going to believe this.'

'Woody?'

'Worse.'

'The new one . . . Gilbert?'

'The Gaffer!'

Ezra feigned surprise. Conrad had told him last night. 'You're just messing me about, man.'

Standing up, Bannister skimmed a small stone across the pool. 'I don't joke about getting shot. She's going to play the smoothy businesswoman who knows nothing about drugs but needs the readies to keep the VAT man off her back.'

'Some businesswoman.'

'They'll sus' her out as the law straight away.'

Ezra adusted his hat again. 'I'm not so sure. Thinking about it, she looks more like a city woman than a cop; most of your lot could've been hacked out of rock. Besides, women are into everything these days. They even run the Mafia protection rackets while their men are doing time. Some of them would chop off your tool just for the pleasure of seeing your eyes water.'

Bannister half-heartedly threw another stone. 'I'm going along as the drug expert.'

Ezra grinned. 'Have to give you some quick lessons.'

They headed back to the car park.

'Earl of Braxford's old pad,' Bannister said, remembering a school trip and pockets full of conkers as he gestured towards the grey stone mansion with its croquet lawns at the front.

Putting a hand on the top of his Derby, Ezra looked up at the imposing building. 'I could get a lot of girls in there.'

'Ezra's Cunt-ry Club?'

'That's it, man. Flashing lights over the main gate. What d'you want me to tell the dealers?'

'As I said. There'll be two of us and I'm the druggie. Say we're not going to let them know anything else about us until after the first deal. If they call it off, they'll lose a big buyer.'

'Sweet talker.'

'You're full of yourself today. Girls turning in a few extra tricks, are they?'

'Best in Westhampton. You should try one. Monica's right for you; trained her myself. Special price to friends.'

Bannister shot him a quick glance, wondering whether he suspected that she had been rabbiting. 'Sod off. I need help, not AIDS.'

'My girls are clean, man. They see the doctor every month.'

'Pox doctor you mean. When's your next contact with Manchester?'

'Said they'd call at two. I'll ring Joan. She's nice and friendly.'

'You stay away from her.'

'She needs a man in her bed at night.'

'How the hell did you work that out?'

'I can tell, it's in her voice.'

Bannister looked down at the fat Jamaican. He didn't underestimate Ezra's instincts for human nature; people were his trade. 'I suppose you'd know all about that in your game?'

'Treat them hard when they're bad, easy when they're good. Like horses, they never forget.'

'Is that how you do it. I thought you were going to tell me something new.'

They reached Bannister's car and the detective opened the door. 'Ring me before three. We've got an important meeting this afternoon and I need to be sure there's a deal on.'

'I'm mister reliable himself, man.'

'You'd better be. The gaffer's mean when she's roused.'

The sergeants' office smelled of warm armpits and stale tobacco. Men never seemed to use their noses, or if they did then they weren't too particular, Molly thought as she told Gilbert to open the window. When he had done so, and she had everybody's full attention, she spoke to them.

'We are about to embark on what promises to be the biggest and most hazardous drug-trafficking operation this department has ever undertaken. Tons of cannabis are being distributed by a gang of traffickers supplied from Morocco. Half an hour ago I received confirmation that the link men will meet Bannister and myself to arrange a test purchase. If things work out, there'll be more deals which should lead us to the star players.'

She paused, giving them time to grasp the scope and significance of the operation.

'At seven tomorrow night,' she continued, 'Bannister and I will meet two men from Manchester outside the Railway Hotel. You'll cover the meet, but you must keep it tight: we've been told that they'll be carrying guns. For reasons I won't go into, I haven't been able to get firearms back-up but units of the Special Patrol Group and Traffic Cars will be on hand to assist. Force Surveillance will video the meet. Bill and myself will be at the sharp end but your part is no less important. If you show out, the whole operation might be blown.'

The room was quiet, as though they had all stopped breathing. 'Are there any questions before I hand over to Sergeant Turner?'

Molly's eyes moved from face to face. 'Just make sure you get it right, and don't do anything that will make them jumpy. If they think they've been lured into a trap, there'll be blood on the pavements. It might be yours.'

11

After the briefing, Sergeant Smith walked into the inspector's office.

'Ah! Gordon. How's things?' Molly asked.

'All right thanks, ma'am. Macdonald's having an uphill struggle with Gilbert but there's hope.'

'Fill me in on the brothel?'

'We've nearly got enough. Be ready to raid it next Wednesday at the latest.'

'Good. Somebody's bound to complain we should've gone in as soon as we heard about it. Have you traced the owner of the house yet?'

'No, ma'am. Council can't help, and no one in the street has seen him.'

'Tell me about the girls.'

'Gilbert calls the fat one Miss Piggy and the other one Kylie. They're both about fourteen.'

'What about the punters?'

'The same as you see around our end of town every night of the week. Most of them arrive by taxi. We know the drivers. They'll be lifted after the raid and done for aiding and abetting.'

'How many punters so far?'

'Seventy, give or take a few.'

'Any particular night?'

'Varies, ma'am. Wednesdays and Thursdays seem favourite for some reason. They've had as many as ten a night. On Tuesdays, there's just one regular. Big guy, about your age. Macdonald thinks he's a professional footballer, but he can't put a name to him yet. More gold chain than Samuel's.'

'Surveillance?'

'Tactical Support Unit have managed to get an endoscope through an air-brick in the back room. That's where Kylie performs. Miss Piggy uses the bedroom. Luckily the Tuesday show's downstairs, so we've got action shots of both of them.'

The telephone rang. 'What is it, Joan?' Molly asked.

'Superintendent Graham from D Division, ma'am. Wants to speak to you urgently about a shebeen.'

'Put him on the intercom. Sergeant Smith is with me.'

The telephone clicked. 'Hello, Molly luv. Still locking them up?'

'One or two.'

'I need your squad, Molly.'

'What for this time?'

'Shebeen.'

'When and where?'

'Saturday night, Cliff Spence's place.'

''Oh no!'' Molly mouthed at Smith.

'Are you still there?' shouted the voice on the intercom.

'Yes, I'm here. That's the biggest blues party in the Midlands, but if you raid it now there'll be all kinds of aggro.'

'Can't be helped, I've had a councillor on my back; a right obnoxious little git. Threatens to raise Cain if I don't do something this weekend. Claims he's a big buddy of the chief's. He gave me a letter from one of the residents. I'll read it.'

'Don't bother,' she replied, determined not to get involved. D Division was the worst division in the force because Graham would never have a go at anything if there was likely to be problems.

'Listen to this,' he continued. ' ''The noise is a solid wall of ear-splitting decibels that upsets everyone in the street. We have to put up with the heavy thumping reggae music, not only on one night, but throughout the weekend. The racket goes on endlessly. We are being driven round the bend''. Did you get that, Molly? If we don't raid it soon, the locals will form a vigilante committee.'

'With respect, sir, *you've* got problems and I suggest *you* do something about it. Like seeing Spence and telling him to pack it in. Better still, stick some of your cars outside his house before the happy party-goers arrive. Most of the big spenders will be from out of town, using stolen motors, and driving whilst disqualified. Once they see your smart blue and whites, they'll disappear like bishops in a brothel raid.'

'So you won't help us then?'

She sighed. 'To be honest with you, sir, we haven't got the time. We're already snowed under. In any case, trying to put a hundred men into a heaving blues party in the middle of the night is asking for trouble. There's better ways of stopping it. What about Noise Abatement? Get the Environmental Health people to serve a notice under the Control of Pollution Act.'

'Come off it, when did you last see anybody from the council at one o'clock in the morning?'

'The Mayor's Ball?'

'Don't start getting funny with me, Miss Watson. You know as well as I do that they're shit scared of going anywhere near a blues party.'

'All right then, grab the sound equipment and arrest Spence for conduct likely to cause a breach of the peace; hit him where it hurts, in his pocket. It's called pro-active policing. You'll get promoted if you pretend to know what it means.'

'Cut it out, Watson. It's down to you because they'll be using drugs.'

'Who says so?'

'They always smoke pot at blues parties.'

'That's a presumption, I need evidence.'

'You're being a bloody-minded woman, Watson,' he bellowed. 'You've done enough shebeens to know exactly what I'm talking about.'

'Well, I suggest there's at least one ambitious chief inspector on your division who has the necessary know-how. If you're so keen, get on with it.'

He lowered his voice and a sixth sense warned Molly that their conversation was being taped.

'So you won't help,' Graham said.

'Yes, sir. Of course I'll help. You can have three of my men for searching and drug enquiries. All you've got to do is organise things and take charge on the night.'

The intercom died, and a moment later Molly switched it off. 'I bet he goes whining to that daft bugger, Davids.'

She stood up. 'You know the real trouble, don't you, Gordon? He's terrified that there'll be racial problems if he doesn't raid Spence's place, and also racial problems if he does.'

'And he's obviously unaware that Cliff Spence is one of your best informants.'

'It isn't only that. Spence is due to be done for something anyway; he's starting to show out. A couple of months inside will restore his credibility and his contacts.'

'If not his faith in human nature.'

Molly sat back in her seat, signalling to Smith that the subject was closed.

'How's the wife?' she asked.

'Like a red balloon and just as cheerful.'

'After three girls, I suppose you're rooting for one with a handle.'

'As long as the little blighter's OK, I don't mind. But you're right, a few more underpants on the line would even things up a bit.'

Molly only heard half of what he said. She was pondering the problems of raiding a shebeen on Saturday night. It was a complication she didn't need.

'Where's the gaffer tonight?' Fletcher asked, looking at his companions around their usual table in the back room of the Shakespeare. It was six o'clock and they were having a quick pint while they waited for the evening traffic to sort itself out.

'Retirement do. One of her old sergeants,' Macdonald replied, wiping foam off his moustache. 'Best brew in the Midlands this.'

'She doesn't have much home life,' Gilbert said, still intrigued by his new boss.

'It's a bloody shame,' Woods intervened. 'She's got a pad worth at least two hundred grand and she's never there.'

'How could the gaffer afford a place like that?' Gilbert asked.

Macdonald studied his beer. 'You ask too many bleeding questions, you do.'

'An old lady left her some money,' Turner volunteered.

'Did she die?' Gilbert asked.

Betraying his envy of Watson's good fortune, Conrad intervened sourly. 'Of course she bloody died. How else do you leave anybody a stack of money?'

'It's not right,' Woods said. 'Not when there's whole families living in one stinking room.'

'Didn't know you were so concerned about the masses,' Conrad mocked.

'Has she got a boy-friend?' Gilbert asked.

'With a body like hers, she should have half a dozen,' Williams said with conviction.

Woods held his pint glass away from his lips long enough

to make a contribution. 'She can have me any time.'

'It's the job she's in love with,' Fletcher said seriously. 'And she's definitely fired up about the trafficking gig.'

Macdonald, the oldest detective on the squad and regarded by the others as something of a father figure, spoke. 'She's the best gaffer you lot will ever have. She may get one on her now and then, like all gaffers, but she's got brains and she backs you up.'

'If the super had had any guts, he'd have put her on a charge for insubordination,' Conrad said, turning the conversation away from Macdonald's support for Watson.

'Davids was right,' Turner declared. 'We can't issue firearms on the say-so of one informant. If we did, we'd be armed all the time.'

'You tell her,' Conrad said.

'Look who's here,' Williams cried, as his partner walked into the room. Bannister picked up a drink from the bar and found a place at the table.

'Don't tell me,' Williams continued, 'Liz's thrown you out because you left her to drown in her hour of need?'

Bannister gulped down his beer, then gazed into the empty glass, his face a picture of misery as they waited for a reply. 'Worse,' he murmured. 'The mother-in-law's moved in.'

Everyone, including the landlord, burst out laughing. Walking over to the bar, Williams ordered eight halves. Passing the drinks along the table, he raised his glass. 'To the one and only Bill Bannister who gets a bollocking from Watty every day and a bollocking from Liz every night.'

'Ah . . .' they all chorused.

Bannister looked up and smiled ruefully before taking a long slow draught of beer.

'That's better, Bill,' Woods shouted. 'Enjoy yourself. You might be dead tomorrow.'

12

'Hello Joan,' Molly said when she arrived at the office. 'Friday already. Where did the week go?'

Joan shrugged. 'The same way as all the others we've worked together.'

Molly was puzzled. The squad secretary's early-morning cheerfulness usually matched her own.

'How long have we worked together now?'

Joan lowered her eyes and pretended to read a statement beside the keyboard.

'Two years.'

'Any regrets?'

'No.'

Molly gave up, knowing that if there was anything wrong, Joan would tell her eventually. They were both lonely women and sometimes they shared confidences.

She did not have to wait long. After she had finished dictating the draft of a drugs lecture for the Rotary Club, Joan told her that she was feeling low because her husband's overseas posting had been extended for a further six months.

Later, when Joan walked into the inspector's office, it was her turn to be concerned. Molly looked ill and she was staring vacantly out of the window. Joan tapped the leg of the desk with her shoe until Molly turned and faced her.

'Sorry, Joan,' she said in a far-away voice. 'I've just had a bust-up with Davids. We've got to do a shebeen tomorrow night.'

'Doesn't give us much time, ma'am.'

'It isn't only that, we're being set up. There's bound

97

to be trouble.'

'D'you want me to come in? Weekend shopping for one doesn't take long.'

Molly looked briefly out of the window, watching the crows as they circled above the trees then settled onto the bare branches. She could manage without Joan, but it would help her to take her mind off an absent husband if she had something to do.

'Yes, that would be very useful, thank you,' Molly said, clearing a space on her desk and reaching for a new folder on which she printed SHEBEEN in bold red letters.

'Anything else, ma'am?' Joan asked.

'No — yes. You could look at Jackman's statement. It isn't up to your usual standard, I'm afraid.'

Perplexed, Joan took the drug file from her boss and started to read the statement as she walked out of the office. She's right, Joan thought angrily, it isn't up to my usual standard — I didn't type it.

The offices were empty when Joan returned from her lunch break. She took a large iron key out of the safe drawer then hurried down to the cellar and unlocked a door marked Confidential Waste. After she had found the black plastic rubbish bag she was looking for, she dragged it up two flights of stairs and into the office. When she tipped the contents of the bag onto the floor, the smell of half-eaten sandwiches, fatty pieces of cooked meat and brown apple cores rose to meet her.

Forcing herself to delve through the stationery, she eventually found what she was looking for, a crumpled typed copy of the statement made by Delroy Jackman shortly after his arrest. Smoothing it out, she saw that half-way down the page the word ''seven'' had been altered to read ''several'' immediately before the phrase ''blocks of cannabis resin''.

Joan compared it with the statement that Molly had complained about, and immediately understood what had happened. Someone had tried to alter the first copy she had typed, but had made such a mess of it they had thrown it away and retyped the whole page. Although the second copy, which Watson had returned to her, looked perfect, a sentence did not make sense because several words had been omitted.

Joan then examined Jackman's original statement which had been taken down by Conrad in his atrocious writing. The inspector often complained about ''Conrad's Gaelic graffiti''. Alterations would normally have been impossible to find in such a mess of untidy strokes and blotchy curves, but Joan knew exactly where to look. Holding the page up to the light, she saw that the word ''seven'' had again been changed to read ''several''.

He must have stolen some of the cannabis and forged the statement to cover it up. Watson had told her that over three kilos of resin had been found at Jackman's house but Joan had no way of knowing how much Conrad had taken before sending the remainder to the laboratory for analysis. All she had typed on the report was the usual ''a quantity of resinous subtance''. Only a forensic scientist was qualified to describe it as cannabis, and to state the exact weight to the nearest gramme.

Conrad would know that with a guilty plea the cannabis would not be required in court, and nobody would bother to check it when it was finally returned from the lab. The forgery, she decided, must be in case of any unforeseen problem, such as a last minute not-guilty plea. Conrad was too cunning to be caught out by something as basic as that. What was he stealing drugs for anyway? Surely not to sell.

She momentarily relived yesterday's caress and her body went cold. What had she been thinking of? Not only was he sly, he was a thief: a bent cop.

Her hands were black by the time she had stuffed the old papers back into the bag and returned it to the cellar store. Soaking her hands in hot soapy water, she wondered what she should do. Molly had got so much on at the moment, what with Bannister's job, the brothel and the shebeen, it didn't seem fair to bother her with anything else. At least that's what she told herself. The truth was that she didn't want to be involved. As much as she disliked Conrad, she wasn't going to be the one to send him to prison.

Carefully folding both statements, she slid them into an envelope which she dropped into her handbag.

Molly lunched in A Division's plush Social Club, mostly paid for by the proceeds of two overworked one-armed bandits. These were now surrounded by the regular group of day-shift workers who took over the machines every lunch hour. She asked Turner if he had seen Bannister.

'Not today, ma'am. Can I get you a drink?'

'Lime and lemon please, Roger.' She looked around the crowded room and wished that the early shift would go home so that she could see who was who.

Turner handed her a drink and they moved away from the bar.

'Thanks, Roger. Bad news I'm afraid. We've got a job on tomorrow night, a shebeen. Tell Smithy as soon as he arrives, then pass the word on to the men. I want everybody in the office at nine tomorrow morning. Get a message to Conrad. He's not having any more time off.'

'Good job we've got no homes to go to,' Turner said, polishing his glasses as he worried about his children who were being looked after by friends and relatives.

The ground-floor briefing room had no windows. Rows of steel-framed chairs faced a small table. Beside it was an old schoolroom blackboard and easel.

Molly, hands clasped behind her back, waited in front of the table. Knowing she had to face an audience and later meet the drug traffickers, she had dressed in a stylish black and white check jacket over a red cashmere sweater. A black skirt and comfortable black shoes completed the outfit.

Sergeant Turner hovered about behind her as the first group of men filed into the room and spread themselves along the chairs at the back of the room. Molly pretended not to notice the nudging elbows and the suggestive sniggers. She knew that once she started to speak, their minds would switch to the operation.

'Right,' she began after most of the seats had filled. 'You all know who I am. Let's see who we've got. Special Patrol Group?'

Inspector Jones, a hulk of a man, stood up. Chest out, chin in, he was every soldier's picture of a drill sergeant.

Molly acknowledged him with a pleasant smile. 'It's good to have you aboard, Dai . . . . Traffic?'

'Sergeant Murphy, eight smart officers and four very clean cars, ma'am,' shouted a completely bald man, who stood up and sat down again in one movement.

'Surveillance?'

There was no response and she had to search the room to find the group of men in the far corner. They could have been taken for electricians, service engineers or gas fitters. One of them touched the peak of his flat cap.

They're so taken with this undercover business, they won't admit even to themselves who they really are, Molly concluded.

She glanced at the wall clock. Where had Bannister got to?

After welcoming the assembled men, she gave them a short introduction to the operation, then stood aside for Turner who started to brief them in his slow, meticulous style. Molly sat in the empty row of front seats.

A short time later Bannister sat down next to her.

'Sorry I'm late, ma'am.'

'What took you so long?'

'You'll have to halt the briefing, ma'am.'

'Halt you, you mean. Time's important in this job.'

'They didn't call Ezra until the last minute.'

'When I say two o'clock, I mean two o'clock!' she said, louder than she intended.

Turner stopped talking and all eyes switched to Bannister.

'The meet at the Railway's off, ma'am.'

Their audience groaned at the unexpected news.

'Quiet,' Molly ordered.

'It's been moved to Birmingham, ma'am.'

'What has? The Railway Hotel or Blackpool Tower?'

Men behind her started to laugh but she turned and cut them off with a stoney glare.

'The meet, ma'am,' Bannister replied. He felt famous and vulnerable at the same time, like the victim at a public hanging.

'Whereabouts in Birmingham?'

'It's outside the Norfolk Hotel, Hagley Road.'

Molly's mind ran through the additional problems as she stood up and faced the room.

'Right! Section Commanders get yourselves a cup of coffee. I'll see you in ten minutes' time. The rest of you be back in here at three-thirty.'

As the room cleared, Bannister waited for his boss to errupt, but she was preoccupied with new plans.

'One sugar for me, please,' she said quietly.

13

Molly and Bannister left Birmingham railway station, riding the escalator into the bright neon of The Pallasades shopping centre. People resting on bench seats stared at the elegant woman and her shabby escort with his long unkempt hair and ragged jeans. The mismatched couple weaved between sales kiosks and plastic trees, then made their way down the ramp into New Street, dodging overladen shoppers and grey-faced office workers as they headed for the taxi rank outside the Midland Hotel. It was a cold, blustery day, with litter swirling about and flags on important buildings flying proud in an east wind that blew, uninterrupted, all the way from the Urals.

'That's better,' Molly sighed, as she shut the cab door, pleased to escape the noise of the traffic and the shrill chorus of squabbling starlings fighting for their favourite roosts.

The taxi pushed into the bumper to bumper stream of traffic that headed towards the Five Ways underpass. Both detectives were quiet, Molly psyching herself up for the meet and rehearsing her lines. She didn't feel afraid of the guns: not that she thought of herself as being particularly brave, but because she was able to shut off that part of her mind. It was only after coming out of dangerous situations that she sometimes had the shakes.

Bannister interrupted her thoughts. 'What did the Birmingham City lads say when you told them we'd be working on their patch, ma'am?'

'Not a lot. They promised to send a van to pick up the pieces if there's a shoot-out.'

'Did they mind our mobiles?'

'Pleased to see them. It seems that their police committee is even tighter than ours. They think the police are so well paid they should provide their own patrol cars.'

'A red band around my old banger would cover up some rust,' Bannister muttered.

As they approached the floodlit Norfolk Hotel, Ezra was standing on the forecourt, holding onto his hat in the strong wind and looking anxiously in the direction of Westhampton. He had not been told that they would be travelling by train and taxi.

Giving the driver an over-generous tip, Molly asked him to return for them at seven.

Ezra moved forward to meet them, his face creased with worry, eyes furtive. 'Over there,' he fussed, pointing towards a black Mercedes parked in the road next to the hotel. 'We've got to join them.'

As they approached, the rear offside door of the car swung open. 'In here,' ordered someone from inside. Ezra pushed down on Bannister's shoulder and then followed him into the back. Molly hesitated, fighting the temptation to look for signs of the back-up team.

'Come on missus, we ain't got all fucking night,' demanded the same voice.

She was still shutting the door when the car surged forward and accelerated past the observation van towards St Augustine's Church, standing on its island at the centre of the junction. The car slewed crab-wise in a racing driver's wheel-lock spin around the church, then powered on towards the end of the road a few hundred metres away. Swerving on two wheels, they turned left into a busy thoroughfare and roared off again, headlights on full-beam. The Mercedes crossed two major junctions, hurtling past braking cars without slackening speed, then turned right into a side road.

The back-seat passengers were tossed from side to side,

Ezra's head bouncing against the roof, denting his Derby. Passing Winson Green Prison, the driver expertly zigzagged through a series of minor roads. Tyres skidded, rubber burnt and pedestrians dived for cover as the Mercedes mounted pavements to avoid the oncoming traffic. Molly braced herself against the back of the seat, trying to work out where they were being taken. Ezra clutched his hat and cursed under his breath.

Suddenly, they slowed and the Mercedes turned into a dark alleyway, so narrow the sides of the car almost scraped along the high brick walls. They were trapped.

The driver switched on the interior lights, then looked round at his passengers. 'Enjoy the ride, folks?' he asked in a strong Mancunian accent. 'I've only been nicked twice for causing death by dangerous.'

His laughter was a harsh, mirthless sound. A purple birthmark completely covered the left side of his face, tendrils reaching out to his ear and across the ridge of his nose. A hulk of a man, his jacket looked several sizes too small for his broad chest and long, muscular arms. Molly guessed he was about thirty.

Dots of light signalled from both ends of the alleyway. 'No sweat, folks. Just a few of the lads making sure you're safely tucked in,' the driver mocked.

The front-seat passenger turned slowly. He was about ten years older than the driver. A short, obese man with greasy black hair and a slept-in suit. Seeing Molly for the first time, he sucked air. 'You're no bleeding drug dealer.'

She sat taller in her seat. 'I don't know who's supposed to be in charge of this circus, but I'm here to trade, not to be bounced around town by a lame-brained driver who thinks he's Nigel Mansell.'

'I tell you, Spider, something's up,' cried the front seat passenger, glancing at the driver.

'Fuck me, Duke, you're right,' he agreed, staring at

Molly. 'She ain't like no dealer I've ever seen before.'

'Come on! Who are you?' Duke demanded. His accent was less pronounced than the driver's and he took short asthmatic breaths.

Molly eyed him coolly. 'Listen, mister whoever-you-are. I deal with professionals, not poseurs. Take me back to the hotel before I lose my temper.'

Spider scowled menacingly. 'How do we know you're not a female fucking copper trying to set us up?'

'She hates the filth. We both do, for Christ's sake,' Bannister intervened.

'At least you're all right mate,' Duke said, taking in Bannister's Mickey Mouse T-shirt and casual dress. Duke scrutinised Molly's face. 'There was a van parked in the road outside the hotel. Green with no windows. Looked like an obs van to me.'

Molly's dead-pan expression gave nothing away. When she was a girl, she had dreamed of being an actress.

'I don't know what you're on about, and what's more I don't care. It's make-your-mind-up time. Talk business, or get me out of here.' The men in the front seats continued to stare at her suspiciously. 'You've got a decision to make, mister,' Molly pressed.

Spider spoke. 'For fuck's sake, Duke, let's get on with it. We'll be here all bloody night.'

Duke's attention moved to Ezra. 'You're quiet. You set this up. Who is this broad?'

Ezra wiped his sweating brow. 'I told you, man, I don't know.' He nodded towards Bannister. 'Ask him.'

'She's all right,' Bannister said immediately.

Rubbing his chest inside a dirty white shirt, Duke coughed. 'We've got some good gear to sell, but we must unload it by Wednesday.'

'How much gear?' Bannister asked.

'Twenty kilos. But that's only the start. Our Arab mate

gets regular deliveries. If you've got the bread, you can have half a ton whenever you want. It's good stuff. Moroccan or Paki black. There's also the red. I don't know what it's called. If you want bush, we can get that as well. I don't like it myself.'

Seemingly at ease, Molly looked at Duke's greasy face. 'I've no idea which dope sells the best, and I'm still not satisfied that I can trust you.'

'Look,' Duke said, 'we don't know you, you don't know us. There's a lot of crooks in this game and we ain't gonna be set up. The deal will be done right. You can trust us, and your money'll be safe.'

'Who mentioned money?' she asked.

Lighting a cigarette, Spider deliberately blew the smoke into her face. 'We've told you,' he said. 'Are you fucking deaf or something? As long as everything's on the level, you've got nothing to worry about.'

Molly spoke to Duke. 'I'm not getting in too deep until I'm sure you're straight. Twenty kilos will be enough for the first deal.'

Duke lowered his voice. 'You listen carefully, Doll. Twenty kilos at ten thousand a kilo on the streets, makes two hundred thousand quid. You can have it for half, less twenty-five per cent. Only seventy-five grand. At that price you'll make a bleeding bomb.'

'Just a minute,' Bannister interrupted. 'What exactly are you selling?'

'Best Moroccan. All you've got to do, mate, is produce the readies. Used notes in different denominations.'

Molly edged forward in her seat, eyes moving from Duke to Spider and back again to Duke. 'Who's the Arab you mentioned?' she asked.

'He gets the gear. There's a few of us in it together.'

'Why isn't he here then?'

Duke's breath came quicker and he started to wheeze.

'. . . . He's in London . . . . You'll meet him when you go down to do the deal.'

Coughing phlegm into the palm of his hand, Duke wiped it off on the carpet covering the transmission tunnel. Breathless, he faced Molly again. 'He . . . won't deal anywhere else . . . scared of being stitched up.'

'Is he all right?' Molly queried anxiously. 'He's not here and I don't know anything about him. Thinking about it, I'd feel a lot better if I knew who you were —.'

'For Christ's sake!' Duke exclaimed. He snatched the half-smoked cigarette out of Spider's mouth and threw it through the open window, hitting the back of his hand on the brick wall as he did so. Cursing viciously he sucked at skinned knuckles. The other people in the car watched in silence, at least two of them seeing the funny side of Duke's self-imposed misfortune.

When he spoke to Molly, his gravelly voice was almost inaudible. 'Look, I'm not happy about this lot. I'm calling it a day. We'll take you back to the hotel, and that's it.'

Molly shrugged as if she had no further interest. 'Suit yourself, I can go elsewhere. I need fifty kilos a month — every month.'

Duke and Spider exchanged looks. 'That's half a million!' Duke exclaimed.

'No it isn't,' Molly parried. 'At your prices it's one hundred and eighty-seven thousand, five hundred pounds. With that amount I'd be asking for an extra discount. Let's say I might be willing to pay a hundred and fifty thousand.'

'I'll see the Arab,' Duke said eagerly. 'How are you going to move all that gear?'

'Don't worry about it. If I didn't have a market, I wouldn't want it, would I?'

Duke laughed, 'Yes, you're right. Look, we've got to trust each other or we won't get anything done.' He nodded at Ezra. 'He's here with you. That's good enough for me.

108

When do you want the gear?'

'Not before Tuesday. I've got business to finish in Carlisle.'

Duke glanced at Spider. 'We've got to go abroad on Wednesday to fix up some more deals.'

Molly made a show of looking through her diary. 'Let me see . . . . Yes, Tuesday's all right. How about one o'clock? I can catch the overnight train and still have time to draw the cash in London.'

'Yeah . . .' Spider drawled. 'One's OK, plenty of folks about then.'

Duke's eyes darted between Molly and Bannister. 'You know the score. The money will be all right because we won't know where it is until the switch.'

'What do you mean?' Molly asked with an exaggerated frown, starting to enjoy her new role even though she was trapped inside the stuffy car.

'The switch . . . . Your mate comes with us to check out the drugs, then he'll take us to wherever you've stashed the bread.'

'I don't understand. Where will the merchandise be?'

Duke's body shook with another bout of coughing, his eyes disappearing into folds of sweaty fat. 'You'll finish me off, lady. It'll be somewhere you don't know about. Same as we won't know where your cash will be. That way there's no chance of anybody knocking you on the head and nicking it.'

'Here, hang on a bit,' Bannister said, lighting up a cigarette. 'Before we start making all these bloody travel arrangements, I think your price is a bit over the top.'

'Don't you start, mate,' Duke said, face pained. He seemed genuinely about to have a seizure. 'It's bad enough with her daft questions.' He crossed his arms over his chest and bent forward.

Molly knew that they'd got him going, but she didn't

believe he'd give anything away. Asthma or no asthma, he wasn't the type who would crack that easily.

When he recovered Duke turned towards Bannister. 'You know the prices, mate. Dealers are paying five grand a kilo down the smoke. You're getting it at three seven-fifty. We're being kosher about this. It's top quality gear.'

Molly unobtrusively waved smoke in Duke's direction, determined to increase the pressure in a final attempt to get something out of him. 'I recall someone mentioning a dealer price of three thousand,' she said.

'Yeah!' Spider growled. 'Before the bleeding Beatles.'

Bannister intervened. 'What's the arrangements then?'

'Do you know London?' Duke enquired.

'No.'

'The Cumberland Hotel is the best place to meet. Do you know where that is?'

'I told you, I couldn't find Big Ben.'

Duke suddenly turned to Molly. 'You're a yuppie. You should know your way around.'

'I do have connections in the City,' she conceded primly, 'but I prefer to keep away if I possibly can. Too many ice-cream-licking, north-country tourists.'

If Duke thought she was having a go at him, he did not show it. 'The hotel's near Marble Arch.'

Checking the luminous hands of her watch, Molly decided that it would be wise to end the meeting while she was ahead. 'My taxi will be waiting.'

'Yes, we've agreed on the time,' Duke said. 'Let our friend here know if you're OK with the Cumberland. We need an answer by Monday afternoon at the latest.'

Spider switched on the ignition and eased the car out of the alley-way. Duke waved at shadowy figures who vanished into the darkness as the car turned into the road.

A short distance from the Norfolk Hotel Molly leaned forward between the two men in the front of the Mercedes.

110

'Don't drop us too near that van you were on about.'

'Why not?' Duke asked. 'We're doing nothing wrong, and I'd like to have another shufti at it.'

Shortly afterwards they arrived at the hotel. There was no sign of the observation van but a taxi was waiting on the forecourt. Leaving the car without a word, Molly and Bannister boarded the taxi.

'New street,' Molly ordered.

As they drove away from the hotel she could see Duke and Spider watching them from the black car which had not moved. Ezra, who'd hardly spoken, was hunched down in the back.

'Thank Christ that's over,' Bannister said. 'I thought we were goners.'

Molly rested her head on the back of the seat and closed her eyes.

'Bloody hell,' Bannister continued, adrenaline still pumping. 'Was I glad to get out of that sodding car. Trapped like rats we were. They're a right pair of head-bangers.'

Molly looked through the rear window. 'Scared stiff, the pair of them,' she said quietly, still trying to make sense of their unusual meeting.

'I'm not so sure. That Spider's a lunatic. Did you see the veins in his neck? Like bloody hose pipes they were. I never thought they'd deal; not after they'd said you were in the job.'

'Greed was the key. Their eyes lit up when I said I wanted fifty kilos a month? After that they couldn't think straight. They would've done the deal on the top of the Statue of Liberty if I'd asked them to. I hope the back-up crew got some pictures. Any sign of Traffic?'

'No one could have kept up with that driver, ma'am. He's out of his skull. When we bombed full-tilt over those give-way signs, I thought we'd had it.'

'What did you think of fatso?'

'He's a cunning sod, ma'am. Mind you, the way he was gasping for breath, I thought we'd end up giving him the kiss of life.'

'It's a good job you're the first-aider,' Molly murmured.

'Sorry about London, ma'am. I was gob-smacked.'

'So I noticed. Don't worry about it. If everything had been too pat they'd have known it was a set-up. Ezra wasn't much help though.'

A police car overtook them, blue lights flashing and sirens wailing as it sped towards the city centre.

'I think Ezra was frightened about something, ma'am. I could feel him shaking. Just wait until the next time he starts telling me about how he's mixed it with heroin dealers in Harlem. I'd be surprised if he's even seen a bloody gun.'

'Neither did we, this time. It might not be so easy in future.' She hadn't been frightened in the car, but now she felt weak kneed and light-headed. She took deep silent breaths, concentrating, counting — five in, five out — keeping her mind occupied.

Bannister licked his dry lips. 'I'm bursting for a pint.'

'It's all that smoke.'

'Sorry, ma'am, but I had to play the part. Thought it might keep Duke coughing.'

'Steady your nerves you mean. I'm surprised he didn't knock the cigarette down your throat.' She had another quick look through the rear window. 'I'm not so sure about that Duke. He talked too much. Most of the traffickers I've ever dealt with have been the strong, silent type who use words as sparingly as I use fifty pound notes. I don't know why, but it didn't feel right, somehow.'

'It was pretty convincing to me, ma'am.'

Molly stared at him, replaying in her mind the haggling inside the Mercedes; Duke throwing in the towel then changing his mind as soon as she had mentioned future deals. They were too keen for her liking.

Bannister wouldn't shut up but she was learning to turn him off.

'Tell you what, though, ma'am,' she heard him say in the distance. 'They've been handled. Sounded like regular CID to me. They knew an obs van when they saw one. Dracula-face shouldn't be too hard to trace. There can't be many guys as evil-looking as him about.'

The taxi passed under the bridge that linked the Hyatt Hotel with the Conference Centre and Molly felt more relaxed. She remembered her last concert in the magnificent Symphony Hall: Simon Rattle, talented and youthful with a boyish smile and that gorgeous bum. Why couldn't she have a super like that?

New Street was now quiet. The shops were shut, the starlings slept. A young couple in matching anoraks held hands and stared at sunny posters in a travel agent's window. Birmingham was a more friendly place at night, she decided.

Alighting from the taxi, the detectives returned to The Pallasades. They then crossed the mall and ducked into a doorway opposite the station escalator. The afternoon crowds had been replaced by bored cleaners operating electric sweepers. A dwindling line of late workers rode down the moving staircase.

Ten minutes later, satisfied that they had not been followed, Molly and Bannister made their way down to the station. They arrived at the platform in time to jump aboard the eight twenty-three to Westhampton.

14

Leaving Westhampton station, Molly made sure that their third taxi of the evening was not being followed. She then slid across the glass partition to shut out the driver and spoke to Bannister.

'The decision to meet in London makes things a lot easier.'

'What will the super say?'

'He can please himself,' she retorted. 'It'll be much easier down there. We can get seventy-five grand from the Met without any trouble. Davids wouldn't let us have seven-fifty; you'd think it came out of his own bank account.'

'Yes, ma'am.' What else could he say? It was a long way from slipping a few quid to a prostitute for information about the vice scene. This was the big time as far as he was concerned. He glanced sideways at his boss, seeing her with new eyes. She wasn't just a looker; she was good, very good, and he was starting to like her.

'I don't think the back-up team had much chance, ma'am,' he said, trying to head off a bust-up when they returned to the office.

'As long as they've got some mug shots it doesn't matter. We must know who we're dealing with before Tuesday.'

Turner was waiting for them in the general office, his look of relief shadowed by apprehension. 'Am I glad to see you, ma'am.'

'Where was that alley-way?' Molly demanded.

'What alley-way?'

'The one we were hijacked to.'

'Traffic never had a chance, ma'am. The Merc went clean off the screen.'

'That's the second time this week I've heard that lame-brain excuse. What do we buy their road-racers for?'

The sergeant held her angry gaze for a moment before taking refuge in the business of polishing his glasses.

Molly frowned at the coats and personal radios abandoned on the desks. 'Where is everybody?'

'SPG and Surveillance have gone home. I've sent the lads over to the Shakespeare for a break.'

'You what? We could've been lying in some dark alley with our throats cut!'

'Sorry, ma'am, we did our best. They must've done a ton down Rotton Park Road. There didn't seem much point in mounting a search after that. We'd only have disturbed you while you were doing the business.'

'Any complaints of dangerous driving?'

'Nothing, ma'am. I checked when I asked Birmingham Control to keep an eye out for the trafficker's motor.'

'Hum, not surprising I suppose. Not for a place that holds formula-two races around the ring road. What did Surveillance get?'

'No good I'm afraid, ma'am. Said it was too dark to take pictures of them sitting in the car, and they didn't get out.'

'Too flaming dark! Haven't they heard of light intensifiers?'

'Sorry, ma'am. Something to do with distance and angles.'

Molly picked up the anxiety in the sergeant's voice and relented. He seemed to have everybody's share of bad luck. 'Don't worry about it, Roger. We'll get them in London.'

A relieved Turner put his glasses back on. 'There is some good news, ma'am.'

'Go on.'

115

'Smithy's dashed off to see his missus. She's had a little boy.'

'Well then, what are we hanging about up here for? Let's go and wet the baby's head.'

The men sitting around the table in the back lounge of the Shakespeare were subdued, expecting the worst.

'Evening Jim,' Molly called across the bar. 'Halves all round, one for yourself, and my usual. Anything to eat?'

'Cheese and onion sandwiches?'

'Great! You'd better do a tray for the gannets.' She left some money on the bar and joined her men at the table. They fidgeted with cigarette packets, boxes of matches, and anything else they could lay their hands on, none of them prepared to look her in the eye. Molly smiled to herself, feeling like a headmistress in a classroom full of naughty boys. 'To Gordon Smith junior!' she toasted, as soon as the drinks arrived.

'The poor blighter will be spoilt rotten,' Macdonald ventured. She knew he would be the first to speak and she could have guessed that Woods would be the next.

'I bet Smithy's already ordered his first pair of soccer boots,' he added.

Williams resolutely put down his empty glass. 'We thought we'd lost you, ma'am.'

'You nearly did. I've never travelled so fast on four wheels in my life. What do you say, Bill . . . ?'

Before he could answer, the licensee arrived with a large tray of food and the squad tucked in.

'I was ready for that,' Bannister announced, having put away his fourth sandwich.

Molly had eaten sparingly, thinking again over the night's events. After an uncertain start it had gone reasonably well. Bannister hadn't let her down, and they'd all but clinched the first deal. But who were the traffickers? They didn't ring true, somehow. Spider was a typical heavy who happened to be useful behind the wheel, and Duke seemed more like a second-hand car dealer than a drug trafficker.

Silence disturbed her reverie and she looked up to find everyone watching her. Pushing away her plate, she marshalled her thoughts.

'Well, you now know the kind of people we are up against. Fortunately there were no shooters and no one was hurt. The meet went well and we've agreed to make a test purchase on Tuesday. Did any of you have a good look at them, or do you have any ideas about their identity?'

No one replied.

'They called themselves Duke and Spider,' she continued. 'Duke seemed to be the guy in charge and Spider was the driver. I'll let you have their descriptions later.' Standing up, she spoke to Turner. 'Get another round in will you, Roger? I'm going to phone Scotland Yard.

As soon as she had gone, Turner faced Bannister. 'Right, Bill, let's have it. What went on in that perishing car?'

Bannister spoke quietly, his mates leaning forward as he gave them a blow-by-blow account.

'It must have been pretty hairy when you found yourselves trapped in the Merc?' Gilbert said when Bannister had finished.

'Too true,' he replied. 'But you should've seen Watty, she never turned a hair. The first thing she did was to give them a tatering.'

'She's good at that,' Woods said.

Gilbert, scavenging bits of onion off the tray, nodded emphatically.

'I told you she'd been around,' said Turner, one of Watson's staunchest supporters since she had helped him to sort out his domestic problems. 'She's the best undercover DI in this force.'

'She must be,' Bannister said. 'She sounded so bloody genuine, I started to believe it myself.'

'What's that?' Molly asked as she returned to the table.

'Talking about old times, ma'am,' Woods lied.

Molly spoke to everyone. 'Don't forget, lads, full turn-out for the shebeen meeting tomorrow morning. It shouldn't take too long.'

She asked Turner and Bannister to join her at a table in the corner. When they were seated, she informed them that she had arranged to be at New Scotland Yard with Bannister on Monday morning.

'Time please, gentlemen,' called the landlord.

'One for the road, ma'am?' Bannister offered.

'No thanks, Bill,' she replied, pleased to have been asked.

15

The man taking his dog for a late-night walk was surprised to see lights burning inside the vacant factory. The biggest building on the industrial estate, its workshop, now an empty shell, was the size of a football pitch.

Peering through a bolt hole, he saw the backs of a large gathering of uniformed police officers who stood listening to a woman sporting a sheepskin coat. She was standing on a wooden pallet at the centre of the workshop, her clear voice echoing through the building. It was not a local accent, the man thought, more like London or the Home Counties. Standing beside her was a small, rough-looking group of men, mostly wearing jeans and casual jackets. They looked like city-centre layabouts. A line of blue Transit vans and a number of cars were parked at one end of the workshop. Clouds of steam rose from a stainless-steel urn on a trestle table piled high with food boxes.

A German Shepherd padded into view less than a metre away from the inquisitive man. Nose in the air and ears pricked, the dog stopped dead in its tracks, then barked furiously at the bolt hole, leaping against its collar and dragging its handler towards a side door.

Outside, the man and his poodle fled into the night. Several men started to follow the dog handler until their sergeants called them back into line.

The woman on the pallet waited until she had everyone's full attention again. Sixty of the one hundred and ten uniformed officers were from the Special Patrol Group; the remainder were drawn from Divisional strength.

'For the benefit of those who don't know me, I'm

Detective Inspector Watson and I'm in charge of the Force Drug Squad.' She gestured towards the men standing beside her. 'Here they are, take a good look. I don't want you pegging them in the mêlée . . . . Not before they've finished their assignments anyway,' she added, in an unsuccessful attempt to lighten the briefing. She cast her eyes over the sea of silent faces and resolved to stick to her script in future.

'As a result of information received,' she continued, 'I have obtained search warrants under the Misuse of Drugs and Liquor Licensing Acts. In other words, we're going to raid a shebeen!'

She noticed a sprinkling of new uniforms and highly polished toe-caps. 'For the benefit of those who haven't done one before, a shebeen, or blues party if you like, is all about making money; lots of money. The organiser will earn a small fortune selling watered-down spirits, beer, and cans of lager at double the normal price. He'll have to pay for the ''sound man'' but if he gets a star performer, followers will travel from all over the country and the party will be going full swing throughout the weekend.'

She thumbed through her notes. 'Tonight's target is an old terraced house which will be packed solid with young blacks, a scattering of toms, and half a dozen drug traffickers. If it's anything like last month's shindig, we can expect top cats from London, Liverpool, Birmingham, Nottingham and Manchester. Local dealers will also be active, selling resin or wraps of bush. If you don't know what cannabis is like already, you will after tonight: the smell will hit you as soon as you enter the house.

Should you come across any Rastas, you might find crack: off-white rocks about the size of a pea. Look out for bent Coke cans with burn marks. They use them to heat up the drug before drawing the smoke through the hole at the top.'

She paused, knowing they were reaching the end of their attention span.

'There are two objectives: obtaining evidence to prove the illegal sale of alcohol, and arresting those in possession of controlled drugs. Users will be welcome, but the people we're really after are the traffickers: the big guys who distribute large amounts of gear around the country. Also the local drug dealers who buy from them. Be on your guard against knives, razors or lino cutters. If anyone's cornered in possession of drugs, they're likely to put up a fight. Team up in pairs, and watch your partner's back.

Once we've got some sort of order in the place, get your pro formas filled in as quickly as possible. If there's any doubt about having the correct name and address, check the voters list. When you're satisfied that you've got the right person, take him or her to the Reception Sergeant and have them photographed. Don't be shy, I want pretty pictures of you standing beside each person you detain. That way, there can be no question of mistaken identity if you're challenged at court in a few months time. Don't forget to take off your helmets.'

A fresh-faced policewoman, standing at the front, raised her arm. 'Do we have to take our hats off, ma'am?' Several men at the back hooted derisively.

'No, that won't be necessary,' Molly said kindly.

She tucked the clipboard under her arm and surveyed the raiding party, willing them to do their best. 'Are there any more questions?'

'How d'you spell resignation?' someone yelled. A number of men laughed, the high-pitched nervous sounds of men about to do battle.

Raising her voice, Molly addressed the assembly. 'A word of warning about the young bucks. Most of them are simply out to listen to their music and have a good time. If you handle them nice and easy with a smile and a joke they'll respond in kind and we should manage to get by without too many problems.'

She sensed that her audience was becoming restless, and noticed some of them edging towards the tea urn. 'Hot drinks, pre-packed lunches, or whatever you want to call them at this ungodly hour on a Sunday morning, are on the table next to the SPG vans. Thank you and good luck.'

Stepping down from the pallet, Molly went over to her squad. 'Off you go,' she said to Bannister. 'Don't forget, we need to know what it's like in there. Make sure Ezra finds out where the takings are kept and who's dealing.' Without a word, the big detective buttoned up his denim jacket and headed for the side door.

'Come on, lads,' Molly said, rubbing her hands together as she led them towards the trestle table. 'Let's get some food before the SPG wolf the lot.'

Collecting a drink and a packet of sandwiches, Molly sat down on the pallet and warmed her hands around a mug of hot chocolate. Other shebeens came to mind and she wondered if she had missed anything in her preparations. She hadn't told the raiding party about the six van-loads of mutual-aid men fully kitted out in riot gear, who were standing by at C Division's headquarters. The raiding party would be more careful if they thought they were on their own.

Only a few selected people knew where they were going. She had used the factory as a rendezvous point to give her team a better chance of surprise. Security was always a major problem; local detectives, in particular, not being averse to tipping off informants who might otherwise have attended the party. It would not be the first time that she had raided an empty house. Local hospitals and the emergency services had been warned in case there was serious public disorder, petrol bombing or looting, similar to that which had followed raids in other parts of the country. The force helicopter with its thirty-million candle-power night sun, seven-hundred-watt public-address system, heli-tele, heat-seeking equipment and infra-red spot-marker was also fuelled up and ready to assist.

Smith joined her. Balancing his paper plate on the wooden slats, he sipped a cup of hot chicken soup.

'Don't mind if I share the top table, do you, ma'am?'

'Make yourself at home, Gordon. The wine waiter will be along shortly.'

'We could've done without this in the middle of the London job.'

'Yes. I hope Bannister's up to it.'

'He'll be all right. He's pretty useful in a punch-up.'

'I need a thinking detective, not a baboon. Which reminds me, how's Gilbert shaping up?'

'It isn't easy. I'm getting into his head. But his body's another matter. Breast-fed on bitter if you ask me.'

Molly gestured towards the table where Gilbert stood alone, making short work of a pork pie. 'He'll end up like a sumo wrestler.'

'You always give me the cream.'

She put her empty mug on the floor. 'That's because you're the best sergeant I've got. How's the offspring, by the way?'

'Very well, thanks. The missus seems more chuffed with this one than all the others.'

'Sorry I had to turn you out. You can have a few days off after we've raided the brothel next week.'

'Job's got to be done, babies have to be born. It's just a bloomin' pest when they happen at the same time,' he replied philosophically.

Molly picked up a sandwich and bit into gristle.

'Your friend Cliff Spence isn't going to be much pleased,' Smith said quietly.

She threw the remainder of her sandwich into a rubbish

box and looked sharply at her dinner guest. 'Spence is no friend of mine. He just happens to be a king rat in the sewers we work in.'

'He'll kick up a stink tonight, all right.'

'There's no choice. I'm doing the job the only way I know. If I don't, then someone will get hurt.'

She heard Conrad's humourless laughter and watched him talking excitedly to a group of SPG men. Earlier she had seen him swallow some pills. Speed, she thought, studying his agitated movements. I know they help him to stay awake, but if I don't put a stop to it soon, I'll end up with a squad full of pill-heads.

Shivering, she rubbed her arms to get the circulation going, and surveyed the gloomy interior of the factory. Men and women, cold and weary after hanging about for many hours, spoke in quiet voices, dozed fitfully in private corners, or slept on improvised beds made from old packing cases and foam off-cuts.

She stood up, stamping her feet on the concrete. 'It's warmer in Siberia, Sarge.'

When Bannister returned, the factory was in darkness, except for a pool of light shining on Watson and a group of section commanders who were bent over the trestle table, studying plans of Spence's house. They straightened up and listened to the detective's report.

'Useless pimp!' Molly shouted when he finished, disturbing some of the sleepers. 'I knew we shouldn't have used Ezra on this job. The one thing I stressed was the need to pin-point the takings, and that's the only flaming thing he doesn't know.'

'Spence usually keeps most of it on him, ma'am. Just leaves a small float in the kitchen,' Smith volunteered.

Molly's eyes steeled with anger but she checked herself,

not wanting to upset her best man before he undertook the most difficult and dangerous part of the whole operation. 'Well, we've drawn up the plan of action, and it's down to you then. Spence knows all about police raids. If we find the cash, he'll cough the illegal sale of alcohol.'

'Right, I'll see you later, ma'am,' Smith said as he nudged DC Gilbert towards the side door.

Molly pulled her coat tightly around her then turned to the section commanders. 'Is there anything else before we start?'

'Don't you worry, gal, it'll go like clockwork,' the SPG inspector assured her.

Molly glared at the dark, rugby-playing head of the SPG. Idolised by his men, he had an irritating air of superiority. The SPG were the hard men of the service, but their positive policing methods had earned them a reputation for being heavy-handed and over-zealous. 'I'm not worried,' she said sharply. 'Just keep your men in check, that's all I ask.'

Jones touched his forehead in mock salute. She ignored the gesture. The point had been made, and she knew that he would make doubly sure his men didn't over-react.

She turned her attention to the others. 'Have your officers in their vehicles and ready to roll at one o'clock. We enter the premises twenty minutes later. Once we're on the road I don't expect anyone to lag behind. It's vital that we reach the rendezvous before we're spotted.' She paused, still trying to think of anything she had missed. There would not be another opportunity to alter the arrangements.

'Right gentlemen, wake up the dead. They'd sleep all night if we let them.'

The factory was in darkness when the double doors were

swung open. Fourteen Transit vans and eight unmarked cars edged out into a cold, moonless night.

The convoy moved slowly off the industrial estate and onto a dual carriageway. Molly, in the lead car, looked behind her, waiting until the last vehicle was lined up on the road. Satisfied with the formation, she nodded to her driver and the convoy picked up speed.

The lights of Westhampton grew brighter and Molly shifted in her seat, hugging the shebeen file to her chest. Her fingers tightened around the hard edges of the clipboard, and her knuckles turned white.

16

Smith and Gilbert approached Spence's house warily. Thick cardboard blanked out the windows, and a deaf man walking past the square, Victorian bay might have assumed the house was empty. The detectives, however, had all their faculties, and knew that the throbbing reggae music came from behind its dark facade.

No wonder there'd been complaints, Smith thought, surprised that the long-suffering neighbours hadn't set fire to the place months ago.

'Don't know how they stand it, Sarge,' Gilbert whispered, as they concealed themselves behind a high privet hedge directly opposite the house.

The sound of the music grew louder briefly, then decreased to its former level, as three black men spilled out of the front door on to the pavement. They looked up and down the street as if they were expecting someone. The dark porch behind them gave nothing away.

Gilbert seemed concerned by the number of cars that lined both sides of the street. 'If the cars are anything to go by, Sarge, it must be jam-packed in there. How does the gaffer expect us to slip unnoticed into a house full of blacks? We'll stick out like polar bears in a coal-mine. And what happens if we're clocked before the lads get here?'

'That's easy. They'll chop you up into little pieces and chuck you into a pot,' Smith snarled, hoping to concentrate his detective's mind on the job in hand.

Gilbert belched noisily, sorry now that he had eaten Macdonald's pork pie as well as his own. 'It ain't right. We should get danger money. Anyway, why couldn't

Fletch do the job? They'd think he was one of them.'

'Shut it,' Smith snapped as he peered at his watch. 'The cavalry will be here in ten minutes. Get ready to go for that door. Don't think, don't speak, just follow me.'

'Right, Sarge!' Gilbert crouched down like a sprinter on the starting blocks.

The three men opposite suddenly darted back into the house, leaving the front door open.

'Now!' Smith rasped, moving quickly from behind the hedge, zigzagging across the road and dodging between cars travelling in both directions. Reaching the other side, he leapt over a stone step into the porch of Spence's house. Gilbert, gasping for breath, caught up with him.

'Shut the front door,' the sergeant hissed.

He waited until Gilbert had done so, then opened the hall door, just enough for them to squeeze through without attracting attention. It was very dark inside the hall, brightened only by sporadic flashes of light from adjoining rooms and a dim glow from the kitchen at the far end.

The detectives kept close to the wall and sidled past noisy groups of blacks. Excited squeals and raucous laughter competed with the thunderous throb of the reggae. Smith wiped the sweat from his face. Time was running out and they had to get to the kitchen before the raiding party arrived. Fortunately, everyone was too high on drugs, too drunk, or too busy enjoying themselves to notice the white men in their midst.

Shuffling past the open door of the front room, Smith and Gilbert saw a mass of moving bodies, their heads seemingly red, blue and green as they bobbed up and down like psychedelic tappets in the flashing disco lights. The stifling air was heavy with the sweet, pungent smell of burning cannabis.

Progress became more difficult as Smith and Gilbert reached the end of the hall where there was more light.

Men carrying cans of lager and spilling frothy beer from plastic pint pots squeezed past them.

Smith stopped as he caught sight of the kitchen. Two shirt-sleeved barmen battled unsuccessfully to keep pace with the constant demands for more drinks. Spence stood behind them looking cool and unperturbed. In his mid-thirties, born in Westhampton of West Indian descent, he was a beautiful looking man with a winning smile and soft, liquid eyes. The biggest ponce in town, he had started selling sex while still at school, forcing his fourteen-year-old girl-friend to masturbate his class-mates at a pound a time. Soon realising that he could make more money, he had taken her to city-centre pubs with outside toilets where she had graduated from oral sex to the full service.

Steering Gilbert into a corner under the stairs, Smith pitched his voice below the racket, a skill he had acquired while keeping observations at hundreds of discotheques. 'There's a stack of beer crates across the kitchen door with a board on top,' he said urgently. 'Two guys are serving; Spence is lording it at the back.'

Gilbert looked over his shoulder. 'That's buggered it, Sarge. We've got to get out of here.'

Smith gripped his arm. 'Stay close. I'll take Spence, you take the barmen.'

'We've been spotted!' Gilbert yelled fearfully as a gang of men bore down on them. 'It's Catweasel and his heavies.'

The sounds of violent hammering and the breaking of glass pierced the air above the reggae. Doors crashed open and shafts of light from powerful hand-held Dragon lamps bounced off ceilings and walls as the police in plain clothes and uniform surged into the house from the front and rear. Shouts and curses filled the downstairs rooms. Partygoers, fighting to escape, threw cans, beer, and plates of curry at the unwelcome intruders. Screaming prostitutes pushed, kicked, and scratched. Catweasel and his mob turned, barged their way through a struggling mass of bodies, then raced for the stairs.

'Come on,' Smith yelled above the uproar. He shoulder-charged through the crowd in front of the bar and dived over the beer crates.

Gritting his teeth, Gilbert followed. He swerved to avoid his sergeant's boots and, losing control, he slid along the improvised counter before crashing into the wall and bouncing into the kitchen. Landing on the edge of a slop bucket, he splashed beer everywhere. He leapt to his feet, as if on springs, grabbed the startled barmen by their shirt fronts, and pushed them against the sink. 'Police! Don't give me any trouble,' he shrieked.

Beer crates smashed onto the stone floor behind them and the kitchen filled with uniforms. The reggae suddenly stopped, to be replaced by the tumult of fighting men and shouted orders. Lights slowly came on throughout the house and the hubbub died down as confused revellers peered bleary-eyed at the mass of blue helmets all around them.

Someone blew twice into a hand-held megaphone, testing it. 'This is a police raid! Remain where you are until an officer has seen you.' The warning was repeated several times before some sort of order was established.

'Please keep calm and settle down,' continued the megaphone in a more conciliatory tone. 'Do as you're told and we can get you off home as soon as you've answered a few questions. Anyone who doesn't co-operate will be arrested for obstruction.'

Molly pushed here way through a group of SPG men and into the kitchen. 'What are you doing down there, Sergeant?'

Smith groaned as he slowly lifted himself off Spence and brushed soggy cigarette ends from out of his hair. 'Making sure he didn't do a runner with the takings, ma'am.'

'You smell like a brewery.'

Wiping a hand across his wet face, Smith glared at Gilbert who turned away and started to search his prisoners.

Molly inspected the dingy kitchen. A chipped cooking pot was tilted over on the ancient two-ring gas stove, with caked rivers of burnt curry forming obscure patterns on the yellowing enamel. The shallow, dung-coloured stone sink was barely visible under an untidy stack of dirty dishes. Beside it was a putrid heap of garbage: the accumulated debris of previous parties. She kicked a dog-food tin at the bottom of the pile and disturbed a rat which scurried across the kitchen floor, then dashed outside through the open doorway. Shaking her head in disgust, Molly looked down at Spence who was sitting in a pool of stale beer, his hand-stitched suit a clinging, brown-stained ruin.

'Drowning in your own greedy effluent is nothing compared with what's going to happen to you,' she said, as he gripped the edge of the cooker and hauled himself to his feet.

Wide-eyed with righteous indignation, Spence's mouth opened and closed several times before he found his voice. 'You're out of order, woman! Your men beat me up in my own place! It's a birthday party for my friends.'

'You're lying, Spence. This is a shebeen, and you know it.'

'I want my lawyer!' he screamed.

'You're running a blues party to fleece your black brothers. If you don't tell Sergeant Smith what he wants to hear, you're in deep shit.' She turned away from Spence. 'He's all yours, Sarge,' she said, walking out of the kitchen as SPG men fell over themselves to get out of her way.

'I wouldn't want to be her old man,' one of them said when she was out of earshot.

'I don't know,' his mate replied. 'She looks like a goer to me.'

131

'She'd bloody murder you.'

The hall had cleared when Molly joined Inspector Jones on the front doorstep. They watched a Transit reverse in the road then drive off in the direction of the city centre.

'Prisoners for obstruction,' Jones informed her.

She nodded, mentally ticking off her "things still to do list". 'Seen anything of my lot recently?'

'Roger Turner and his crew dashed out soon after the raid started,' an SPG sergeant standing behind them offered. 'Chased some guys who had jumped out of the back bedroom window.'

'Thanks,' Molly acknowledged. 'Any problems, Dai?'

'Few banged heads and a bit of damage. Some of my boyo's got involved in a little altercation. Your dealer friends were a tiny bit shy about what they had in their pockets. They've been taken to hospital for treatment. Nothing for their loved ones to fret over.'

'I wondered what the pitched battle in the back room was all about. Where are they now?'

'Your Sergeant Conrad and his crew have taken them to the lock-up.'

'Would you mind giving the control room a bell and telling them to stand down the emergency services and the reserves?'

'What reserves?'

'Just do it, please, Dai.'

She walked back into the hall and almost collided with Gilbert. He spoke to her in a hoarse whisper. 'Sergeant Smith says to tell you that we've found the takings. They were in a handbag on a peg behind the kitchen door, underneath an old coat. He hasn't had time to count it yet, but he said I was to say one thousand two hundred and twenty-two pounds because you wouldn't know any different.'

'Well done,' she said, remembering the confusion of her own early days in the CID. She moved on and walked into the back room which was brightly lit with two-hundred-watt lamps fitted by the SPG. There was an old wooden table in the corner, and upturned chairs lay scattered about. Empty cans, plastic pots and half-eaten curries cluttered the table and every available ledge. Uniformed officers with clipboards were being harangued by mouthy, white toms spitting abuse. ''Raz clazz'' was their favourite insult: equating their captors to a soiled sanitary towel.

'Nearly finished in here, ma'am,' said a sergeant who had once boxed light-heavyweight for the force. He raised his voice for the benefit of the toms. 'Just a few hangers-on asking for a night in the slammer.'

'Before you leave, Sarge, make sure there's a thorough search by a scenes of crime officer.' Molly crossed the room and kicked a couple of empty Red Stripe cans along the cheap yellow lino. 'And get somebody to bag these cans and plastic pots. At least we'll have some idea how much booze Spence has sold.

There was no furniture in the front room and the smell of curry was stronger because most of it had finished up on the floor. After picking her way carefully through the mess, Molly examined the eight-foot amplifiers. One was lying on its side surrounded by broken glass; the other was tipped over onto its front exposing a tangled mass of multi-coloured wiring so that it looked like a disembowelled robot.

'What happened here?' she demanded, seeing a constable on his hands and knees under the bay window.

'Collecting evidence, ma'am.' He stood up, palm outstretched to show her a handful of cannabis resin. 'There's at least forty deals here. Saw a guy throw them away, but we couldn't get through the crowd quick enough to catch him. Bloody bedlam in here it was, ma'am. Plenty of joints, though.'

'Who did the demolition job on the sound equipment?'

'SPG. They couldn't find the switch in the dark. You said you wanted the sound off as soon as possible.'

'I didn't say wreck the flaming things. They're expensive pieces of kit. Have they been searched for drugs?'

'Don't know, ma'am.'

'Then make sure they are . . . and then tidy them up a bit.'

Leaving the room, she ran up the stairs. 'Any action up here?' she asked a slovenly-looking constable who rose wearily from a chair at the end of a dark landing.

'Some blokes jumped out of the window onto the brewhouse roof. Dog got one. They've taken him to the District. The others legged it.'

Molly frowned at the bedroom doors hanging off broken hinges. 'Who smashed these doors in?'

'Dunno. Suppose they couldn't find the keys.'

The man's uniform jacket hung open and his shirt spilled out of his trousers.

'Ma'am!' Molly shouted. 'And smarten yourself up, for goodness sake.'

'Sorry, gaf— ma'am,' he spluttered, jumping to his feet and retreating in one movement as he fumbled with the buttons of his jacket.

Molly went into the back bedroom and leaned out of the open window. The outhouse roof was a metre below the window ledge. When she turned, she saw the sagging ceiling and the torn rose-bud wallpaper. The constable, looking somewhat smarter, had followed her into the room. He stood sheepishly on the opposite side of a large cast-iron bed.

Molly stepped forward and pulled back the tattered grey eiderdown. 'Christ!' she exclaimed in astonishment. The mattresss was covered with layers of twenty-pound notes.

She did a quick calculation. 'There must be at least thirty grand here. Get Inspector Jones.' The constable gaped at the money. 'Move!' she shouted.

A few seconds later, Jones rushed into the bedroom. 'What's the pan—? Blood-y hell, boyo, you've hit the bleeding jackpot!'

'Somebody's been expecting a big drop tonight. I want this money photographed, and I want it counted. SOCO can also dust that window frame while they're at it.'

'Anything to help the Drug Squad, ma'am,' Jones smiled casually, serving notice that he was not going to jump about for someone of the same rank.

Her face hardened. 'I want every note checked for prints, but that'll have to be done later. You stick to that money. Once SOCO have got their pictures, take it to Prouds Lane. Obtain a signature and make sure it's locked in the safe. Fingerprints will want to take it away later, but that'll be Division's problem.'

'Would you like me to rewire the house at the same time?' He asked sarcastically. Her eyes blazed at the implied challenge to her authority.

Jones raised his arms in a gesture of submission. 'I'm not asking for a fight, Molly. We're on the same side, remember? Just slow down a bit. You're starting to run people ragged.'

She knew that the Welshman was right, but she wasn't going to admit it. She wanted the job done properly and was determined that there would be no mistakes. Her voice was dangerously low. 'I know what I'm doing. If they're a bit ragged, good. That's how I like it. Keeps their minds working. Even that man of yours, guarding the landing, showed a spark of life before he went to sleep holding up the wall. If I were you his feet wouldn't touch.'

'That's my decision,' Jones snapped back angrily.

She tensed like a boxer trying to anticipate the next

straight left. But the response she got was more devastating than any punch would have been.

'If you must know, that's PC Rawlings.' Jones continued quietly, 'His little girl died of cancer on Monday. She was three years old. I don't think he's slept since. He's come to work today to stop himself going mad.'

Shaken, Molly paled, falling back a step and leaning against the ragged rosebuds. 'I'm sorry, Dai. I didn't know.'

Jones stood very close to her. 'I've told you before, Molly, ease up a bit. Three years running the Drug Squad is getting to you.'

He was right, of course, but what could she do about it? She wasn't going to give in to Davids and ask to leave the CID. She pushed herself off the wall. 'I'm going to see how the squad are making out with the prisoners.'

She stopped at the door. 'Thanks, Dai. We'll have a tot one of these days. There's a lot of catching up to do.' After a final glance at the money, she left the room and walked down the stairs.

The old house was quiet and peaceful, a few men and women remaining, searching for evidence and collecting exhibits. Standing beside a sergeant on the front doorstep, Molly felt the chill of the night. Low clouds overhead were tinged with the amber glow of urban street lights. A solitary police car waited at the kerb, the intermittent gabble of its radio breaking the silence.

The houses all around were in darkness but she knew that people inside had enjoyed the show. Spence had made their lives a misery and something had been done about it at last.

'What's the time, Sarge?'

'Three o'clock, ma'am. My missus will think I've got another woman.'

'Many prisoners?'

'Seven to your lads, including the three for the illegal sale of booze, that is. Six to Plain Clothes for using drugs. Ten to the SPG for public disorder, resisting arrest, obstruction, and assault. One to the Dog Section for arguing with a German Shepherd, ma'am.'

'Could've been worse, I suppose. At least there's been no serious injuries. At one time I thought we were in for a full scale riot.'

'You did the right thing, ma'am. Went in hard and hit 'em before they knew what time of day it was.'

She smiled wryly. 'That's the theory. Sometimes it works. I'm going to the lock-up. Warn everyone to be in the canteen for a debrief at three-thirty.'

'Yes, ma'am,' replied the sergeant, putting up a salute as she climbed into the police car.

'Never seen you do that for a woman before,' said a grey-haired constable who was his regular crown-green bowls partner.

'What's the difference? There's not many gaffers like her about, Bob. She'll be the last one to go home tonight.'

'What night?' grumbled the constable.

137

17

Molly pushed her way through the doors of D Division's headquarters. The square goldfish pond, sunk into the grey marble floor, brought back happy memories of her Junior CID Course, and the day she had stood in line with male colleagues to be reprimanded for a series of drunken escapades following an hilarious end-of-course party.

They'd all been on a high before a drop of alcohol had passed their lips. It was the day when they got their final results. Everyone had done remarkably well, and she had come top of the course. Tradition making no allowance for sex, she had been carted shoulder-high around the playing fields, tossed onto the gardener's compost heap, and then hosed down in the men's showers. They had made it! They were going to be detectives. It was a delightful, wonderful feeling that would surpass the joy of all future appointments and promotions; it was a time that none of them would ever forget.

The training superintendent had never found out how many of the men had emptied their beer-laden bladders into the pond at four o'clock the following morning, and he had been careful not to include her in that part of his tirade, but rule five of a yellowing notice was dedicated to their memory: "Students must not pollute the fish pond".

She had qualified in heavy boozing on that course. The only woman in the group, her fellow students had spent almost every night trying to get her drunk. Thanks to her time in the Navy, a strong constitution and thirsty houseplants, they had not succeeded — until the final night.

Her course report had described her as a "good mixer who would hold her own in the company of criminals".

At the time she had thought that the compulsory tours of the dirtiest drinking dens in the city — anyone who stayed behind had little chance of joining the CID — were just an excuse for the instructors to enjoy a night's drinking at the students' expense. Now, with seven years CID experience, she could hold her drink as well as any man, and occasionally found it useful.

She walked into the interview room to find Turner and his crew lounging around a table littered with empty cups and biscuit wrappers.

'What's this then?' she asked angrily.

They sprang to attention, a chair crashing to the floor behind Fletcher.

'Bloody hell!' Woods cried out as he sucked a burnt finger and stamped on the cigarette end he had been hiding behind his back.

She waved them down and Fletcher gave her his chair, collecting another one from the next room.

'What's going on?' she demanded.

Turner adjusted his glasses. 'I don't think you'll be disappointed, ma'am.'

She glanced at the men around the table seeing for the first time the smiles in their eyes. 'Why not?'

'There's a friend of yours in the traps.'

'Who?'

'Catweasel.'

'Catweasel?'

'Yes, ma'am.'

Her face lit up. 'Tell me more.'

'We'd got half-way along the hall when someone upstairs yelled down that three guys had done a runner through the back bedroom window. We turned and fought our way through an army of SPG men who were still pouring into the house. By the time we got out of the front door, the three guys were racing up the hill. We chased them as far as the waste ground at the top of the road but when we got there they had vanished. Me and Woody kept watch while Fletch returned to the house to round up some help.

When they came back we surrounded the area and sent the dog in. He made straight for the bushes next to the old Methodist chapel. Like a hairy Exocet, he was.' Turner took off his glasses and cleaned them on his shirt.

'Go on,' Molly prompted.

'The dog flushed them out in no time, ma'am. Sank his teeth into Catweasel's arm and wouldn't let go, even though he was being belted about the head with an old chair leg.'

'Any injuries?'

'The dog complained of a headache; Catweasel was upset about his shredded leather coat. The other two ran straight into the arms of the SPG.'

Putting his glasses back on, Turner blinked as if testing them. 'Trouble is, they weren't carrying any gear and they're screaming for their solicitors. We were having a breather when you arrived, ma'am.'

Molly rubbed her hands like a Red Indian making fire and looked at the men around her. 'Catweasel, at last! We've got the bastard! Well done, lads. There was at least thirty grand in the back bedroom. He must have been calling to collect his money before making the drop. All we need now is the gear. Where's the man I asked to check the cars?'

'On his way in, ma'am. I don't know whether he's found the Jag.'

'Catweasel's too crafty to leave drugs in his own car, but you never know, they can't be far away. Keep at him and join the debrief as soon as you get something. I'll see him myself later.'

Molly next visited the custody suite where she found

Bannister writing prisoners' details in his pocket book.

'Some right beauties here, ma'am.'

'Have they admitted supplying?'

'They won't admit it's Saturday.'

'It's Sunday . . . Where's Conrad?'

'Interviewing,' Bannister replied without taking his eyes off the custody record sheet.

After satisfying herself that everything was under control, Molly left the custody suite and walked into the barn-like canteen. She was met by the familiar rustle of nylon coats as the waiting officers struggled to their feet.

'Don't get up,' she said quickly, stopping them.

The SPG had been in action for eighteen hours, including a difficult local derby involving baton charges against fighting fans at the South Bank end of the city football ground. The men looked dirty and dishevelled, and they smelled of sweaty serge.

'Sergeant Turner's team have gone to check out a motor, ma'am,' Bannister offered, seemingly less tired than his companions. She hoped he hadn't picked up Conrad's pill-taking habits already.

'What motor?'

'They didn't say, ma'am.'

Molly said a silent prayer. She knew it had to be the Jaguar. They must find something, if only enough to hold Catweasel for a few days. There were so many crimes they wanted to put to him, and several neighbouring forces would be sending people to interview him about offences in their areas.

Smith, seeing a new paleness in his boss's face, asked her if she felt all right.

'Of course I'm all right. What were the takings?'

He examined the back of his hand. 'Two thousand four hundred and thirteen pounds, sixteen pence, ma'am.'

The suggestion of a smile lifted the corners of her mouth.

'Your educated guess was only half wrong then?'

Smith shot an accusing look at Gilbert who concentrated on picking his fingernails.

Raising her voice, Molly addressed the whole group. 'Can I have your attention, please?' Most of them looked towards her, but some appeared to be in another world. Two SPG men, leaning against each other for support, snored in unison. A sergeant brought them back to life with cruel kicks to the shins.

'Thank you all for your efforts. There were some good drug arrests and we have more than enough evidence to prove the alcohol offences. I asked for restraint and, apart from a little over-enthusiasm in switching off the sound and opening bedroom doors, I'm grateful for the manner in which you conducted yourselves. Is there anything you wish to add, Mr Jones?'

Responding with a slight bow, and appearing to accept the compliments as personal, he looked across the room at his band of loyal officers. 'Only to say, boyo, that the highly trained Special Patrol Group is always pleased to work with the Drug Squad, and we look forward to the next punch-up.'

'Thank you, Dai. Are there any questions?'

The door opened and Turner, followed by his team, tumbled into the room. Broad smiles split their faces but she ignored them, not wanting to keep the uniformed men back any longer.

'All right,' she said. 'Drug Squad stay where you are. The rest of you get off home, and drive carefully.'

There was a noisy scraping of chairs and a shuffling of feet as the room quickly cleared.

Molly joined her squad sitting around a table near to the door. 'I gather you've got some good news for me, Roger.'

'How about ten kilos of cocaine and, wait for it . . .

thirty kilos of crack,' Turner replied smugly.

'Where?'

'Hidden in the Jag.'

'What did Catweasel say?'

'Denies that it's his gear; claims that he's never seen it before.'

'How's it supposed to have got there?'

'Usual thing — we planted it.'

Molly laughed. 'Even Complaints wouldn't believe we could come up with that much gear.'

Her laughter was only partly sardonic. It was marvellous news. Not only had they got the man she'd been after for a long time; there would be national publicity. Every drug squad in the country had been trying to make the first sizeable crack bust. It was the drug that had caused horrendous problems in the States, and squad chiefs knew it was only a matter of time before crack spread to the UK.

'We also found a bunsen burner and a couple of cooking pots in the boot, ma'am,' Turner added. 'They were still wrapped up. Purchased in Liverpool, according to the stickers.'

'He wasn't travelling in hardware, Roger. He was getting ready for a cooking session. Cocaine to crack in about ninety minutes. Catweasel was boasting in the Green Parrot about retiring and buying a mansion. The only place he's going to is Her Majesty's Prison, Winson Green. With his record he should go down for at least nine years. After that, they'll deport him to wherever he came from. Congratulations, the Gaming Team. I'll have to move you all over to drugs if you keep this up.'

Some instinct caused her to glance in Conrad's direction. His expression was venomous and he immediately buried his head in a sauce-stained newspaper. His plans to get rid of Woods and Fletcher had suffered a major set-back, but she knew that he wouldn't give up.

She returned to the debrief. 'Well done, everyone, it's been a good operation. You can forget page three tomorrow, Woody. Read about yourself on page one instead.'

'*Then* I'll look at page three,' he replied, joining in the laughter.

'Make sure you get a telex off, Gordon,' Molly said to Sergeant Smith. 'Send it to the Chief Constable, National Criminal Intelligence Service, and the Press Office. "Arresting officers, Detective Sergeant Roger Turner, Detective Constables Peter Woods and Tony Fletcher, Westhampton Drug Squad." '

The canteen clock moved forward with a tired click and the hour hand quivered at four.

'This is no place to be on a Sunday morning,' she continued. 'Finish whatever you were doing then book off duty. With the exception of Sergeant Conrad, who will be standing by at the office, and those on brothel obs, you can all have Monday and Tuesday off. Bill and myself will be in London.'

'It's all right for the chosen one,' Williams said, hand on his mate's arm as they left the canteen together.

Molly held Smith back. 'Where's Spence?' she asked, as soon as they were alone.

'End cell, ma'am. Said he's going to kill you.'

'He's only joking. We're the best of friends.'

'It didn't sound like that to me. He was like a raving lunatic. If all the things he said about you could be proved you'd get life.'

'He'll calm down. I'll go and see him shortly.'

'I think I'd better go with you.'

'Don't you fret, Gordon. Me and Spence go back a long way. And in any case, you've got a baby to go home to. I'll see you when I get back from London. In the meantime, tie up the loose ends here, will you, please?'

'I'll come back straight after the morning service,' he grinned. 'Best of luck down the Smoke.'

'Thanks. And thank you again for a good job tonight. This squad of ours is starting to motor.'

'Well enough for you to spend more time at home,' he replied seriously. 'If you don't, you'll wilt like those roses you used to bring to the office.'

She frowned, surprised at the sudden turn in the conversation. 'I'm OK. Locking up traffickers like Catweasel does me more good than a month of days off. But you're right about the roses. If we keep on at this pace much longer, they'll die of neglect.'

His expression did not change. 'D'you remember Tommy Hinds?'

Molly checked her watch. There was no time for reminiscing. 'Traffic sergeant, wasn't he? Had a heart attack, about two years ago?'

'That's right. Worked himself to death. After he went, they replaced him with two sergeants and two PCs. Most people in the force can't even remember his name.'

'You should take up the church, Gordon. They'd love you in the pulpit.'

He shook his head and stood up. 'I'm not joking, Molly. We're all like poor old Tommy Hinds. No one gives a shit when we've gone. Only the family's important.'

After he had left she stayed in her seat, lingering in the quiet solitude of the canteen. . . . What family? There's only me and Holmes. My last affair was a right flaming disaster. Not only did the creep have another woman in tow, he "borrowed" my credit card to pay for his pleasures.

After a few moments she stood up and spoke to the empty canteen in a firm determined voice. 'Bugger men, it's the age of the single woman. What's wrong with freedom and independence?'

145

18

'All right, Cliff?' Molly asked, as she opened the cell door. Spence was leaning against the far wall, feet crossed and head resting on his chest. At the sound of her voice he shot forward, face twisted in a savage manifestation of his hate.

'All right? I'm over the fucking moon!' he screeched. 'You raid my place with half the bastard police force, beat up my best customers, lock up the biggest dealer in the country, smash up my home, steal my life's savings, insult my friends, throw me in the pissing can and then you have the fucking nerve to stroll in here like you were going to a monkeys' fucking tea party and ask me if I'm all fucking right! Jesus woman, if this was Jamaica I'd cut your white limey throat and feed you to the hogs.'

She shut the door and walked away, howls of protest chasing her down the passage. As she passed the duty inspector's office her name was called. It was Joe Christian. They had joined the job together. His nose gets larger and his cheeks a little redder each year, she thought. No wonder they always ask him to be Father Christmas.

'How's it going, Molly? A nice, good-looking woman like you shouldn't be mixing it with druggies. It's time you got yourself a real job, something with a bit of dignity.'

'I like my job.'

'You probably do, but it's inside that counts. It'll get all tight and twisted, so that one day you'll snap like McEnroe's racket.'

'You're the third person who's said something daft like that tonight. Apart from suggesting I'm ready for the crem', is there something I should know about?'

'Yes, I've had to keep one of the prisoners back. A black kid. Said he's an international athlete. Thought you'd like to have a word with him. Claims that your Sergeant Conrad planted him.' Misinterpreting her pained expression, he shook his head. 'Yes, I know Molly, that's what they all say. This one's different. I think you should have a word with him before I make it official.'

She hesitated for a moment. Everybody complained these days: their solicitors advised them to. It delayed the prosecution and cast doubts on the integrity of police witnesses. It didn't matter whether the allegations were true or false. The prisoner was no worse off, and he had the satisfaction of getting back at the officer who arrested him. But it wasn't the complaint itself that had affected her, it was the mention of Conrad's name. She had suspected for some time that he had been planting drugs. Perhaps this was the opportunity she had been waiting for.

'Where is he, Joe?'

'First cell.'

Molly opened the heavy door and confronted a tall, slim youth. Obviously distressed, his whole body shook and his eyes moved about restlessly as if seeking a way out of the cell.

'I understand you wish to make a complaint against one of my men,' she said.

'Who are you?'

'Detective Inspector Watson, Drug Squad.'

'I want to speak to a uniformed inspector. You won't take any notice.'

'Time's on our side. Try me.'

He hesitated, then spoke in a quiet, nervous voice. 'I've never seen any drugs before. I'm an athlete, a runner, I don't even smoke. What use is that stuff to me?'

'People who go to shebeens stay up all night, dance, drink, smoke pot and, if they've got any energy left, find

themselves a woman. Sportsmen go to bed early and sleep.'
He moved his weight from one leg to the other and she
pressed on. 'You were found in possession of cannabis
resin. It didn't appear out of nowhere.'

He closed his eyes, and she waited. A few minutes passed
in silence. Then, with a sharp intake of breath, he opened
his eyes and stared at her.

'Look,' he said wearily, 'I'll say it again. I never had
any drugs. I wouldn't use them if they were given to me.
I hope to run for England one day. If I get into trouble
with the Sports Council they'll ban me for life. Do you
honestly think I'd waste years of training for a cheap thrill?
I'm not interested.'

'We're all human, we make mistakes, we try things,'
she said in a neutral, interrogator's voice. 'What were you
doing at the shebeen?'

'Don't know. Interested, I guess.'

'I'm told you're alleging that Sergeant Conrad planted
drugs on you.'

'You said that. I said I hadn't seen the drugs before.'

'What happened when he arrested you?'

'He put his hand in my coat pocket and took out a piece
of brown stuff. It looked like pipe tobacco to me, the stuff
they cut up. I'd never seen it before, I swear to God.'

'Is that what you said to the sergeant?'

'Yes.'

'What did he say?'

'He laughed in my face, and kept on laughing, like a
crazy man. If you ask me he'd been drinking or something.
He was certainly not right in the head.'

'That's another serious allegation.'

'I'm telling it right. My future's on the line, my whole
life. If I'm done for having drugs it's the chop. There'll
be nothing left. I may as well be dead.'

Walking across the cell, she opened the door. 'You'll

be bailed shortly. Stay away from shebeens and keep up the training.'

He closed his eyes again, head resting against the wall.

Leaving the cell block, Molly went with Christian to the custody suite and searched through the exhibits until she found the matchbox-sized block of resin Conrad claimed he had found on the prisoner. Turning it over, she saw faint traces of blue paint.

'This must be taken to the lab first thing tomorrow morning, Joe,' she said, handing over the exhibit. 'I want a chemical and physical comparison made with the cannabis found at Delroy Jackman's house on Monday. Tell the lab that the officer in that case is Detective Sergeant Conrad. I'll give them a ring late Tuesday or first thing Wednesday, after I get back from London.'

The dusty old wall clock chimed five times but it was barely audible over the strident ringing of the bell to number-one cell. Jack Spoon, the custody sergeant, shook his head in exasperation. A big, bald-headed man, his black belt stretched around his mighty girth like a ribbon around an Easter egg.

'Don't you think you'd better go and see him, ma'am? He's been ringing that bloody thing non-stop for at least half an hour. My head's splitting.'

'He's slowing down.'

'So am I'.

Molly picked up the keys. 'No staying power, that's your trouble Sarge.'

She returned to the cell block, not looking forward to her confrontation with Spence, but aware that it had to be done and that she must come out on top if she was to get him working again. Putting an eye to the Judas hole, she watched Spence pacing up and down, yelling at the walls and stabbing the air with his hands like a tick-tack man minutes before the start of a race. Unlocking the door, she walked in.

Spence whirled round and faced her accusingly. 'Where the fucking hell have you been? I've been ringing that fucking bell all fucking night.'

She calmly removed a piece of cigarette packet that was jamming the bell button. 'If it had been left to Sergeant Spoon, you'd have stayed here forever.'

Spence shook with fury, strings of saliva slithering down his chin and soaking into his shirt. Molly thought he was going to have a fit.

'I want out!' he shrieked. 'And I mean now! You fucking woman pig!' Eyes protruding, his hands clawed at the air. 'Pig! Pig! Pig!' he yelled.

Molly froze, then something snapped, releasing the fierce demon within her. With lightning speed, she kicked off her shoes, half turned, then hammered her right foot into the soft flesh between Spence's legs. His mouth gaped in a soundless scream and he collapsed onto the floor in a wave of excruciating pain; drowning in a blood-red sea of nausea.

As Molly stood over the writhing prisoner, iron-hard hands clamped her wrists from behind. 'He's not worth it,' the custody sergeant breathed into her ear.

He held her steady until her arms stopped shaking and she felt the coldness of the concrete through her stockinged feet. When her breathing slowed the sergeant relaxed his grip, allowing her to break free.

'Thanks,' she murmured, still seething with anger as she shuffled back into her shoes.

'I'll give you thirty minutes to get him out of here,' Sergeant Spoon said sternly. 'Otherwise, I'm sending for the police surgeon.'

Molly bit her tongue and fought for control. 'Fix up the paperwork, I'll bring him along shortly.' Molly waited until the sergeant had gone, then filled a bucket with cold water. She'd bring him round all right.

Spence pulled himself into a sitting position. Legs wide apart, he winced with pain. 'Why'd you hit me?' he groaned, sucking breath.

She dropped a wet cloth into the bucket and stared down at him. 'Nobody talks to me like that.'

He cried out, fingers exploring his swollen testicles. 'You've ruined me for life,' he groaned.

'Drink!' she ordered, holding out a mug.

He took it from her and did as he was told.

Sitting beside him on the wooden bench, she allowed him more time to recover.

'Why did you raid my place?' he asked, wiping his wet face with the back of his shirt sleeve.

'No choice. Refused at first, but Division moaned to headquarters. They ordered me to do it.'

'You said you took no notice of them.'

'They pay the wages.'

'Why didn't you tip me off?' he asked cautiously.

'No point. The neighbours and local bigwigs would've kept on until it was done. You wouldn't have stopped, you've been making too much money. It was a case of sooner rather than later.'

'Where's my bread?'

'Big deal in the offing, was there? A certain Mister Catweasel?'

Spence stared sullenly at the floor. 'You're not supposed to ask questions like that. We had an agreement.'

Jack Spoon had been right, she thought. She shouldn't have hit Spence, but it had been satisfying all the same. It was a trick she had been taught in the Navy. "A man's Achilles' heel is his balls, and a woman's best weapon is her foot" the petty officer in charge of the unarmed combat course had said, as a line of wrens had practised on stuffed dummies until they could hit the right spot in the blink of an eye.

She turned suddenly and glared at Spence. 'Don't start getting lippy with me.'

He flinched and ducked away from her. 'Why couldn't you have done it nice and easy? We've conned the woollies before.'

'This involved Division. They don't understand informants and undercover work. They think we use crystal balls and radar to detect drug offences.'

'There was no need to shout at me in front of my people; I'm important. I lost height, woman.'

'It had to look good. Someone will tell the superintendent everything that was said, word for word.'

'I thought he was your friend?'

'He is but he wants to be a chief super so that he can run his own show.'

'You could have told him about all the good work I do for you guys.'

'He wouldn't have taken any notice.'

Spence didn't believe her. All the dealers knew that her greatest pleasure was putting them away. They joked that it was the only thing that turned her on, saying that she had an orgasm every time she felt a collar.

She scared the shit out of everybody in the business and she'd been in charge of drugs for too long. The top people were usually promoted before they learned enough about the game to be dangerous, but Watson seemed to have been about forever. She was a woman, and women didn't understand the finer points of business. No one could get close enough to make her see the way things worked in other cities. She could have been rich if she'd played her cards right. Errol Garwood had tried to enlighten her, but he'd ended up with two years chokey for Conspiring to Corrupt a Police Officer. They all knew that there would be no peace as long as Watson was around. It had been suggested that they pay someone from London to end their

152

troubles permanently.

He gasped, hands between his legs, 'I think I'm ruptured.'

'You'll live . . . Your place was overdue. Even your old pals were wondering how you'd got away with it for so long.' Standing up, she took hold of his elbow. 'Come on. Let's get you out of here. You'll feel better after a few hours' sleep.'

Molly parked her car in a quiet back street and handed Spence a packet of cigarettes from the carton she kept in the glove compartment.

'What'll I get?' he asked.

'I'll have a word in the Magistrates Clerk's ear and fix up a nice friendly Bench. You won't go down, I can promise you that.'

'What about the fine? That's a pretty tough court.'

'About a hundred pounds for the liquor offences to make it look respectable. You'll get that back in one quick deal, and I needn't touch you for another two years at least. You can forget the other offences — insufficient evidence.'

'What about the blues? It's a nice little earner.'

'Not any more it isn't. You've got to keep moving. But if you had a real brain, if you were really clever, you'd pack it in. Your girls earn more in a week than I make in a month.'

'When do I get my money back?'

'That thirty grand the tax man knows nothing about?' she murmured thoughtfully. 'I'll have to think about that one. If I need it for evidence, it may be months, years even.'

'You'll put me out of business, woman.'

'When you've pleaded guilty and started to be more helpful I might be able to let you have a few hundred now and then. Just to show how grateful I am.'

'But I need the money now,' he cried in alarm. 'How am I going to live?'

153

She looked at the trembling wreck beside her. What would his women think of him now? 'It's drug trafficking money. The judge can make a confiscation order if I decide to tell him about it. And if you don't come up with something tasty in the next couple of weeks, I might just do that.'

'Ah, come on,' he cried. 'And what about the takings and the booze? It's a sale or return: the man will want his money or the drinks.'

'I'll write to the Police Benevolent Fund,' she replied shortly.

'You're being too hard on me, woman. I can't survive in this town any more.'

'If you start working, you can.' She wound down the window to let out the smell of stale beer. 'Information is what I need, and you're going to start giving it to me, understand? Like who's running that teenage brothel you were so keen to tell me about?'

'I'll find out and let you know,' he mumbled unconvincingly, turning his head as a car drove by.

He made sure that the road was clear, then opened the door. 'I'd better be off, the town's waking up.' Getting out of the car, he yelled in pain as his foot hit the pavement. Quickly recovering, he staggered along the footpath for a few metres then vanished into a dark passageway between the houses.

Molly reached for the ignition — damn! She'd forgotten to see Catweasel. It would have to wait. Even DIs had to sleep sometimes.

Moving through the gears, she headed for Coovers Wood. Holmes was staying with Joan until she returned from London, but she was missing him already.

19

Sunday night, Saturday night, what's the difference? Nobody goes to church any more, Conrad thought as he drove around Westhampton's vice area.

Approaching the Red Cow, he saw a group of prostitutes standing on the corner. A tall, black woman who had the advantage of seeing the punters first; a slim smart-looking woman wearing a shiny leather suit; and a short, fat woman in a long white coat, looking like a pregnant school-crossing warden. Perhaps it's the only way she can get the motorists to stop, he speculated. It was a raw night and they stamped their feet like a trio of mismatched Morris dancers.

Passing the District Hospital, Conrad searched for Ezra who would be ramrodding his girls and scouring the area for "new meat". He was always on the look out for girls who were foolish enough to think they could work without a minder.

A couple of toms in short skirts moved out of the shadows; they knew an expensive car when they saw one. He drove past them and parked at the top of the street. He could wait. On a Sunday there were no vice patrols who might report back to Watson. The job couldn't afford to pay for the overtime.

A dark Granada pulled up at the kerb and one of the women got in. It moved away, brake lights flaring as it hesitated at the junction, then turned right.

Conrad took a couple of tablets out of a brown paper bag and popped them into his mouth, swilling them down with mineral water from a large bottle he kept in the car. He was always thirsty these days, he thought, knowing it was the pills. He was taking too many: twenty, even thirty on some days. Conrad the junky. What a bloody awful joke that was. And when would it end?

It was his own fault. He should've stayed as he was; birds, boozing and work, and in that order. In those days he couldn't have cared less what kind of car the neighbours had on their red-block drives, or where they'd got their sun-tan. The old man and the wife had changed all that. They'd nagged and nagged until he'd finally fallen into line and become a victim of the ''big con''. Now he had all the essentials of a miserable, top-of-the-shit-heap, suburban life. A crippling mortgage, a flash motor on the never, and wallet full of plastic cards he couldn't use.

He lit a cigarette, finding it more difficult than it used to be because his hands shook.

As if that wasn't enough, he thought, taking a deep drag. There would never be the two point three kids every family was supposed to have. He'd been firing blanks, and that was all he'd ever do. Mary hadn't said a lot. They rarely spoke anyway. She'd spent more time at her mother's and was hardly ever in when he got home. He thought she'd found herself someone with real balls, and now he wished to Christ she had.

He closed his eyes, trying to shut out the memory of the unopened boxes and cartons that filled the attic: baby dresses, first shoes, nappies, creams, rattles and a dozen other things that babies needed. She'd spent her time in baby shops and the big stores, indulging a phantom child. He owed thousands. The banks and building societies were threatening to report him to the chief if he didn't cough up by the end of the month.

Feeling hot, he switched on the ignition, then pressed a button which opened the sunroof.

A chief superintendent at least, his father had said he would be. Fat chance now. . . . And there'd never be a law degree. He'd forgotten to take his tablets with him when he went into the exam room. Without them, his mind hadn't functioned and he'd spent most of the time staring at a blank piece of paper.

What would his old buddy, skinhead Davids, say? The superintendent had promised him the Drug Squad if he helped him to get shut of Watson. Now it was a matter of life or death. He had to have her job so that he could control the scene, milk the dealers, and sell enough gear to pay off his debts.

He sighed, deeply, head back, watching cigarette smoke as it curled through the open roof into the blackness above him, wishing there was another way. He hadn't felt like crucifying anybody since his own troubles had started to multiply — not even Watson. A few months ago he would've cheerfully choked the life out of her to get his promotion. Now he didn't have the stomach for it. She wasn't too bad, a bit smart-arse maybe, but he'd known worse.

He clenched his fist and pounded the leather-bound wheel. His life was falling apart. He had to survive. He must finish Watson.

There was a tap on the driver's window, and on the other side of the tinted glass he saw two circles of mascara above a thick red gash, like an evil apparition. He shook his head, thinking for a moment that he was hallucinating. 'I'll have to pack in these bloody tablets,' he murmured.

The red gash split to reveal nicotine-stained teeth. 'D'you want business, mister?' the woman asked, hard eyes calculating the asking price.

'Go away, you stupid old bag,' he shouted.

A small van, bearing the name Frederick Swartz Anti-Friction Metal Parts Company stopped a short distance down the road. A woman with the body of a girl stepped out. She waited until the vehicle had gone, looked up and down the street, then walked slowly along the edge of the pavement. Conrad recognised her. It was Monica, one of Ezra's girls.

A dark shape emerged from behind a parked lorry and snatched the bag from Monica's shoulder. Fascinated by the silhouettes in front of the sodium street light, Conrad watched the struggling figures, one big and fat, the other small and puny. A scream of terror was silenced and Monica fell backwards over a low garden wall.

Throwing the bag after her, Ezra stuffed something into his pocket, tapped the top of his Derby, and strolled towards the Saab.

As soon as he was aboard, Conrad drove off. He stopped behind the bus depot a few streets away.

'What's she been up to?' he asked.

'Nothing, that's the trouble. Twenty quid for two hours. It's not worth paying her rent. She'll put me out of business if I don't sort her out soon.'

'D'you want me to have a go at her?'

'You're welcome. She needs to be taught a few tricks that'll bring the punters back for more.'

Conrad lit another cigarette and puffed furiously.

'Are you OK?' asked Ezra, straining to see him in the poor light.

'Don't worry about me, Watson's the one with the problems. She's really got herself and most of Scotland Yard in a spin about Tuesday's deal. Is everything fixed up?'

'Hope so. At least she's agreed to cough up seventy-five thousand quid. My cut's a third.'

'Less ten grand.'

'You said five.'

'That was before I knew how much you were making. If we're going to carve up this city, we've got to share the spoils, old mate.'

'What if it fucks up? I'll end up in the can, not you. That Watson woman's sharp. She scared the shit out of me in Brum. The guys from Manchester weren't too happy about her either. They thought she was a cop as soon as they saw her. If it hadn't been for me, they'd have scarpered.'

Conrad grabbed the bottle and drank more water, spilling some down his shirt front. 'Ah, shut it. You get up my prick sometimes. She wants to set up a really big deal so she can get into the headlines and be made up. It's only a test purchase as far as Watson's concerned. She'll simply grab the gear and hand over the readies.'

'If it goes wrong, it won't take her long to work out that it was me who set her up.'

'Don't be daft. You're only the messenger. It'll be the Manchester goons she'll be after. By the time she realises what's hit her, they'll be out of the bloody country.'

Ezra grunted, as if winded. 'I hate Tuesdays. Everything really bad that has ever happened to me, happened on a Tuesday.'

'You worry too much. With Watson out of the way, we can lean on the dealers and make a bloody fortune.'

Conrad laughed, loudly, more in hysteria than good spirits.

20

Bannister sat opposite his boss, who was studying a street map of the West End. She's like one of those birds in the glossy magazines, he thought, liking her black outfit and the silver earrings. They'll be fighting over her down the Met. He picked up the *Sun*, glanced at the front page, then threw it down again. He was too keyed up to read. They would soon be working with detectives at Scotland Yard, the birthplace of crime detection.

Molly folded her map. 'Have you packed your other clothes?' she queried. Bannister's single-breasted suit was long past its best.

'Thought I'd dress up for the Yard, ma'am. This rig only sees the light of day at weddings and funerals.'

She kept her thoughts to herself, not wanting to upset him.

'Have you been to Scotland Yard before, ma'am?'

She looked out at bare winter fields overhung with dark clouds. 'It's "New" Scotland Yard, and yes, I have. The last time was after some Swedish porn merchants had flooded the country with dirty books. They'd shipped them over in containers marked "Open University".'

Bannister grinned. 'They'd certainly educate some. What d'you think about the Yard, ma'am?'

'Don't get excited about that place. It's just a jumble of offices full of Met bobbies with inflated egos. . . . Civvies too, come to think of it. They're even worse. Most of them have been there for so long they can remember Sherlock Holmes.'

'Can they . . .?' he half-asked, before the stupidity of

160

the question dawned on him. 'I thought it was the Mecca of crime detection.'

'So do a lot of people.'

He wondered what she had against the Met, and hoped the lads would find time to take him on a tour of the West End clubs.

Molly occupied her time thinking about Conrad; the theft of Jackman's cannabis, the planting at Spence's shebeen. What else had he been up to? She looked at Bannister. Did he know what was going on? He may be inexperienced, but he was nobody's fool.

The Intercity rattled through Milton Keynes station.

'Ever been to London?' she asked.

'No, ma'am. Stuart Williams told me that they call gaffers "guv" and sergeants "skipper" as in ships.'

'They do a lot of daft things in the Met. And stop calling me ma'am. You might do it when we're with the traffickers.'

Leaving the train at Euston, they joined the other passengers as they streamed off platform six into the large open concourse with its giant flip-over destination boards.

'Where to now, m—?'

'The Tube. St James's Park.'

They rode down the double escalator, then followed the signs to the Northern Line platform. A train arrived as they reached the platform and they squeezed aboard.

'Our timing's smack on today,' Bannister said, hanging onto a safety strap and surveying his fellow passengers. He smiled at a pretty brunette who was standing directly in front of him. Although she was close enough to kiss, she cut him dead. Unabashed, he contemplated the other passengers; some reading, some knitting, some staring fixedly ahead like wax models. Their only common bond seemed to be a steadfast resolve to ignore each other.

The train stopped and started at white-tiled urinal-like stations. Doors opened, doors closed; breathing people out, breathing people in. Goodge Street, Tottenham Court Road, Leicester Square and Charing Cross. All lined with the same gaudy pictures advertising toothpaste, Concord, Canada and mint-flavoured condoms.

The Westhampton detectives emerged from the underground at St James's and turned into Broadway.

'Over there,' Molly called above the roar of the traffic. The world-famous address was a disappointing building: rows of uninteresting windows, boxed in lines of colourless concrete and reflecting London's sullen sky. Only a revolving stainless steel sign on the forecourt relieved the monotony. It had three sides, each bearing the legend ''New Scotland Yard''.

'That's an impressive name-plate, ma'am.'

Molly smiled ruefully. She preferred things of style which had been worked by craftsmen. 'Do you think so? It reminds me of a tired piece of cheese.'

They walked past a queue of cars, security guards with long-handled mirrors searching underneath each vehicle before allowing it to be driven into the underground car park.

A royal blue chauffeur-driven Jaguar stopped outside the main entrance.

'Christ, that's our Chief Constable!' Bannister exclaimed, stopping to watch a tall man unwind himself out of the passenger seat.

'Cool it!' Molly cautioned, nudging Bannister forward.

The chief looked at them, a brief shadow of surprise crossing his distinguished features. 'Cleaning up Soho, Watson?'

'Not quite sir. We're following up a drug importation racket.'

'Good, let me know how you get on,' the chief said pleasantly, transferring his attention to a short, midget of a man with bright red hair and coat-hanger epaulettes that made him look comic rather than superior.

'Is that the commissioner?' Bannister whispered in awe.

'One of his underlings.'

Bannister stepped back to let the two men pass.

'Get off my foot, you great oaf!' Molly gasped as the heel of his shoe crushed her toe.

'Sorry, ma'am.'

They entered a large grey and white marble foyer and approached two security guards who were sat at the reception desk, patiently dealing with enquiries from a queue of visitors. Waiting their turn, the detectives showed leather-bound warrant cards and one of the guards entered their names, ranks and numbers in the visitors' book.

Taking the lift to the fifth floor, they then made their way along a corridor similar to those at their own headquarters. Bannister glanced through open doorways as if hoping to see world famous crime-busters sitting around boardroom-sized tables discussing incidents of national consequence. But the rooms were empty and sparsely furnished, the desks buried under piles of paper, like CID offices anywhere.

Molly stopped outside a door marked "SOU".

'Sorry,' Bannister said as he bumped into her back.

She spun round angrily. 'For goodness' sake, settle down . . . You're like a flaming buffalo stomping about the place.'

Satisfied that he had got the message, Molly opened the door and led the way into a spacious but austere office. Two men seated behind a black-topped conference table rose to greet them.

163

'Inspector Watson and DC Bannister from Westhampton? Good morning. I'm in charge of the show — James Cranleigh-Smythe. This is my skipper, Dave Stockley. You spoke to him on Friday, I believe.'

'Pleased to meet you sir,' Molly said, leaning over the table to shake hands with the detective chief inspector and the well-built, ginger-haired sergeant who towered above him like a bodyguard.

'Shall we start by cutting out the formal stuff?' Cranleigh-Smythe said. 'It's James and Dave.'

'Molly and Bill,' she replied guardedly.

The chief inspector gestured towards the chairs in front of his visitors. 'Sit down, please. Take the weight off your feet and tell me all about it.' He had the deep, articulate voice of a man who never for a moment doubted his own authority. Tall and slim, with fine, aristocratic features and watchful grey eyes, his black hair receded slightly and was cut in the military, short-back-and-sides style. His suit was dark blue and he wore a Police College tie. She decided that he was about ten years her senior.

Outlining the events of the previous seven days, she described Ezra, the men from Manchester, and the contacts they'd had with them. Taking care to keep to the facts, Molly carefully trod a neutral line: not playing things down, but avoiding exaggeration and over-optimism.

When she finished, Cranleigh-Smythe remained silent for some time, as if mentally analysing the information. Finally he spoke. 'Do you think we have enough to let the test purchase run?'

'That's what I had in mind at the beginning,' she replied, 'But it's too risky. We don't know enough about the traffickers and I've still got my doubts about the informant. He's far too vague for my liking. We'll just have to arrest them and go from there. They might put in their supplier if we talk to them properly. It's been done before.'

Stockley intervened. 'We're dealing with this kind of thing every day. Just leave it to us, gal.'

Molly's expression could have split mountains. 'Don't you dare patronise me, Sergeant!'

The big man coloured and blustered an apology, looking to his boss for help.

Cranleigh-Smythe's eyes sparkled but his voice was as smooth as a diplomat's. 'We'll be very pleased to work with you, Molly, and I'm sure you're right. We can't afford to take chances. What do you think of these men from Manchester?'

Molly was not that easily pacified and she answered his question coolly. 'They're not like any drug dealers I've ever dealt with.'

Cranleigh-Smythe turned to Bannister. 'What about your contact, Bill?'

'Ezra's well into the scene, sir, but I've only used him for a few weeks. My DS handed him over to me.'

'Rather unusual, isn't it?'

'The sergeant said he wanted to help me, sir. Give me a good start like.'

'Very noble of him, I'm sure,' Cranleigh-Smythe replied without conviction.

He turned back to Molly. 'Is there anything else I should know about, Molly?' He loved the name and was fascinated by the freckles which seemed in keeping with her fiery temper.

'No, I don't think so. That's about it.'

Straightening out a desk blotter, he sat up in his chair. 'Well, we can certainly help to accommodate your Manchester friends and relieve them of twenty kilos of cannabis. All we need now is the commander's OK to borrow the seventy-five grand.'

'There is one thing I'd like to know before we start,' Molly said quietly. 'Who am I dealing with? Until last

Friday I'd never heard of the Special Operations Unit.'

'We're rather new, actually. Not many people *have* heard about us. We like it that way. There's a hundred or so of us at the moment, which may seem a lot, but we sometimes work all over the country, and abroad; Common Market countries mostly — Spanish sunshine and Italian tavernas if we're lucky,' he smiled. 'Our work involves a wide variety of unsavoury, and if I may say so, rather delicate, mostly clandestine operations. Stuff which I'm sure you wouldn't expect me to elaborate on. Covert operations, keeping an eye on certain politicians, that sort of job. Anything that's too sensitive for others to handle. If you need a bench-mark, then I would say we are somewhere between the Special Branch and the Crime Squad. Buying and Surveillance are the units that will assist you tomorrow.'

'Buying?' she frowned.

'Yes. We call every operation a ''buy''. Bullion, counterfeiting, prohibited weapons, stake-outs, whatever. They're all buys. We set up our own jewellery shop last year. Half the house-breakers in town sold us their loot. Most of them are now behind bars and their solicitors are screaming *agent provocateur* at the Court of Appeal.'

'Thanks for putting me in the picture . . . James.'

'My pleasure. We just happen to be between buys. The Drug Squad are so tied up at the moment they're in grave danger of disappearing down their own hooka pipes.' He gathered up some of the papers he had been going through with Stockley. 'I'm getting decidedly peckish. Would you like to sample Scotland Yard's à la carte specialities and meet Dave's Dragoons?'

'Only if they're friendly.'

They walked in single file through a self-catering canteen and into a dining room which was more in keeping with a four-star hotel than a police headquarters.

Bannister looked incredulously at the pink drapes and starched white tablecloths. 'Are DCs allowed in here?'

Cranleigh-Smythe spoke over his shoulder. 'It's a democratic institution, Bill. The troops use this place more than anyone. With all their overtime they can afford to.'

He led them to a window table overlooking Victoria Street. A strikingly attractive woman in her mid-twenties, and two men who were obviously in the autumn of their service stood up.

Cranleigh-Smythe stretched out his arm as if to embrace them. 'May I introduce the lovely Patricia Gerrard, one of my best undercover agents. Ably supported, I may add, by Graham Fothergill, generally known as Squint and his long-suffering pal, Cliff Rawlings. They have been with us since the start, and are in constant fear of having to return to the helmets where they might have to do some real work for a change.'

Fothergill was a short, wiry man with a protruding Adam's apple and a puckered, permanently puzzled expression. His partner was tall and stocky with the brooding, full face of an Italian film idol who had gone to seed.

Cranleigh-Smythe gestured towards the visitors. 'Detective Inspector Molly Watson and Bill Bannister, Westhampton Drug Squad.'

They shook hands all round then sat behind oversized menus bearing the crest of the Metropolitan Police.

After the wine had been poured Cranleigh-Smythe tapped the table for attention. 'First, a warm welcome to our friends from the Midlands. I'm sure we can make their stay a memorable one. Next, I would like to wish our lovely Patricia a very happy birhday.

'Happy birthday,' they chorused, raising full glasses.

'Thank you,' she replied, beaming at her boss.

The food arrived, the wine flowed, and conversation

came easily. Not one for idle gossip, Molly sized up the other diners and was impressed. In amongst the small talk they asked the right questions about the task ahead and seemed keen to get on with it.

After liqueurs she looked pointedly at her watch. 'That was an excellent lunch, thank you James, but I'm afraid we'll have to contact Ezra. You'll see him tomorrow,' she said for the benefit of the others. 'He's short, fat, black and fifty. Always wears a Derby hat.'

'Sounds too good to miss,' Fothergill laughed.

Before they left the table, Cranleigh-Smythe told his detectives to be in his office at six o'clock that evening.

21

An hour later, Molly and Bannister rejoined Cranleigh-Smythe and his skipper at the conference table.

' . . .so the Cumberland's out,' Cranleigh-Smythe was saying. 'Any ideas, Dave?'

'Royal Court's the best, guv. They owe us for the dipper job.'

'Good idea.' He looked thoughtfully at Molly.

' . . . Piccadilly.'

'Dipper?' Bannister queried.

Cranleigh-Smythe smiled benignly. 'During a stake-out for a counterfeiting team we picked up a gang of Colombian pickpockets who were using the hotel as a base. They had more cheque books and credit cards than Barclays.'

'Not to mention a suitcase stuffed with nicked jewellery,' Stockley added.

'Yes, management thought we were super-cops and gave us the freedom of the hotel. Until Squint's dog chewed up a Persian carpet, that is. When did the Manchester people say they wanted to do the switch?'

'One o'clock tomorrow afternoon, guv,' Bannister replied.

Cranleigh-Smythe doodled on his memo pad. Circles. He always did circles, circles and more circles, progressively smaller. Someone had told him it was a subconscious longing to return to the womb.

Running out of clean space, he tore off the top page and binned it before looking up. 'I think we should agree to their time but insist on the Royal Court. See to it, Skip. Adjoining rooms and the usual surveillance. Make sure it's on video this time. I'll go and squeeze seventy-five grand out of the commander.'

He then spoke to Molly, leaning unnecessarily close. 'I'll see you back here at five.'

'The original action man,' Stockley said after Cranleigh-Smythe had left. Molly gave the sergeant a questioning look. Was he being disloyal to his boss or simply trying to help her to understand him? 'He seems to know what he's doing.'

'And where he's going, ma'am. We rate him, even though he never lets up.'

'Where did he get a name like Cranleigh-Smythe?'

'His mother's family were big landowners in Kent. A while back, mind you. Four centuries, give or take a few generations. We call him Cranny.'

'What's he doing in this job?'

'He's the youngest son. It used to be the church or the army; things must be changing. Anyway, it's the Met's gain. He'll be running the whole show one day.'

Molly saw that Bannister was having difficulty keeping his eyes open. 'Come on, Bill. Geriatrics nod off after lunch, detectives on the threshhold of international fame make telephone calls. Contact Ezra and tell him that we'll see them at one o'clock tomorrow at the Royal Court. When you've done that, call the office and find out if there are any messages. I'm going out to stretch my legs.'

When Molly returned she found Bannister in earnest conversation with Pat Gerrard who had perched herself on the edge of a desk.

'Evening, ma'am,' Gerrard said cheerfully, tugging down her short skirt before making a quick exit.

Molly closed the door behind her. 'You want to be careful there.'

'Just passing the time of day,' Bannister replied truculently.

'Fresh air would have done you more good than chatting her up.'

He looked pointedly at the dark green Harrods' bags. 'Enjoy the walk, ma'am?'

'Never mind about that. Have you talked to Ezra?'

'Yes. They've agreed to the Royal Court but threatened to blow apart anyone who gets in their way. Said they know the hotel and will meet us in the Spanish Bar.'

'Any news from Dinsall?'

'Sergeant Conrad's done all the usual checks on the car and the Manchester guys' descriptions, but they've drawn a blank . . . .'

'Go on,' she demanded, sensing that he was holding something back. He hesitated, seemingly unsure of himself. 'Come on,' she insisted, 'we haven't got all day.'

'Superintendent Davids paid a visit. He did a wobbly when he found out we were in London. Said to tell you that you're not running your own private army and you've no right to go chasing all over the country without his say-so. Wants to see you the moment you get back.'

Davids hadn't been anywhere near Dinsall since he had made an inspection after she first joined the squad. Why should he decide to visit today of all days?

Someone must have tipped him off . . . and she had a good idea who it was.

'There's more, ma'am.'

She looked at Bannister's serious face and waited.

He swallowed hard. 'Catweasel's escaped from Central Lock-up. Jumped Sergeant Spoon and marched him out of the custody suite with a knife at his throat. No one dared to stop them and once they were outside Catweasel hopped into a waiting BMW.'

'Is Jack Spoon all right?' Molly asked, anger gripping

171

at her insides.

'Didn't say, ma'am. His pride must've taken a tumble. Stickler for the rules, is Jack.'

'Yes, I know,' Molly replied. 'Is that it?'

Bannister bit his lower lip, colouring slightly.

'Go on then,' demanded Molly, becoming more annoyed by the minute as she thought of Catweasel. 'No. Don't tell me, I can guess — Spence's shebeen.'

'The same as Jackman's raid, ma'am. You're being served forms for burglary, assault and malicious damage.'

'At least they're flaming consistent. Who's complaining? It can't be Spence.'

'Sound man. He's quite well known in the music world, by all accounts. Reckons those speakers were worth fifty grand. His agent is sueing for a lot of bread.'

Bannister couldn't bring himself to tell her about Conrad's snide remarks. ''Your old woman wants you to ring her urgently. She must be missing her home comforts already.'' Hearing Conrad's coarse laughter, he had slammed down the phone. When he'd tried to ring Liz the line had been engaged.

'I've got the seventy-five grand on the understanding that it's guarded by an armed man at all times,' Cranleigh-Smythe announced after the small group had reassembled. 'How did you make out, skip?'

'Couldn't be better, guv. Rooms on the seventh floor, and whatever else we need.'

Cranleigh-Smythe turned to Molly. 'Manchester?'

'They've agreed to the Royal Court. Said they'll meet us in the Spanish Bar.'

Stockley let out a hollow laugh. 'That's appropriate, ma'am. Blood-spattered matadors and dying bulls all over the place. Put you right off your steak and kidney, I can

172

tell you.'

'I hope we don't add to the carnage,' Molly murmured, still fuming over Catweasel and not happy about the guns. Villains who carried pieces were prepared to use them these days.

'What are we going to call this operation, Molly?' Cranleigh-Smythe asked.

'Operation Moscow,' she replied sharply.

He raised an eyebrow but made no comment.

Arrangements for the switch had been finalised when the three SOU detectives joined them at six o'clock. Cranleigh-Smythe gave them a brief outline of their plans and invited questions.

'What about control, guv?' Rawlings asked.

'First floor office across the road from the hotel. We'll call it Kremlin Control.'

'Will they be wired up for sound?' Gerrard asked.

'No, far too risky. The bad guys use scanners these days.'

'Shooters are a bit over the top for drug dealers, aren't they guv?'

'Not any more, they're not. I've arranged for ninjas to be in the vicinity of the hotel, and one will be with the money at all times. Firearms officers,' he said after seeing Bannister's puzzled expression. 'We'll also have TSG back-up nearby.'

Molly's dark look stopped Bannister asking what TSG meant. The Territorial Support Group was the SPG under another name. It was changed after a series of complaints about their heavy-handed methods. The first choice had been Fast Action Response Team, until controllers had started to use the initials with obvious glee.

Fothergill jerked his head in disgust. 'Isn't that typical. Special protection for the cash; passing attention for the

173

workers. They should get their priorities right.'

'They can replace you at anytime, Squint. Seventy-five grand is a little more difficult,' Cranleigh-Smythe said.

'I'm not so sure, guv', Rawlings said seriously. 'He's unique — no pockets.'

'If it wasn't for me, mate, you'd die of thirst,' Fothergill shot back.

Cranleigh-Smythe winked at Molly, then stood up and stretched his arms like a gymnast limbering up. Molly, never long off her feet, stood up beside him.

Two for a pair, Bannister thought. Over-active gaffers who can't keep still for a minute.

Resting his hands on the back of a chair, Cranleigh-Smythe addressed them. 'The traffickers were pretty nifty at Birmingham and I want to cover all the angles. Think about what I have said, and if you see any flaws in the arrangements or have any useful ideas, let me know before tomorrow's briefing. We certainly need a command performance from you, Bill. Get it right tomorrow and we'll strike a medal.'

'Can I pin it on his chest, guv?' Gerrard asked impishly.

'Boy-friend giving you a party tonight, Pat?' he countered.

'Rather be at work, guv.'

The chief inspector frowned for a moment. He tried not to make special allowances for DC Gerrard. At times she was a teaser but mostly, like other women in the job, she preferred to talk like the men, drink like the men, and curse like them, until you started to believe it; even with good-lookers like her. But he was careful not to, having learned that inside they were more vulnerable than men in a number of ways. He never ceased to be amazed at their commitment and their bravery, but he knew that at times of sudden emotional pressure or physical stress, they could crack like crystal. He wondered whether Molly fitted this

174

role model. She seemed to be one of a growing number of women who could be totally effective and at ease in the macho world of crime while still retaining their femininity.

'In that case, we can introduce our guests to the doubtful pleasures of the Tank. Fancy a drink, Molly?'

'Not really, but I'll enjoy the company.'

Bannister glanced upwards as if expecting the roof to collapse.

The Tank, Scotland Yard's watering hole, was in the basement of the building. Men in suits, and occasionally a woman, stood about in groups, ignoring the furniture as they enjoyed a few wind-down drinks and swapped stories about their latest bust, or bragged about how they had destroyed a defence barrister at the Old Bailey. It was a time to relax before the crawling queues of traffic or the push and shove of the Underground. It was also a daily meeting not to be missed: detectives picked up more information over a pint than they ever did at formal crime conferences. Cranleigh-Smythe's little band forced their way towards the bar.

Bannister, feeling hot in the warm, smoky atmosphere, looked about him and wondered which group was the Murder Squad, the Flying Squad, or the Robbery Squad.

Arms encircled him and soft hands crossed his chest as Pat Gerrard pressed against his back, her firm breasts demanding to be noticed. 'I need someone strong to fight off all these big hairy CID types,' she said in a hushed, silky voice.

A fine film of sweat appeared on Bannister's brow and his imagination went into overdrive. 'I'm your man,' he managed.

Pat dug her chin into his back. 'You're my special birthday treat.'

He held her hot hands and frantically trawled his mind for ways to get rid of his boss. 'How am I going to escape from Watty? She's already accused me of chatting you up.'

'She's only jealous.'

His face creased. 'Never thought of that. D'you think so?'

'Drinks up!' Cranleigh-Smythe called, 'I've bought a pint and a large scotch for everyone. Save struggling back to the bar for a refill. Swap what you don't want.'

Concentrating on full glasses they moved towards the side of the room.

'Happy birthday, Pat!' Cranleigh-Smythe said, kissing her on the cheek.

'Time you joined the WI,' Fothergill said with a wicked grin.

'If I was as old as you, Squint, I'd take up knitting,' Gerrard replied. When the sarcasm and the insults were flying she always gave as good as she got.

'You certainly can't get any bigger,' Fothergill laughed, leering at her blouse.

'Leave her alone,' Rawlings threatened, placing an empty pint glass on the floor and starting on another he had exchanged for a whisky.

'D'you want me and DC Gerrard to have a nose at the Royal Court tonight, ma'am?' Bannister asked Molly as soon as the idea struck him.

'Certainly not,' she snapped, finishing Rawling's whisky. 'The first time you'll see that place will be at lunch-time tomorrow — with me.' As Bannister ambled away, Molly cast an eye over the long black hair tumbling down the back of Gerrard's stylish leather jacket. She also noticed the skin-tight Levis, pointing at shapely ankles balanced precariously on extra-high heels.

'That woman could be earning a fortune in the fashion business,' she said quietly to Cranleigh-Smythe. 'Does she have any problems?'

'With the men, you mean? When she started, a sergeant

176

suddenly lost all interest in his work. Had to get rid of him in the end. She's good at her job, especially in the West End.'

'Will you recommend her for promotion?'

'She won't even take her exams. I've given her every encouragement but, like a lot of good detectives, she doesn't want to move.'

Molly watched Gerrard slide her hand into Bannister's trouser pocket. 'She's certainly got the hots for Bill Bannister. I hope she doesn't eat him alive — not before tomorrow, anyway.'

'Hum! I'm rather surprised. She's usually very discreet.'

There was an awkward silence. 'Perhaps she's just being friendly,' he continued. 'We like to look after our visitors from the provinces.'

'Excuse me while I take the straw out of my hair.'

He held her forearm. 'No offence meant, Molly. . . . I was on the point of asking you out. I know an enchanting little Italian place. The patron is a personal friend of mine, and his wine is superb.'

'Come off it, James. You just want to screw me.'

Thrown off balance, he finished his drink and reached for another.

'Sorry,' she apologised. 'It's been a long day. A long week, in fact. Yes, I would love to go out with you, but first I need to change my clothes.'

'I'll see you to your rooms,' he responded brightly. 'It's only a section house I'm afraid, but it's the best one we have.'

22

Molly couldn't remember the second bottle being tipped on its head but she did have a vague recollection of Giovanni popping the third.

When she had arrived at the restaurant, he had leaned over his enormous paunch and kissed her on both cheeks, his curly black moustache tickling her nose. His equally fat wife and spindly teenage daughter were summoned from the kitchen to shake her hand and nod respectfully before being ushered back to the pasta.

The wine was strong and dark. "From my brother's vineyards in Barolo" the proprietor had explained, rolling the word around his tongue as if the place itself was a delicacy.

Cranleigh-Smythe had chosen well, and Molly wondered how many other women he had lured into the warm, intimate booth tucked away among the hanging wine bottles and trailing fish nets.

Half-way through the starter — mushrooms in olive oil bombarded with diced pecorino — he had invited her to tell him all about herself.

"Oh, no," she had replied coyly, playing the courting game. "You first."

He seemed to enjoy talking about himself and his family. The country house, parents working in the city, pater's private club and prospective knighthood. His chummy public school days: summer hols on pater's yacht, winter hols on the pistes. She had actually yawned while he and his daredevil friends cramponed up the Eiger.

"I say, Molly, I'm not boring you am I?" he had said.

Although she'd denied such a suggestion, he had retreated into his shell and remained there until they were well into the *brasato*.

It was different now. The table had been cleared, the red candle was a shapeless stump, and they had slipped into that melancholy state on the edge of inebriation. She looked at the man across the table, thinking he was a dream in his dark blue jacket, white shirt, and silk, abstract tie. She was past caring now, but when he had picked her up, she'd felt a mess. There'd been time for a quick shower but her normally well-behaved hair was making some sort of protest and sticking out all over the place, and the beige, wool-crêpe suit she'd bought at Harrods, for the Police Surgeons Conference, was not really suitable for evening wear.

Molly stifled another yawn, wishing she didn't feel so tired. The strain of the last few days was beginning to tell and she was finally admitting to herself that she needed a break. Fat chance, she thought; not until this job, the brothel, and Conrad had been dealt with.

'Tell me about it,' coached the cultured voice.

'What?'

'Whatever's bugging you.'

'Is it that obvious?'

He reached for her hand. She nodded, more to herself than to him. His hand was warm and comforting, the nails perfectly manicured.

Not accustomed to sharing her problems, and certainly not with a high-flying detective chief inspector from New Scotland Yard, Molly felt her way slowly at first, then she suddenly gathered momentum so that the words gushed forth as if someone had opened the floodgates. She told him everything about her battles with Davids; his outdated ideas and attitudes, his prejudices against anything new and his stifling of initiative and progress. She also told him about Conrad's corruption.

When she finished, he did not try to advise her or offer easy solutions. 'I'm sure you'll work it out, Molly. Just remember who your friends are.'

Feeling better, she pressed his cool hand against her hot cheek.

'You're a very attractive woman,' he said softly.

She laughed. 'I was right about your intentions this afternoon.'

A shadow crossed his fine features.

'I'm sorry, James, she said hurriedly, 'that was unfair. It's just that I'm no good at relationships; never have been. I don't want to go soppy on you but I was brought up in a children's home. They don't teach you how to love in those places. I've tried. Oh, how I've tried. I'm just no good at it.'

She looked into his eyes to gauge his reaction to her outburst, but saw only the flicker of candlelight. 'D'you understand what I'm saying?' she asked, a note of desperation in her voice.

'Some of it, the home, possibly. I've always thought they were like public schools: huge monolithic buildings, in the middle of nowhere, so that you think they will gobble you up and no one will ever know about it.'

She gave him one of her best smiles. 'Something like that.'

Giovanni floated in and out of the booth, leaving a pot of steaming coffee and a plate of almond macaroons.

'Will you beat them?' Cranleigh-Smythe asked.

'Who?'

'Davids and Conrad.'

'God knows. Conrad, possibly, but how do you beat a superintendent? I think I'm OK with the chief. At least he put me in charge of the most difficult department in his force.'

180

'Does it work?'

'Of course it works. I've got the best squad in the whole country. And I can do the job in my sleep.'

His smile was gentle. 'They tell me you're a little tartar when roused.'

'No I'm not,' she snapped back.

He continued to smile.

'Well, a little,' she conceded. 'Sometimes. It's the best way to get things done. I let go with both barrels before they know what's hit them. After the initial shock they accept it. I think they prefer it that way. At least they know where they are.'

'And your fellows?'

'My who?'

'The other inspectors.'

'Most of them are great. One or two of the older guys can be funny: they can't stand to be shown up by a woman.'

'Um, I know how they feel.'

'I'm sorry, James. You've been wonderful, tonight has been my best for ages.'

'Is the job worth all the aggravation?' he asked.

She paused, thinking it through, finding it hard to concentrate. 'I always thought so, but lately I'm not so sure. There was a time when I would have rowed the Atlantic to be a chief super. But I'm changing, I'm beginning to think there must be more important things. My life seems incomplete. Maybe I need something else. . . family of my own perhaps.'

He kissed her hand. 'Perhaps I should take you home.' Cranleigh-Smythe parked his Rover outside the section house. Molly kicked off her shoes and curled up on the leather seat beside him. London's traffic was light but continuous: a city not wanting to sleep.

He told her about his broken marriage. His wife couldn't

stand his long, irregular hours at work. Bored and revengeful, she had taken up with a city stockbroker. One night when he returned to their apartment the furniture had gone and there was the proverbial note on the mantlepiece. That was three years ago, and he had not heard from her since.

They had been talking for an hour when a police car drew up in front of the Rover. A big man stumbled out of the back and a woman with long hair followed. Taking his arm, she guided him up the steps and pushed him through the door into the building.

'Oh, my God!' Molly exclaimed. 'That wreck out there is the star of tomorrow's show.'

James tapped the digital car clock. 'Today. In less than ten hours you'll both be on your way to the meet. I must go now I'm afraid.'

Surprised and disappointed, Molly looked away. She had been prepared for some time to tell him that she was no good at one night stands, but she would have liked to have been asked.

'I promised to see some of my chaps who are on a dicey job,' he continued. 'Home Office dirty tricks, actually.'

'You'd better go then,' she said quietly.

'Sorry, but it's very delicate.'

'There's no need to apologise. Just make sure that they don't do a Stalker on you.'

He nodded. 'Don't worry, I've got a safe-deposit box full of insurance.'

Impulsively, she reached across to give him a peck on the cheek. But he held her, surprising her with his strength and the gentleness of his kiss.

'Thank you, James,' she said a few moments later. 'Thank you for everything.'

Reluctantly, she left him and made her way into the section house.

23

Bannister groped for the alarm clock and batted bleary eyes at dark curtains framed by the pale morning light. His clothes trailed over the back of a chair, and on the dressing table, his shoes were heels up like sinking ships.

He rolled out of bed and threw open the curtains anticipating London in all its glory, but seeing only grey, grime-stained walls criss-crossed with black pipes and square ventilation shafts that were close enough to touch. Lowering himself onto a window seat, he craned his neck to see a postage stamp of dark cloud. How the hell did I get here? he asked himself.

Scraping a canal through brushless shaving cream, Bannister thought of Pat. He moved his head to one side, scanning the room through the mirror, half expecting to see her bra straps dangling over the end of the bed.

'Bastard,' he cursed, after slicing into his top lip.

He couldn't remember much about his night on the town. They'd finished up in a night-club close to the Elephant and Castle, and had a meal. Chilli-fry and pitta bread, somebody making his into a sandwich. The owner of the club was a former DC in the Murder Squad. He and Dave Stockley had joined the CID together, cutting their teeth on the vice and squalor of Soho. Anecdotes about their early adventures had flowed as fast as the whisky. A beer man himself, his memory of the night was a confused blur with only brief patches of lucidity.

He finished his shave, put on his druggie outfit, then stuffed his suit into a travelling bag.

Bannister met his boss at the bottom of the stairs,

appearing not to notice the bottle-green Yves Saint Laurent suit she had spent three months overtime on. She needed to convince the doubting drug traffickers that she was a high-flying businesswoman.

'All right, ma'am?'

'Good morning, Bill,' she replied cheerfully. They entered the small basement dining room and sat at a red formica-topped table.

The section-house cook, a female Frank Tyson, barged backwards through the kitchen door and turned towards a group of white-shirted duty men. Carrying two plates of steaming food in each hand, she waddled across the green vinyl floor and banged their breakfasts onto the table.

'Hey, Gertrude!' shouted one of the men. 'Did you bring these black bangers all the way from Zulu Land?'

Fat arms folded, she stared down at him. 'I'll report you to the Race Relations, you white honky trash!'

'Come here and let's make piccaninnies,' he laughed, hopelessly trying to encircle her wide girth with his arm.

She swatted it away. 'Man, you ain't got the tools. If you's in stud, they'd shoot you and sell your skinny carcase for dog meat.' His companions rocked with laughter as she followed her huge chest back into the kitchen.

Molly sent Bannister to order breakfast.

The cook eyed his crumpled jeans and dirty T-shirt. 'Can't serve you till I knows who you is.'

He flashed his warrant card. 'I'm a detective . . . from the Midlands.'

'You's not supposed to bring your floosie in here.'

Bannister coloured, not daring to turn around. 'That's my boss.'

The cook's bovine nostrils flared. She thought she'd heard all the excuses.

'What's for breakfast?'. Bannister asked.

She pointed at the chalked menu. 'Detectives are

supposed to be able to read.'

He asked for full breakfasts, then retreated to the table.

'At least one woman can resist your charms Billy Boy.' Molly said. She felt good. Her evening out with James had recharged her batteries. What would she have been like if she had spent the night at his place?

Leaving the section house, the Westhampton detectives paused on the steps to watch London's traffic: swarms of busy black cabs carrying cross-legged businessmen; lines of red double-decked buses full of strap-hanging secretaries. Shop fronts were night-bright under an overcast sky and passing pedestrians leaned into a biting north wind.

'Well, Bill. It's a week since we first heard about our friends from Manchester. Today we'll find out who they are and what they're up to.'

A cab stopped at the kerb. 'Inspector Watson?' called the driver.

'Who's asking?'

'Mr Cranleigh-Smythe. Sends his regards and asked me to pick you up, ma'am.'

'That's thoughtful of him,' she said, climbing aboard, followed by Bannister.

Heading south, and crossing the Thames at Tower Bridge, they passed the stern of HMS Belfast, once a proud fighting ship, now a sad stationary museum. Molly looked hard at Bannister, noticing the cut lip and the dark patches beneath his eyes. 'Didn't let the squad down last night, did you?'

'No ma'am. I think they'd have been proud of me.'

Traffic had thinned and the streets were narrow when the taxi suddenly ducked into a passageway between derelict buildings that had shards of glass where the windows had once been. They rattled across a cobbled yard, then drove into a warehouse, roller-shutters clanking to the floor behind them.

Molly sprang forward in alarm and was about to tackle the driver when she caught sight of Cranleigh-Smythe standing outside a Portakabin.

'Pleased to see you, Molly,' he welcomed.

She smiled briefly, checking her new surroundings. 'Good morning, James. I thought for a minute we'd been hijacked again.'

'Our humble home, for the time being at least: we keep moving.' Workmen in overalls pushed trolleys laden with cardboard cartons, stacking them in colour-coded bays. A fleet of Renault vans with Santana Supplies painted on the sides filled one end of the warehouse. At the other end, there was a mezzanine floor with a cinema-style balcony.

'It's certainly big enough,' Molly said, noticing for the first time the men and women who were watching them from the balcony. 'Are that lot up there waiting for the second feature?'

' "That lot up there" are my stake-out team, sizing up a frightfully stunning city businesswoman and a small-time drug dealer from the Midlands,' he replied with a gracious smile. 'They'll have the colour of your eyes and length of your skirt by now.'

Cranleigh-Smythe signalled for his officers to disperse. 'Come on, Molly, it's time you visited the ops room.'

The Portakabin was surprisingly large. Four tables marched down the centre and folding chairs lined the walls.

'Morning, guv,' croaked a voice from the far end of the room. Seeing Stockley, they walked towards him and stopped in front of a table covered with used bank notes.

'Christ!' Bannister exclaimed.

'Bent money,' Cranleigh-Smythe offered. 'See all the different bank stamps? On the last job it was a quarter of a million. We're sure to lose it one day.' He sorted some of the bundles into their different denominations.

'Let's count it, skip. Where's the ninja?'

'On his way, guv.'

'Enjoy yourself last night, Bill?' Cranleigh-Smythe asked, glancing at Molly.

'Super . . . thanks, guv.'

'Where did you finish up?'

As Bannister struggled to find a plausible answer the door opened.

'Constable Sippits, PT17, guv,' declared a fit-looking man with close-cropped grey hair who casually nudged his sports jacket to show the butt of a shoulder-holstered 9mm Glock semi-automatic. 'I've been told I'm not to let that money out of my sight.'

'Good. You'll be with Sergeant Stockley. He has the same instructions.'

Molly and Bannister watched the SOU men count the money into a black suitcase.

'There you are, Molly,' Cranleigh-Smythe said when they had finished. 'Seventy-five thousand pounds exactly.'

As if on cue, the taxi which had picked the detectives up from the section house returned with two motorcycles, their noisy engines resounding through the warehouse.

'Who're they?' Bannister asked after the din had subsided.

'That's the cavalry,' Cranleigh-Smythe replied. 'The stick insect in green leathers with Ace Courier Services on the back is Walter. The young fellow in the Hell's Angel's outfit and Brixham Chapter colours is known as Killer. You've already met Bert the Taxi. Let's go and join them. They're playing an important role today.'

When the introductions were finished, Molly checked the Hackney Cab badge on Bert's blue suit. It looked genuine enough. I should have realised that he was a member of the SOU when he picked us up, she thought.

Watching her closely, Stockley smiled. 'He makes more money out of the fares than he gets paid, ma'am, and it's tax free.'

'Anything for a crust,' Bert said.

The men in leathers leaned on their machines and Bert sat on the luggage platform of his taxi. Walter passed around the Bensons.

'I'll warn you now,' Molly said to them. 'If they use the Merc, you won't keep up with it. They're surveillance conscious and very fast.'

'Don't you fret, ma'am. We've never lost anyone yet,' Walter grinned condescendingly.

Molly's face darkened and they saw the steel in her eyes. 'I'm not worried, but you'd better be. That driver's a maniac.'

Cranleigh-Smythe, overhearing the exchange, smiled briefly. The tiger was back, he thought.

'What's your rig, Walter?' asked Bannister, trying to cool things down.

'Suzuki 125,' he replied, hand moving along the petrol tank like a man stroking his mistress. 'Best machinery for beating the traffic.'

'What about you, Killer?'

'I can leave the old geezer standing,' he boasted, side-stepping to avoid Walter's riding boot. 'Harley-Davidson Low Rider, 1000cc. I'd come to work if they didn't pay me. Nothing gets away from this beauty,' he added, giving Molly a meaningful look.

Leaving them to tune their engines, Cranleigh-Smythe took his visitors back to the ops room. After the final briefing, Cranleigh-Smythe stood up. 'Well, this is it folks. Any questions before we get things moving?'

Molly rubbed her hands together. After seven days hard work things were about to happen. 'Let's get on with it. I've got a couple of Mancunians to straighten out.'

Cranleigh-Smythe handed Bannister a black suitcase then escorted the Westhampton detectives to the taxi.

188

'Good luck, Molly, and be careful,' he said seriously.

A man in brown overalls pulled a rusty chain hand over hand, like a sailor hoisting the ensign at daybreak. Men working in the warehouse stopped what they were doing and watched as the roller shutters rose.

Bert switched on the ignition and the taxi, followed by its motorcycle escort, moved out into London's sobering daylight.

24

They had left early to allow for traffic problems but the short journey into the West End was uneventful and there was time to spare. Driving past the Houses of Parliament and down The Mall, they stopped outside Buckingham Palace, Bert giving them the commentary he had perfected for the day when he hoped to ply his own cab.

Not that any of it registered with Bannister who felt shattered after a night's eroticism such as he'd only dreamed about. He had a splitting headache, his stomach was in ferment, and he felt that his bowels could make a fool of him at any moment.

Molly asked him if he was feeling all right.

He forced a grin. 'Yes, thanks ma'am.'

'Just make sure you are, that's all. And for goodness' sake, drop the ma'am.'

The taxi pulled into the kerb. 'Royal Court,' Bert announced. 'That'll be seven quid, please, ma'am.' Molly gave him a look of disbelief. 'Got to keep up appearances, ma'am.'

She handed over the exact fare.

'May I take your baggage, sir?,' offered the doorman, resplendent in his olive-green coat and matching topper trimmed with gold. Beneath the hat were the swarthy features of DC Rawlings.

Grateful for any help he could get, Bannister swung the suitcases in the doorman's direction, but Molly stopped him.

'No thank you,' she said crisply. 'My man's perfectly capable of carrying it himself.'

The briefest flicker of amusement showed in Rawling's eyes before he respectfully touched his cap and led the way up the granite steps of the elegant Edwardian Hotel.

The ornate, blue-carpeted foyer was luxurious. Shops and boutiques lined both sides and a theatre-looking office faced them. Potted greenery, interspersed with pink marble statues, shone in healthy splendour under a magnificent stained-glass dome.

The receptionist's automatic smile of welcome changed to a look of disapproval as her eyes moved from the smartly dressed woman to the handsome young scruff who accompanied her. Checking the reservation, and seeing that it was an afternoon booking only, the receptionist nodded imperceptibly. She removed a room key from the board and handed it to Molly.

'I hope madam finds her short stay satisfactory,' the receptionist said with a barely concealed tone of disapproval.

Molly smiled sweetly, 'I can't fail, darling.'

'What was all that about?' Bannister asked as they walked towards the lift.

Molly chuckled. 'Women's talk. Don't worry about it.'

Bannister frowned but his attention was immediately distracted by someone standing beside the lift. He was sure he'd seen her at the SOU base. She had one of those figures you don't miss, not even in his fragile condition.

When they reached the seventh floor, a man with a vaguely familiar face was standing in the corridor, ostensibly reading a brochure. Molly unlocked 737 and walked into the room.

'Good afternoon, ma'am,' Stockley said as he walked through a door from the adjoining room to greet them. 'Our friendly manager's popped in to make sure we've got everything we need. He said that the guys from Manchester booked in yesterday and have been hanging about in the

191

foyer like TV detectives.'

'That doesn't surprise me.'

They were joined by a pasty-faced man with fleshy red lips and rounded shoulders. His huge stomach hovered above his belt like an avalanche waiting to happen. Molly decided that he could be an old thirty-five or a young fifty.

'This is Chris Collins, Technical Support Unit,' Stockley said. 'He's not too bad for a civilian.'

Collins had a shrill, effeminate voice. 'You've come just in time — if you'll excuse the expression. Can you find the bug?'

Molly, amused but not showing it, nodded to her detective who started to search the room, looking behind the curtains and other likely places.

'Chris, you'd better tell us where it is,' Molly said. 'We haven't got much time.'

'There you are, my dear,' he declared triumphantly, removing a matchbox from the dressing table and pushing out one end to show the miniature transmitter.

Molly glanced at Stockley. 'I hope they don't ask for a light.'

Bannister heaved the black suitcase into the wardrobe then lowered himself into a comfortable chair. Like a tired child, he closed his eyes and went to sleep almost immediately.

Checking her watch, Molly spoke to Stockley. 'Do me a favour, will you, Dave? Find an empty room for the great lover here and lay him out on the bed. If he doesn't die on us, make sure he's back here and ready for action in thirty minutes' time.'

'Busy night, ma'am?'

She gave him a wry smile. 'His body obviously had difficulty coping with his carnal ambitions.'

After they had left, Molly surveyed the room. Behind the ritzy entrance it was like most hotels owned by the multinationals: functional utility. She rearranged the chairs so that when the money was counted, she would have her back to the window with a good view of the whole room, including both doors.

PC Sippits arrived with an armful of radios. 'Checked and working strength nine, ma'am,' he reported with the air of a man wound up for action.

Stockley returned, felt under the bed, then pulled out a black suitcase which was identical to the one Bannister had left in the wardrobe. When he opened the suitcase, they saw that it was packed with bundles of notes wrapped in clear plastic bags. Molly examined a few of the seals knowing that she would have to accept Stockley's word that it was the seventy-five thousand pounds they had counted out at Special Operations.

Closing the case, Stockley pushed it back under the bed and they made themselves comfortable while they waited for further instructions.

Twenty minutes or so later, the telephone rang. Stockley grabbed the receiver. Sensing the growing excitement, he paused before passing on the message.

'All units ready. Commence Operation Moscow.'

'Do your magic on super-sleuth, will you, Dave?' Molly said. 'I need him on full power for six hours. After that he can sleep for a month if he wants to.'

Stockley produced a small packet of amphctamine sulphate. 'Every good doctor keeps his medicine handy, ma'am.'

A few minutes later Bannister, grinning sheepishly, filled the doorway. The pupils of his eyes were like ink pots.

Molly shook her head in exasperation. 'The little boys' room is over there,' she said, gesturing towards a door next to the wardrobe.

Bannister walked stiffly into the bathroom, closed the door behind him, then smiled dreamily into the mirror.

Stockley's concoction coursed through his system and he felt better by the minute. Flicking his long straw-coloured hair over the collar of his denim jacket, he noticed the bruising on his neck where Pat's lips had held him like a leech.

'Right, our kid,' he muttered to himself. 'Today you become top gun, or you plod the beat for the rest of your life.'

Opening the door, he came face to face with Molly.

'I don't know what you've been doing in there,' she said angrily. 'It's nearly one o'clock.'

He tried to pass her but she stopped him. 'If they ask where I am, tell them I'm putting the money away and will be down shortly.' Their eyes locked and Bannister was surprised by a sudden softening in her voice. 'Just be yourself, Bill. If you start acting like a Hollywood secret agent, you'll be so busy trying to remember your lines your mind won't be on the job.'

He hesitated and she patted him on the back like a manager sending her fighter into the ring. 'Go to it,' she said quietly. 'Let's show them what a good team we are.'

Elated, he strode jauntily down the corridor. Well out of hearing, he smiled to himself and used his inspector's favourite phrase; 'don't worry about it.'

25

Bannister stepped out of the lift and drifted over to the jeweller's shop. Who could afford to pay five years salary for a diamond necklace? he wondered.

Making sure that Special Operations had time to pick him up, he strolled into the Spanish Bar. Inside the door, he stopped and looked around him, getting his bearings like any new resident. It was a large room with orderly rows of oak tables, each having its own red-shaded lamp and sets of place mats showing bright Iberian scenes. The white plaster walls were livened with bold pseudo-Spanish murals of black blood-splattered bulls charging skinny overdressed matadors.

Aware that he was being watched, Bannister resisted a natural inclination to check out the other occupants and made his way to the bar.

'Pint of bitter,' he ordered a little too dramatically. Recalling Watson's advice, he urged himself to stay cool.

His drink appeared. 'Will that be all, sir?'

Bannister's head jerked up in surprise and he saw Pat Gerrard smiling across the counter at him. She was dressed in the hotel uniform, her figure prominent under the gold blouse and green necktie. Lost for words, he fumbled with his money, then paid her for the drink. When she gave him the change, she gently squeezed his hand.

'Are you joining us mate? Or are you here for the view?' asked a rough Manchester voice. Bannister picked up his drink and turned. 'Come on,' Spider said, 'let's get moving.'

Bannister followed him down the side of the room, past

the life-sized matadors, killing swords poised to deliver the *coup de grâce.*

Sitting at a corner table at the rear of the room, Duke watched his approach. So did a slim, dark-skinned man of about forty who was sat beside him. Opposite the two men Bannister could see the unmistakable back of Ezra.

'Get in there, mate,' Spider ordered, indicating a vacant seat next to Ezra who looked grey and frightened under his Derby. Carefully placing his glass on the table, Bannister sat down.

'Pretty-boy here is a fast mover,' Spider grinned. 'Trying it on with the barmaid, he was.'

'Where's your boss?' Duke demanded.

'Upstairs sorting out the money.'

'She bugs me. What's a doll like that doing in our business?'

'I shouldn't worry, she'll go easy on you.'

'Don't smart-arse me, kid.'

Feigning indifference, Bannister studied the middle-aged man sitting opposite him, noting his beady brown eyes and large hooked nose. He was painfully thin, and his suit seemed to be made of silk. A dazzling row of diamond rings fought for pre-eminence on the bony fingers of his right hand.

'This is Isha, the Arab with the gear. He's really a Syrian — from Syria,' Duke said with a false little laugh.

'There is nothing to worry about, my friend,' Isha said in too-perfect English. 'We are all nervous because this is the first time we have done business together. Everything will be all right when we are better acquainted.'

'What's your gear?' Bannister asked quietly.

'Best Moroccan. Come and see it. You can taste it. You can smoke it . . . Do any test you like. Have you got the seventy-five thousand pounds?'

'I've already said, it's upstairs.'

196

Duke stiffened. 'She's here.'

Feeling strangely detached and at ease, Molly advanced on the corner table. She could see the men watching her and felt like a model on the catwalk.

'D'you get that outfit? D'you see those gold buttons? They must be the real thing,' Duke muttered to the dark-skinned man sitting next to him.

'I thought she was short of money.'

'Not that kind of bread. She does deals worth millions for Christ's sake. What d'you think of her?'

'We shall see. She certainly has expensive tastes.'

'I thought she was a cop at first, but she's got too much style. Like a thoroughbred, if you know what I mean, and she's prepared to put up a hundred and fifty grand every month. That's a lot of bread.'

When Molly reached the table, Spider pointed to a chair beside Bannister. 'Sit next to your flunky,' he ordered.

Ignoring him, Molly sat alongside Duke from where she could see the whole room.

Leaning across Duke, Isha shook her hand. 'I am happy to meet you, madam. It will be a pleasure to do business together.'

Molly managed a smile. The man's hand felt like a dead fish and his eyes were everywhere, probing, as if he were trying to do an instant body and mind scan.

Duke intervened. 'Just a little warning before we start. The big guy sitting near to the bar is the "minder". He has orders to shoot if there's any trouble.'

Patently unconcerned, Molly glanced at a tall, thick-set man with a round shaven head and a full, black beard. His lumpy face looked as if it had been used as a punchbag, and he wore a blue open-necked shirt under a black leather jacket which hung away from his fat gut. The pint glass in his hand seemed more like a child's teacup.

'Surely you don't feel threatened by me, do you?' she asked with mock surprise.

Duke scowled. 'Have you got the money?'

'There's seventy-five thousand in a room upstairs if you want to check it.'

'Later will do.' Duke took a twenty-pound note out of his top pocket and passed it to Spider. 'Get everyone a scotch — doubles.'

'Perrier for me,' Molly said. 'And don't forget the ice and lemon.' Spider's comment was inaudible.

Some of the tension appeared to leave Duke and he leaned back in his seat. 'Well, there's one thing for sure, you can't be the Old Bill. They're all piss-heads!' He started to laugh, then gripped at his chest as he broke into a spasm of coughing.

Soon recovering, he wiped his mouth with the back of his hand. 'Your mate can come with us to see the gear. Until he's satisfied it's good stuff, there's no point in checking the money.'

Molly took her time in answering. She had to protect the commissioner's money at all costs, and she had to get the traffickers and their gear back into the hotel where the SOU could spring an ambush. 'I'm new to all this and I don't follow. What are you thinking of doing?'

Isha's brown eyes were intense, calculating. 'We will take your friend to where he can examine the merchandise. You must understand that once he has accepted the bag, he will have to carry it himself. That way, if there is any cheating, he will be the only person arrested.'

Bannister pushed his chair back to let Spider pass with a tray of glasses.

'You can't be too careful in this game,' Duke said, eagerly picking up his drink and taking a large swallow of whisky.

Molly sipped her Perrier, knowing that she must keep Duke under pressure if she was to persuade him to return to the hotel with the gear. 'Which is exactly why I'm not going with you. I've already been for a ride around one cit—'

'What's the matter with you?' Duke cried. 'We haven't asked you to come with us.'

'It could be a trick,' she said, motioning towards Bannister. 'He's not carrying a bag of cannabis around London, and I'm not leaving this hotel with seventy-five thousand pounds. If you want the money you must bring the drugs back here. Otherwise the deal's off.'

She swirled ice and lemon around her glass and waited for a reaction.

Surprisingly, Duke turned to Ezra. 'What d'you think?'

The man under the brown Derby humped his shoulders.

Spider leaned towards Molly. 'Why should we waste twenty kilos of good shit just to set you up? It's the deal of the century, for fuck's sake.'

'All right, cool it,' Duke cut in before taking over again. 'If it'll make you happier we'll bring him back here ourselves. But you must be outside the hotel with the money. When we return, your mate will get out of the car with the gear. You will then hand over the money as we drive past. That way we'll all be safe.'

'No,' she said immediately. 'If you want the money, you'll have to come up to my room and collect it.'

Duke wiped the sweat from his brow. 'You must think we're round the bend. No one takes those kinds of risks in our game.'

'My friends,' Isha soothed. 'We cannot continue like this. Why not split the difference — meet in the foyer?'

'Suits me,' Molly said, silently cheering, but being careful not to appear too eager. 'As long as my man comes back with you.'

Duke grabbed at his glass and as he drank, whisky ran down the folds of his chin and splashed onto his chest. He glared aggressively at Molly. 'I'm warning you, doll. If there's any funny stuff, you're both finished. Dead. Blown apart! Kaput!'

Molly put on a show of complete indifference to his threats, casually looking around the room. It was filling up. The overworked temporary bar staff gave no sign that they were controlling a hidden video camera and a directional microphone.

'My friends,' Isha said expansively, 'I suggest we make a move.'

Taking his lead, they all stood up and filed out of the Spanish Bar.

When the group stopped in the centre of the foyer Molly spoke to Duke and pointed to a seat that faced the entrance. 'In half an hour from now I'll be sitting there with the money. If you're not back in forty minutes, the deal's off.'

26

'Let's get going,' Spider said, shouldering his way through the revolving door.

Bannister started to follow but Isha held him back. 'Do not look so worried, my fine friend. Nothing will go wrong.'

'It's all right for you, but I don't know London, I don't know you, and I don't know the Manchester guys.'

Isha moved closer. 'Take no notice of them, they are nothing. Mouth and muscle, but no brain.' He glanced over his shoulder at the Minder who was closing up but still some distance behind them. 'I have taken a liking to you, my friend. Once this is over we will deal direct. There is no need for the others. We can make more money, you and I.'

As they hurried down the steps, the doorman saluted smartly and wished them a safe journey. Duke, Spider and Ezra were some distance down the road, standing beside a car — the Birmingham Mercedes.

Duke opened a rear door as they approached. 'Get in,' he ordered Bannister. Ezra followed the detective and the door was slammed shut behind him. Duke then went round the back of the vehicle, climbed in, and sat on the other side of Bannister. Isha sat in the front next to Spider.

Trapped between fat, Bannister thought, relieved to hear the throaty rattle of Bert's diesel-engined taxi and the quiet put-put of Walter's two-stroke Suzuki.

The car moved forward, turning left once and then again, circling the hotel. Picking up speed along the curve of Regent Street, and passing the Cafe Royal, they swung into Piccadilly Circus. Bannister noticed the Boots all-night chemist where addicts queued into the early hours for their methadone scripts. He tried to work out where he was being taken, conscious that Isha was watching him closely through the vanity mirror.

'That's it,' Duke said. 'A couple of trips around the West End to make sure there's no tail, then we'll show you the gear.'

Bannister felt queasy, only partly due to his over-indulgence the previous night. It was the Birmingham meet all over again.

They turned into a side road, speed increasing. Spider kicked down on the accelerator, dropping the automatic into second gear while maintaining the revs so that the car surged forward. Ezra's body went rigid as he grabbed at an armrest.

At a Give Way sign ahead of them a milk float stopped. Spider overtook it, two-tone horns blaring as he aimed the speeding car at a banner-waving procession which was crossing the mouth of the junction. Chanting changed to screams and terrified demonstrators scattered in all directions. Swerving to avoid a push-chair and a horror-stricken young girl who had fallen into their path, the car skidded across the wet surface and bounced off a parked lorry. Fighting the wheel, Spider regained control as they hurtled on towards the next crossroads.

Bannister looked back in time to see a baby being snatched from the push-chair and the young woman rising to her knees. Broken placards, smashed umbrellas and personal effects littered the road. People, now receding rapidly into the distance, shook their fists.

'Geronimo!' Spider yelled, throwing back his head in a frenzy of madness. 'That made the stupid bastards jump!'

'Look out!' Isha screamed, cowering under his arms as they shot through red lights and collided with a cyclist, knocking him high into the air.

Bannister gripped the front seat and pulled himself forward. The big men on each side of him were thrown across the vacant space, complaining bitterly as they collided.

The tyres squealed in protest as they slewed around a corner then shot forward again, Spider's fiendish laughter ringing in the ears of his passengers.

'No fucker's following us now!' he shouted.

Straightening himself out, Duke reached for the collar of Spider's polo-necked jumper, pulling and twisting it in one savage movement. 'Stop the car, you stupid fool!' he bellowed.

Eyes bulging, Spider struggled against the ligature. His foot slipped off the accelerator and he groped for the brake pedal. The car bounced along the gutter and slithered to a stop.

Heads dropped. Isha sighed with relief. Ezra farted, long and loud. Bannister opened a window.

Keeping the pressure on Spider's windpipe, Duke spoke quietly into his ear. 'Now, brain drain, drive on slowly and get us back into the traffic so's we look like all the other bleeding cars. Go on, before the whole Metropolitan Police Force turns up.'

They moved forward, slowly. It was several turns and about a mile further on, before Duke released his hold on Spider and ordered him to stop the car.

Duke got out and inspected the damage. He pulled a broken handlebar from behind the front bumper and threw it into a nearby builders' skip. Spider joined him, rubbing his neck as he stared sullenly at the dented bodywork. Moving out of earshot, they squared up to each other. The men left in the Mercedes, seeing contorted faces and the angry gestures, could only guess at what was being said.

Isha spoke to Bannister. 'I am sorry, my friend. That was very dangerous.'

The detective felt ill, wishing he could jump out of the car and run to the nearest toilet. 'The man must be out of his sodding mind,' he said through clenched teeth. 'He could've killed us all for a few kilos of bloody cannabis. That cyclist's a gonner.'

'No, my friend, I saw him get up.'

'Thank Christ for that.'

The Manchester men returned to the car.

Duke eyed Bannister suspiciously. 'He thought we were being followed. Two men in suits in a plain car. The passenger was using a radio, and they were hanging back, like they didn't want to show out.'

Bannister shrugged. 'So what? They all wear suits down here, and who hasn't got a poseur phone?'

Back in the flow of traffic, he looked for road signs and street names which might give him a clue to their destination. They passed Victoria Station and drove along Grosvenor Place.

'Where are you taking me?' Bannister asked as they approached a green, open space and a stretch of water.

'Never heard of Hyde Park?' Duke asked.

'You haven't buried it, have you?'

They laughed, seemingly enjoying themselves.

Isha turned in his seat. 'We did not tell you before but there is no harm now that we are friends. The cannabis is in the boot. It has been there all the time.'

'You must be off your bloody rockers. What would you've done if the law had stopped us?'

'About three years,' Spider grunted, back to his loutish self.

Bannister glared at the bull-neck above the seat in front of him. Thirty years wouldn't be enough for you, he thought, looking forward to the time when Spider was in the traps.

They bumped over the narrow Serpentine bridge, then

pulled into the restaurant car-park.

'Don't move,' Duke ordered. 'I want to see if we're being followed.'

The powerful engine ticked over quietly. Several couples strolled around the lake, apparently untroubled by the fine rain. A tramp, sitting on the wet grass beneath the bare branches of an oak tree, drank from a blue meths bottle.

After a few minutes, Duke got out of the car and opened the boot. Removing a brown holdall, he passeed it to Isha who placed it on the floor between his feet then opened the zip. Bannister stretched forward and saw that the bag was full of muslin-covered blocks about the size of a thin paperback.

'There you are, my friend,' Isha said. 'Twenty kilos of the very best Moroccan.' He handed a block to Bannister who saw the red Arabic lettering and the distinctive 00 mark that signified the highest quality. Isha then cut the block into two halves and showed Bannister the brown coloured substance inside the muslin.

Duke's head suddenly whipped round. 'What's he gawping at?' he cried out, calling their attention to a man sitting behind the wheel of a car only a few feet away.

'Move it,' Duke yelled.

Spraying gravel as the tyres dug into the loose surface of the car-park, the Mercedes shot away at full throttle towards the Kensington Road.

Bannister looked back through the rear window. There was no sign of the car. 'Looks like you spooked,' he remarked casually, knowing that Watson would have said something similar.

It wasn't until they reached heavy traffic and edged towards the hotel that Duke spoke. 'You've seen the gear now. I told you it was good stuff.' He tapped Isha on the shoulder. 'Let our mate here have a gander at the rest of it.'

Isha handed over the block he had cut open.

Bannister examined it. 'Seems OK to me. Let's see the rest.'

'Give him the bag full,' Duke ordered.

Isha heaved the holdall over the front seat. 'Have you got any pocket scales with you?'

Shaking his head, Bannister delved into the bag, trying to estimate the number of blocks. Duke moved over to give him more room and invited him to count them.

'I need a smoke,' Duke said, holding out his hand.

Isha gave him a piece of resin the size of a thumb-nail. Cutting it up into small flakes with a pocket knife, Duke mixed it with tobacco, using papers from his top pocket to make a show of rolling a reefer.

Bannister watched the awkward sausage-like fingers through the corner of his eye, and knew immediately that Duke didn't normally roll his own.

Lighting up, Duke inhaled deeply before collapsing into a fit of painful coughing. Thumping his chest with annoyance, he slowly recovered, wiping tears from the folds of flesh around his eyes.

'This bloody asthma will finish me before the bastard cops do,' he moaned. 'Can't even enjoy a joint any more.' He turned to Bannister. 'Here, mate, you've earned a blast. It's too much for me.'

Bannister snatched at it. Hands shaking, eyes closed in faked ecstasy, he took a long, slow draw, filling his lungs.

'I can see you're on the scene, mate.' Duke grunted, taking the reefer from him.

The inside of the car was unbearably hot and it reeked with the smell of cannabis. Bannister, unable to think clearly, sweated freely. Throwing the few blocks he had checked into the bag, he fell against the back of the seat. 'I can't be bothered to count all this lot,' he mumbled. 'I'll take your word for it.'

Duke laughed, his face bright red. 'Guaranteed the best, mate.' He leaned across Bannister and slapped Ezra's fat stomach. 'I knew this guy wouldn't let us down.'

'Gimme that joint,' Ezra pleaded. Duke gave him the reefer.

'Pass me the bag,' Isha said.

Duke took the holdall from Bannister. He was heaving it over the front seat when the car ahead of them swerved to avoid a jay-walker. Spider slammed on the brakes and Duke fell forward, blocks of cannabis cascading over Isha as the boot lid of the car flew open. Horns blared all around them, impatient drivers gesticulating as they tried to pass the stationary Mercedes.

'Shut the boot,' Duke shouted.

Spider ran to the back of the car and slammed the lid down. Jumping back into his seat, he knocked the auto gear into Drive, then quickly rejoined the moving traffic.

Bannister shook his head, trying to clear it. They're all out of their stupid skulls. Watty will never believe any of this. It's crazy; a sodding travelling circus.

'If you don't want to attract attention, get rid of that fucking joint,' he yelled. 'The whole city can smell the bloody stuff. It only needs a copper on point duty to notice, and we've had it.'

Duke slapped his knee. 'You're all right, you are, mate. One of the boys.'

Isha, having put all the blocks back into the holdall, turned to Bannister. 'Are you satisfied with the cannabis?'

'It'll do,' Bannister replied.

'What do you mean "it'll do". It is top quality,' Isha pressed. 'Forty-four half-kilo blocks. We always give our best customers a few extra.'

Bannister blinked at the faces spinning around him, feeling the effects of Stockley's cocktail and Duke's joint. 'We'll have to move it. She'll be gone if we're not back in time.'

'Silly cow,' Spider mumbled.

Bannister wiped his sweating brow. 'You'd better believe her. She's a hard woman.'

'Give's you a hard on, more like,' Duke said. 'Does she do a bit — for friends like?'

'Not for me she doesn't.'

'I bet she's good in the sack.'

'Yeah,' Spider scowled. 'Over her fucking head.'

Duke laughed. 'She soon sussed you out, you daft pratt.'

Seconds later the Royal Court came into view, and Bannister sighed with relief.

27

When Molly returned to Room 737 she called Cranleigh-Smythe, bringing him up to date and asking for an ambush in the hotel foyer when the traffickers and Bannister returned with the drugs. Cranleigh-Smythe agreed but insisted that the money must not leave the room under any circumstances.

She then kicked off her shoes and found a chair, resting her head on a soft cushion and preparing herself mentally for the next encounter.

'Message from control, ma'am,' Stockley announced. 'They've lost the Merc'. Said it ploughed straight through an anti-abortion march. The mobiles had to stop or they'd have killed somebody.'

My worst fears may have been realised, Molly thought without satisfaction.

'Bill's arse must be going fifties and fives,' Stockley laughed.

'That's neither funny nor useful,' she snapped, her own trip inside that car still fresh in her mind.

'Sorry, ma'am. No offence meant. Cranny says that the man whose's supposed to have the gun has stayed behind. He's prowling up and down outside the hotel.'

Molly looked at Collins who seemed very sad as he stared at his matchbox on the dressing table. 'Pity you won't have a chance to use your gadgets, Chris.'

The TSU man let out a little sigh. 'Just my piffling luck, deary. Never mind, you may need me one day; life's full of sweet surprises.'

'I hope Bill's all right,' she said, picking up her shoulder-bag and heading for the bathroom.

Stockley sat down in the chair she had vacated. 'She's a cool one,' he said to Sippits. 'I don't care what Cranny says, I'm not letting her go down there without firearms back-up. The least we can do is give her some cover. Follow her to the foyer and stay close. But for goodness' sake, don't let her see you or she'll do her nut. Me and Chris will look after the money.'

'Great,' Sippits exclaimed. 'I was trying to work out how I could get into the action.' He took the pistol out of his shoulder holster and checked the magazine.

'Anything new?' Molly asked as she emerged from the bathroom.

Stockley didn't recognise her perfume but he guessed it was expensive. 'Nothing, ma'am. They still haven't found the car. Surveillance are going spare. They'll pick it up, though. Their reputation depends on it.'

'And mine,' Molly said, lifting the black suitcase out of the wardrobe. Identical to the one under the bed, it was, however, stuffed with newspapers.

A short time later Molly sat down on the seat in the centre of the foyer. She faced the main entrance, the black suitcase at her knees. Hazy light from the dome above filtered through the leaves of a palm tree and illuminated her fair hair giving her an unreal, almost angelic aura, so that no man could pass her without a glance of admiration.

Six or seven people sat about reading magazines or talking quietly. Several more were waiting to check in, and a young couple were holding hands behind a bust of Prince Albert. Molly, not bothering to guess how many of them were from Special Operations, kept her eye on the door.

Outside, the Mercedes stopped a short distance from the hotel entrance. A taxi drew into the kerb a few metres behind. Opposite the taxi a motorcycle courier in worn green leathers, carrying several large envelopes, peered at a list of companies on a brass name plate. A Hell's Angel pulled up in front of the Mercedes and examined the front wheel of his Harley-Davidson.

Standing behind the net curtains of a first-floor office above the street, Cranleigh-Smythe watched the big man with the beard saunter along the pavement. 'Target arrived with escorts, Minder approaching,' he broadcast in measured tones.

Three of the men inside the Mercedes scanned the quiet street, searching for signs of danger. Ezra stared vacantly ahead. Bannister, opening a door, took great gulps of air and said a silent prayer of thanks.

'There's no one about,' Duke said, dismissing the taxi and the two motor cyclists. 'No filth, anyway.'

Isha glanced over his shoulder. 'Your man's here.'

Duke spoke to Bannister. 'Come with me.'

The relieved detective stumbled out of the car onto the pavement and stretched his aching limbs.

Isha joined them. 'Here you are, my friend,' he said, handing Bannister the brown holdall. 'The big fellow will look after you. They are worried that you might be foolish enough to run away before they get their money. Move carefully, or they will shoot you.'

Bannister let his knees buckle under the weight of the bag and dropped it onto the pavement, pretending that it was too heavy for him to carry. 'I can't manage it.'

'I knew you were a bleeding poofter,' the Minder said, picking up the holdall as if it were a handbag.

Pleased that it had been so easy to put the Minder in possession of the cannabis, Bannister fell in beside him as they followed Duke to the Royal Court.

'Stop here,' Duke ordered, when they reached the entrance.

211

Climbing the steps, he strode past the doorman then pushed through the revolving door into the foyer. Seeing Molly, he stopped, beckoning for her to follow him. She shook her head and stayed where she was.

Moving backwards, Duke retreated through the door and rejoined the two men waiting outside. 'She's on the seat,' he wheezed. '. . . In the foyer. She's got a suitcase by her legs.' He gripped the Minder's arm. 'Take laddo here with you. Make sure there's money in the case before you hand over the gear . . . and don't let her give you any of her lip. Just get the money and run for it. . . . The car will be waiting for you at the bottom of the steps.'

'Right, Duke. I'll knock her teeth down her throat if she gets funny with me.'

Duke looked down the street and signalled to Isha who was standing beside the car. 'Off you go,' he ordered the Minder. 'I'll be right behind you. If there's any trouble, hang onto the bag and get out quick.'

Molly braced herself, pulse racing and breath shortening, as first Bannister and then the Minder entered the foyer. Duke followed, head bobbing up and down as he tried to see over the shoulders of the big men in front of him. He was using them as a shield while making sure he had a clear run to the door.

With Bannister at his side, the Minder cautiously approached her, eyes fixed on the suitcase beside her legs. Deadly calm, and ready for the action that was about to occur, she took hold of the handle and stood up. The Minder faltered slightly then drew so close that she could smell his bad breath. His eyes held hers only briefly, and she saw that he was sweating profusely.

There was a tremor in his voice when he spoke. 'Put that case on the seat and open it — slowly.'

Molly dropped her handkerchief, a pre-arranged signal that caused the men and women standing or sitting nearby to spring into action and hurl themselves at the four people near to the seat in the centre of the foyer.

Alarm filled the Minder's face, and in that moment his muscles bulged and his whole body seemed to inflate as he prepared to defend himself. Three men hit him simultaneously, shouts of defiance dying in his throat as he sank to the floor under their combined weight.

Duke dashed for the door but didn't make it, disappearing under a mass of flailing arms and legs.

A statue toppled over, hitting the back of the bench seat and beheading itself. The head rolled across the carpet. Fighting men and women cursed, and residents stood and gawped.

Still playing the part of a drug dealer, and feeling a hand on her shoulder, Molly turned and fled, weaving between potted plants, then charging into the ladies hairdressing salon, running over outstretched legs as women trapped under driers screamed for help.

Seeing a door at the back of the room, Molly barged through it and found herself in a dark corridor of rough breeze-block walls. She then ran towards a chink of light at the opposite end of the corridor and kicked open the fire-doors. Suddenly she was in the street, squinting in the midday sun.

Without pausing to see if she was being followed, Molly continued running, thankful she had not worn her high heels, as she sped past flower-sellers and ice-cream kiosks, weaving in and out of bemused shoppers who couldn't understand what the tall woman with the fair hair was fleeing from.

Turning a corner, and looking for somewhere to hide, Molly dashed into a public toilet, pushing open the door of a cubicle and collapsing onto the vacant seat. Leaning back against a wall decorated with obscene, crudely drawn figures, gutter poetry and telephone numbers, she slowly recovered her breath while trying to shut her ears to the woman in the next cubicle who had obviously been over-indulging herself.

Sitting up, Molly suppressed a cry of distress as she saw a small tear in the sleeve of her jacket, and white paint marks on her skirt. It was the most expensive suit she had ever bought, and now it was ruined.

28

Inside the SOU base Bannister could hardly contain himself. He wanted to shout out his joy. They'd done it; led a gang of international drug traffickers into an ambush, arrested them, and seized their gear. He was bound to get a Chief Constable's Commendation at the very least, and the judge would surely thank him personally for his amazing courage and determination in the face of insurmountable odds.

Wait until Liz hears about it! She'll be shouting her mouth off all over the place; cutting articles out of the newspapers: "Undercover detectives smash international drug cartel." She'd phone the whole family, and everyone else she could think of who had half an hour to spare. "They couldn't mention Bill's name, of course," she would say in hushed tones. "But my Bill was the one who arranged to buy the drugs off them; he was on the inside you see. Down in London, it was. Very scary I can tell you. He could have been shot dead. In fact, and this is only between you and me like, he cracked the whole gang single-handed. That woman gaffer of his just sat about in a posh hotel. Bill should get a medal from the Queen, and I should get an invite to her garden party at the Palace, but he'll have to be an unsung hero because he can't say anything about his work; like those SAS chaps. Don't breathe a word mind you, just keep it to yourself. I shan't tell another soul, not even Mum."

As Bannister paced around the warehouse, he wondered what had happened to the SOU and the gaffer. He didn't have long to wait. The side door opened and Molly, looking as cool and composed as ever, walked into the base.

He ran forward to meet her. 'We've done it, ma'am!' he said. 'We've beaten the bastards!'

Pleased to see him safe, she shook his hand but did not respond to his high spirits. Something troubled her; an itch she couldn't scratch. It had gone too smoothly, almost as if they had wanted to be caught. Drug traffickers were devious devils and they could usually smell a trap miles away. She glanced down at her suit, thankful that her emergency repair and the paint didn't show up in the warehouse light.

'Did we get them all?' she asked thoughtfully. There was still a lot of work to do. The trafficker's homes had to be searched and associates must be brought in for questioning. There was also a cache of drugs that had to be found.

'Can't say, ma'am. I belted up the stairs when the Met lads pounced. The last thing I saw was that Minder guy being pole-axed by Pat's swinging handbag. Must've had a brick in it.' He burst into raucous laughter and she searched his face. His pupils were still enlarged.

Yes, Billy Boy, she thought, you're going to suffer when Stockley's speed wears off. She didn't know about the reefer.

'Came back on a magic carpet, did you?' she asked.

Bannister grinned. 'Felt as though I could've. Scarpered into Piccadilly Circus and grabbed a taxi. Arrived a few minutes ago.' His expression clouded. 'I hope Ezra got away. Pals of that Manchester pair will put his head in a bone crusher if they catch him.'

'I shouldn't worry about Ezra,' she said. 'He's a survivor. In any case, they should all be inside by now.'

'That Spider's a real head-banger.'

'Bad, was it?'

'Like Birmingham on the big screen. It's a miracle he didn't kill somebody.'

'You'll have to tell me all about it one day. Where's the SOU?'

'Don't know. A guy in the kitchen said he's expecting them at any moment.'

'Who's he?'

'Warehouse foreman, or at least that's what he calls himself. Sounds like he's been in on the job to me. Police pensioner or something.'

'Is there anything to drink around here?'

'Tea?' He led her through a door marked Spare Parts and introduced her to the foreman who handed over a thick canteen cup. Bannister watched with amusement as his boss screwed her face around the tepid brown liquid.

'Crew room,' the foreman said. 'They doss about and play cards in here. Sometimes they even do some work. It's not much of a place, but they treat it like a pig-hole, so it's all they deserve.'

Molly wished she had brought her skeepskin coat. It was colder than an abattoir. Stained wooden tables were covered with an assortment of clothing, newspapers, McDonald's bags, dirty cups and overflowing ash trays. No one would have guessed that it was the home of the most highly trained squad in the Met. Only the telephone handset in the corner, polished by constant use, could be called clean.

'It's a change from yesterday,' Bannister said cheerfully. 'I don't suppose this place has ever seen a wine bucket.'

'They're back,' the foreman said as the roller-shutters started to rise.

Standing outside the crew room they watched a Rover, two Santana Supplics vans, half a dozen motorcycles and Bert's taxi drive into the warehouse, filling it with noise and choking exhaust fumes.

Cranleigh-Smythe emerged from his Rover, to be followed by a stream of men and women who jumped out of the vans. 'They're here!' he shouted, striding towards the crew room.

'How many prisoners?' Molly asked before he had chance to speak again.

'Four, all guests of Her Majesty at Piccadilly Central.'

'What about Ezra?' Bannister asked.

'He's got to be the fattest man to have run a four minute mile. Scooted down the road towards Trafalgar Square and vanished into the crowds.'

'Guns?' Molly queried.

'Not even a water-pistol.'

'Good,' she said doubtfully, wondering why not. Traffickers didn't bluff about carrying shooters: they did or they didn't.

SOU detectives from the vans crowded around her, shouting their congratulations. She shook hands and forced a smile. 'Well done,' she said, several times.

'It was a good job,' Stockley beamed, 'You should be pleased with Bill.'

'Yes, of course. I'm grateful for everyone's efforts. If there was a bar around here I'd buy you all a drink.'

'You're on,' he grinned, holding out his hand. 'There's an off licence around the corner.'

She dug into her shoulder-bag, then gave him a wad of ten pound notes. Those standing around them knew immediately that it was party time, and they cheered as they pushed past and went into the crew room.

'It went very well, James. . . . I'm grateful,' Molly said. They were sitting at a table some distance from the others, drinking scotch out of paper cups and eating corned beef sandwiches provided by the foreman.

'The lads enjoyed it, Molly. It was a little easy one for them. They usually have to do months of observations before jumping a team like that.'

'The motorcyclists had a tough time,' she said pointedly,

immediately regretting it.

'Yes, you said they would. Killer was livid, I can tell you. I thought he was going to murder his mate.'

'What happened?'

'Killer was about to follow the Mercedes through the procession when Walter ran him off the road and into a car-park.'

'They seem all right now,' she observed, motioning towards Walter and Killer who were sharing a joke over their whisky. 'What have the prisoners said?' Time was slipping away and she was keen to get on with the follow-up enquiries.

'Don't know yet, Molly. I've sent an interrogation team to interview them. As soon as they get anything useful we'll be told.'

'We need to search the prisoners' houses before anybody knows they've been lifted.'

'You're right of course, but they haven't even been ID'd yet. I've sent the best interrogation team in the business. They've been used in Northern Ireland. It's a science these days but I'm afraid it does take time. All we can do is wait.'

Molly's face made it plain that she was not impressed; she preferred to do her own interviewing. There were too many "experts" about these days. She believed that when it was your own case, you never gave up until you got results. It was personal, a battle of wits you had to win. It was also a matter of pride within the CID: a detective's reputation was based on his or her ability to obtain confessions. It was an art learned from the more experienced people in the department; a mixture of cunning and psychology, threats and promises.

Cranleigh-Smythe stood on a bench and called for attention. 'Congratulations to the Westhampton Drug Squad,' he said, smiling down at Molly.

She rose to her feet immediately. 'And the SOU. You're

a great team and I'm proud to have worked with you. Thank you.'

The men around her cheered and bottles of whisky circulated the room as everyone settled down for a session.

The party was in full swing when Cranleigh-Smythe called out in the manner of the House of Commons' speaker: 'Order! Order! Order! Is there any member present who witnessed the whole of today's proceedings?'

'I did, my lord,' Fothergill answered with equal solemnity. His mates were silent, waiting eagerly for one of his famous impromptu performances.

'Will the Honourable Member please stand.'

'I am standing, my lord!'

The crew room filled with laughter.

'Order! Order! Order!' Cranleigh-Smythe shouted, both hands in the air. 'Will the Honourable Member from Paddington Green inform this House of the events which took place at the Royal Court Hotel at two o'clock this nineteenth day of the month of February during the reign of Her Majesty Queen Elizabeth the Second.'

Fothergill stood on a bench. 'Your servant, my lord,' he bowed, gripping the lapels of his jacket as he looked around and watched more whisky bottles nodding their way through the crowd below him.

'Honourable Members,' he began, lowering his cup to intercept a passing bottle.

'Get on with it, Squint,' yelled someone from the crowd.

'Get 'em off,' called another.

'. . . 'Orrible Members,' he continued in his best town-crier's voice, enjoying centre stage and determined to make the most of it. 'Big, brave, Bill here . . .' A rousing cheer interrupted him and those nearest to Bannister slapped his back.

Fothergill waited until he had their full attention. 'Big, brave Bill here walked chin-high towards the Royal Court accompanied by the scourge of the south seas, the infamous pirate, Blackbeard!' Fothergill's audience cheered and waved their cups in the air. He paused, dramatically.

'. . . They were followed by none other than the cunning, conniving Captain Crook, ready to show his stern sheets at the first sign of trouble. Spinning around in the revolving doors, they spilled out onto the fo'c's'le, like sailors thrown from the spokes of a rogue capstan. Sitting before them on the quarterdeck was the one and only, the impressive, the immaculate, the bu'iful — Molly Watson!'

More cheers and she raised her cup in acknowledgement.

Fothergill lubricated his voice box. 'Blackbeard and the dastardly Captain Crook hove to and took their bearings. Blackbeard suddenly pointed to the quarterdeck. ''There she blows, Cap'n'' he growled, ''right between the landlubber's legs''.' Stopping for another gulp of whisky, Fothergill asked, 'What do you think they had spied?'

'Hairy pie,' someone shouted.

'Order! Order! Order!' Cranleigh-Smythe barked above the laughter. The noise slowly died down.

'No, my hearties! Something far more exotic.' Fothergill held them in suspense while he finished his drink. 'Gold . . . Not one thousand, not two thousand, but seventy-five thousand pieces of eight. At the prospect of riches beyond their dastardly dreams, Blackbeard smacked his lips and the greedy cap'n danced a joyous jig behind him. Throwing all caution to the winds they rushed for'ard at a great rate of knots. Big Bill never wavered but held his position on Blackbeard's starboard quarter. Suddenly they were there.'

Fothergill stopped again: the storyteller's final pause. ' ''Yo-Ho-Ho!'' cried Blackbeard. ''hand me that treasure, shipmate.'' Molly stood steadfast, eyeball to eyeball with the fearsome prancing pirate. Suddenly, he dived for the booty —'

The telephone rang and there was a universal groan of disappointment. Cranleigh-Smythe spoke to the caller, then thanking the person on the other end of the line, he put down the receiver, looking first at Molly and then Bannister. The expression on his face told them that the news was not good.

The DCI spoke quietly. 'That was the leader of the interrogation team. The prisoners are insisting that it's not cannabis, but a worthless substitute.'

There were gasps of surprise and murmurings of shock around the room.

'Of course it's bloody shit!' Bannister exploded angrily. 'I smoked the fucking stuff!'

Cranleigh-Smythe gave him time to adjust to the new situation. 'They claim they set out from the very beginning to con someone out of seventy-five thousand.'

Molly nodded, to herself mostly. Now she knew why the job hadn't felt right. It had been a sting. They'd done quite well, she thought, remembering the hungry act they'd put on when she'd mentioned that she wanted huge amounts of cannabis every month. But she had outsmarted them and they'd been arrested for their trouble. . . . Was Ezra a part of it, or had he been duped?

Cranleigh-Smythe sighed with relief as the enormity of the near-miss hit him. 'Thank God we didn't let it run. You were right, Molly. If we had, we'd have lost the money and I'd have been finished.'

She thought back, going over the signs that had made her doubtful about the deal. That first meeting. The unnecessary and dangerous drive through Birmingham. The melodramatics and the arguments inside the Mercedes. Spider's loud, uncouth mouth. Duke's anxiety and his lack of knowledge about drug trafficking. Ezra's silence and his obvious fear in the presence of the two men from Manchester. Isha's suggestion that they do the deal in the foyer of the hotel and Duke's sudden eagerness to agree. No genuine trafficker would have walked into a hotel with twenty kilos of cannabis, no matter who was carrying the drugs.

It was all there. She had suspected from the very start that something was wrong. But what else could she have done? She had had to follow it through and see what was at the end of it all. Now she knew: they were a gang of fraudsters, con-merchants trying to take advantage of the drug scene without understanding its rules and its language, and yes, its sophistication and culture.

'When will we get a lab report?' she asked.

'Half an hour. The gear's being rushed over for analysis right now.'

Molly already knew what the result would be. She faced the men and women gathered around her.

'You have locked up four con-men who were stupid enough to think they could trick us into parting with the commissioner's holiday money.' They received her statement in silence. The mood had changed. Whatever the woman inspector from the Midlands said, they had gone after drug traffickers and their pride was hurt.

'They'll be charged with conspiring to steal seventy-five thousand pounds,' she continued briskly. 'It's been a pleasure working with you and I wish you every success for the future. Thank you.'

When she had finished speaking the room was so quiet that for the first time Molly could hear the barges on the Thames. Cranleigh-Smythe rose quickly to his feet and added his thanks before dismissing his team.

After they had drifted away, Molly turned to Fothergill who had made no move to leave, but was sitting alongside her, mumbling into his scotch and bemoaning the abrupt end of his monologue.

'Come on, Squint, finish your tale,' she encouraged. She

wanted to know more about Ezra — he was the key. He was the one who had told Bannister about the gang from Manchester. Was he in it with them, or was someone else behind it all? She had her suspicions, but she had to be certain.

Fothergill cleared his throat. 'There's not much to say really, ma'am. You and Bill shot off in different directions as soon as we jumped them. The fat guy came easy enough but the Minder went spare, threw the lads about like powder puffs. Pat Gerrard saved the day, like Boadicea riding into battle she was. Clouted him in the north and south with her specially loaded handbag.

After that it was easy. They tell me that outside, the Green Bean strolled over to the Merc with a handful of brown envelopes and asked the driver who lived across the road. Before he realised what was going on, Walter had snatched the keys out of the ignition. There was a bit of a scuffle, but the lads soon sorted it out. The Arab guy stuck his hands in the air like a prisoner of war. Said they were his friends.'

Cranleigh-Smythe answered the telephone again. 'It was henna,' he said after speaking to someone at the laboratory.

'What's that?' Bannister asked, no longer caring what his boss thought.

'Indian hair dye. It looks exactly like cannabis,' the chief inspector added. 'There's often a few blocks of henna in a consignment. It's a way for the workers to supplement their meagre wages. A real trafficker wouldn't bother. Cannabis is so cheap to buy from the producer, it's not worth the trouble.

I don't know about this lot, though. Perhaps Isha imported it specially; the customs wouldn't be interested. . . . There's one good thing. The London druggies should be grateful to you, Bill. If that stuff had been knocked out on the streets, there would have been all kinds of trouble.

Not that your Manchester lot would have lost any sleep over it.'

'Bastards!' spluttered the dejected Bannister.

Cranleigh-Smythe and Molly stood up as one and strolled out of the crew room together.

'Time I had a few words with the Manchester trio and their Arab friend,' Molly said.

'Yes. I must get back to Scotland Yard and give the chief his money back. What a bloody delight that will be. Are you stopping tonight, Molly?' he asked hopefully.

'Sorry, James, I can't. There's a teenage brothel and a certain squad matter that needs urgent attention. If you don't mind I'll the phone the office before we go to Piccadilly Central.'

'Feel free. It's been jolly good working with you. Don't forget, if you ever need any dirty work doing, we're the people.'

'I'll remember that, James. Thank you for everything.' She put a gentle emphasis on the final word.

Cranleigh-Smythe's melancholy was written large on his face. 'I should thank you, Molly. I enjoyed our night out together.'

'I'd . . .' Molly started to say, when a noise caused her to look round and see Fothergill stagger to the door behind them and hang on to the frame, his eyes blank and uncomprehending.

The chief inspector shrugged, a mixture of resignation and sorrow, before giving her a farewell smile and moving towards his car.

She watched him drive away in the Rover, wondering if she would ever see him again, disappointed when he didn't look back. She had fancied him from the moment they'd first met. It had always been like that, some kind of chemistry telling her immediately that she wanted a man. If it didn't happen straight away, then it never would. With

James it had been instant and very strong, and she knew they would have been terrific in bed.

She stood still until the shutters had clanked to the floor, then turned and went back into the crew room. Bannister was quietly drinking his way through a neat line of partly filled paper cups.

'Come on, Bill,' Molly urged with a sad shake of her head. 'That's not the answer. We've still got some work to do.'

It was five-thirty when she telephoned Dinsall.

'Oh, it's you, ma'am,' Joan answered in a flat voice.

'You're working late.'

'Yes, ma'am.'

'Is anybody with you?'

'Sergeant Conrad.'

'Are you all right?'

'Yes.'

'Any messages?'

'Only a personal one from Sergeant Turner.'

'Go on.'

'He wants to see you urgently.'

'Any idea what it's about?'

'He asked me not to say anything, but his wife's come back and she'll only stay if he leaves the squad.'

'Tell him I'll see him in the morning.'

'Yes, ma'am.'

'Sure you're all right, Joan? I can hardly hear you.'

'Yes, ma'am.'

'You sound on edge. Is Holmes behaving himself?'

'. . . I'll have to go,' Joan whispered before the line went dead.

Molly stared thoughtfully at the buzzing ear-piece, then put down the receiver.

'Trouble, ma'am?' Bannistser asked.

'I'm not sure — but something's wrong.'

29

Molly and Bannister followed Stockley down the steps of Piccadilly Central police station. They were met by the smell of fresh vomit and the curses of the custody seregeant who was dragging an unconscious prisoner along the tiled floor. After dumping his charge into the drunk cell, he brushed red and brown chunks of regurgitated stew off his shirt, then returned to his desk.

'If you've come to see this afternoon's prisoners, help yourselves.' He unhooked a heavy bunch of keys from his belt and threw them to Stockley. 'There you are. I'm going to have a bloody shower.'

'Where's the interrogation team?' Stockley shouted after him.

'Said they'd gone for a break. Usually means the bar of the Pen and Wig.'

Stockley led the way along a dark passage lined with iron-studded cell doors. Beside each door was a caged wall light and beneath it a small name board. Finding the cell he was looking for, he released a catch which opened the food trap. He then stood to one side so that Molly could see the prisoner.

Spider was flat out on the wooden bench. Mouth wide open, he was snoring loudly. The patch on his face looked black in the half-light of thc cell. On the floor was an empty tin plate and an overturned enamel mug. A river of tea meandered across green-painted concrete towards the grated gutter.

'Home from home,' Molly muttered, leaving the flap open so that Bannister could see him.

In the next cell, Isha was seated on the toilet, trousers around his ankles. A shaft of light from a barred window shone onto the newspaper resting on his bare legs. He casually flicked the ash off the end of his cigarette and smiled up at them.

'Ah, my friends from the Midlands. Come and join me in my temporary abode. We have plenty of time to negotiate a few more deals. Sorry I am unable to offer you a cup of coffee.'

Overcome by the stench, Molly stepped back and collided with Bannister who had bent down behind her to look into the cell. Her elbow had smashed into his nose. 'I wish you'd watch where you're flaming well standing,' she shouted, striding off in search of the next cell.

Bannister groaned in pain and his eyes watered.

'Never mind,' Stockley comforted. 'You'll be an inspector one day.'

'Not like that ignorant cow, I won't,' Bannister snorted, wiping away the tears and walking unsteadily out of the cell block.

As Molly bent forward to look into the third cell, the opening filled with the bruised and puffed-up face of the Minder.

'You, you bastard! Duke said you were a fucking copper.'

'You should have stayed at home — collecting scrap,' she goaded.

'I want to complain,' the big man yelled, hitting the inside of the door with his fists. 'I was attacked by one of your fucking policewomen.'

'Tough,' she said, slamming the food trap shut so that his beard was caught fast in the door.

'Help!' the Minder squealed.

'Looks as if he's bumped into a wall,' Stockley remarked casually.

Molly rubbed her hands together as they approached the end cell. 'Let's see what Manchester's royalty has got to say for itself.'

Duke was sitting on the floor with his head buried in his hands. His braces, tie and shoelaces had been removed to prevent him from injuring himself.

'Open up,' Molly ordered Stockley, butterflies in her stomach.

Stockley turned the key and pushed the door. 'You've got a visitor,' he announced, as Molly walked into the cell.

Duke didn't look up. 'You don't have to tell me, I know who it is.' An untouched plate of food, solid in a ring of white fat, lay beside him.

'What have you got to say for yourself?' Molly asked.

Slowly, Duke raised his head, his piggy eyes looking as if they had been sand-blasted. 'I always knew you were the filth.'

'That makes you an even bigger fool than I thought you were,' she said in a level voice. It was an anticlimax. All the things she had planned to say didn't seem to matter any more.

He dropped his head again and started to cough. She turned to leave the cell.

'Hold it!' he called out, the effort sending him into another fit of coughing. Molly motioned to Stockley, who left.

Duke spoke in a slow gasping voice. '. . . I don't normally make deals with cops, but I might . . . if I knew what the hell was going on.'

'You tell me.'

'That's the trouble, I don't know. That shit-bag Ezra has stuck it up me. But that's only half of it. . . . He tried to do you as well.' Duke coughed again, and she waited.

'. . . It's stupid. We'd promised him twenty-five grand to fix up a punter who'd take that duff gear off our

229

hands . . . So you tell me . . . Why was he trying to con you? Not for the few measly quid you pay snouts, that's for sure . . . I've sat here trying to figure it out. It doesn't make any sense. The man must be off his rocker or something.'

'Did he approach you?'

'Yeah. I'd met him in a club — Brum. Used a couple of his girls for jobs . . . Nothing heavy,' he added quickly. 'This one night he came in all excited. Said he'd heard we were trying to move some bent gear, and he had a well-healed customer who didn't normally deal and would be easy.'

'When were you going to pay him?'

'As soon as we'd got away from the hotel. He wanted to be dropped off in Mayfair. I don't know where he was going after that — but it wasn't back to Westhampton.'

Duke rose slowly from the floor, hitching up his trousers as he walked towards her. 'That Ezra's a right pillock. I'm warning you, if you don't get him first, he's dead.'

Molly pushed open the cell door. 'I'll see you in court.'

'I don't care,' he shouted as she walked away. 'Just nail that fucking bastard Ezra!'

Molly found Bannister on the custody sergeant's stool.

'You look awful,' she said. 'You should sleep at night.'

'And avoid sharp elbows,' Stockley added quietly.

Bannister said nothing; they were both wrong. He had remembered yesterday's message to contact Liz urgently. After a tirade of abuse for being a day late in returning her call, Liz had told him to ring his ''girlfriend'' who was desperate to speak to him. It was the call to Monica that had made him feel bad.

Leaving Piccadilly Central, the three detectives stood on the entrance steps for a few moments, enjoying the early evening air. Wispy clouds raced across a darkening sky. A double line of schoolgirls in brown uniforms and round hats chattered along the footpath. Molly wished she could join them. She felt a need to be with decent, everyday people for a change.

Stockley drove them to Euston Station. As they were boarding the train, he handed Molly an envelope. 'The guv'nor said I was to give you this, but it's not to be opened until you're on your way home.'

She smiled, holding the envelope and feeling better. 'Thanks, Dave. If you ever find the nerve to venture north of the Watford Gap, come and visit us.'

'I might just do that one day. In the meantime, someone's got to do the sodding paperwork.'

30

Bannister, worn out and unusually quiet, stared into the middle distance.

Molly saw the despondency in his face. 'I'm sorry about the nose, Bill,' she said belatedly.

'It's all right, ma'am.'

Molly felt a stab of conscience as she watched the lights of suburbia fade into the darkness. She hadn't visited her parents' grave in Highgate Cemetery. They would not have believed that after all this time she would still be fighting the world on her own.

Bannister broke into her thoughts. 'I'm sorry if I nearly landed you in it. The sergeant said that Ezra was straight, and I believed him.'

'You did very well today, Bill.'

'I'll be more careful next time. No one's going to catch me out like that again.' He shot out of his seat and ran towards the toilet.

Pleased to be alone, Molly opened the envelope that Stockley had given her. Inside, she found a colour photograph of a Cotswold cottage. She turned it over and read the neat writing on the back.

Molly,

Spend a few days in the country with me. It's a delightful place. We could talk, walk, eat good food, drink good wine — and get to know one another. Just give me a call.

Best wishes, James.

'Doesn't seem long since we were heading South,'

Bannister said as he returned to his seat.

'It was yesterday,' she replied, suddenly hot and flustered as she stuffed the photograph into her shoulder-bag.

A few minutes later Bannister produced his official pocket book and thumbed through the pages. 'Ma'am,' he said in a small voice. 'I think you should read this. Last Thursday's entry. Under "Drug Destruction."'

Without a word, she took the book from him and started to read.

'When you've finished that, ma'am, there's something else I think you should know about.'

She looked up briefly. He seemed to have aged in the last few days.

When she had finished reading the bold, child-like print, she closed her eyes for a moment, then went over it again. Slowly this time, reading several passages more than once.

Bannister waited. The train stopped, several passengers disembarked, and it pulled away again.

'You know how serious this is, don't you?'

'Yes, ma'am.'

'Why has it taken you five days to tell me about it?'

'Didn't know how to, ma'am. I've never shopped anybody before.' He paused, his face looking as if it was about to crumble. 'And in any case, I was involved. I had helped him.'

'What's different now?'

'I don't care about myself any more. It's wrong, and we've got enough problems without having people like him in the job.'

'When did you make the pocket-book entry?'

'Immediately after the drug destruction. You and Sergeant Conrad went to HQ to see about the firearms team.'

Molly leaned back in her seat. Theft, planting, and now more theft and forgery of the Drugs Register. What else had Conrad done?

Bannister squared his shoulders. 'There's more, ma'am. While you were seeing Duke and his crowd at Piccadilly Central I telephoned Monica, one of Ezra's girls.'

'I know who Monica is.'

'Anyway, she's been in a panic, trying to get in touch with me since Monday morning.' He hesitated. 'You're not going to like this, ma'am.'

'I don't have to,' she said shortly.

'Before we left, I asked her to find out about those blokes from Manchester. She'd discovered that Ezra was expecting a big pay-off for a drug job in London. And what's more, he intended going to the States after he got his cut.'

'How much?'

'Twenty-five grand.'

The respectable residents of Coovers Wood had mostly gone to bed when Bannister pulled up outside Molly's mock-Georgian house. She made no effort to get out of the car and they sat in silence for several minutes. Bannister blinked and bit his tongue to keep himself awake. He'd crashed out on the train immediately after telling his boss about Ezra, but it hadn't helped. He felt as though he could sleep for ever.

When Molly spoke, her voice was vibrant with hate. 'I'm going to destroy Conrad. He has no place in this job; he's a vile, evil man. But first we must raid the brothel. I don't want you to say anything about what happened in London, especially not to your sergeant. If anyone asks, we arrested four men on a conspiracy charge and Ezra was allowed to escape. That's all they need to know. OK?'

Bannister, struggling to keep his eyes open, managed a tired nod.

'After that,' she went on, 'I go for Conrad. I haven't worked out how I'm going to do it yet, but you can be sure there'll be no mistakes. He may be clever and he may be cunning, but I'll beat him this time. I must.'

31

Molly would not have slept soundly had she known what happened after her telephone call to Dinsall.

Much to Joan's surprise, she had enjoyed being in the office with Conrad. Feeling a closeness to him that she would not have believed possible, she had soon forgotten her worries about the forged Jackman statement. There had not been much work to do and he had filled the time on Monday by telling her stories. Funny, and sometimes sad, they made her laugh and cry at the same time, arousing emotions that had not been touched since her husband had gone away.

At five o'clock he had taken her home, but refused her invitation to stay even though she offered him a drink and a meal, thinking it would be nice to have some male company in the flat for a change. She did not see him again until late on Tuesday when he seemed more subdued, as if there was something on his mind.

Slowly, she had got him to talk. It was Mary, his wife. She had been caught shop-lifting at a shop called Todlers Togs. One of his mates had telephoned him and he'd been at South Road police station all morning. Close to tears, he had told her everything about his marriage. The pressures to go for promotion, to have a bigger house and a bigger car than everyone else; Mary's shopping for the baby they could never have and the enormous debts which hung over him like the sword of Damocles.

Feeling sorry for him, Joan put an arm around him and his head rested on her shoulder as they stared at the flames of the old gas fire and day turned to night.

Then, after he had been for a wash, he changed. He was suddenly full of bounce and energy, as if given a new lease of life. He told her more stories, but they were smutty tales like she imagined men told amongst themselves. And he couldn't keep his hands off her, so that she wanted to get away from him and go home.

Later she became really frightened. Still sitting in front of the fire she caught his reflection in the metal surround. The friendly smile had gone, replaced by a lust-filled, leering mask. Alarm bells sounded and she needed all her will-power to control the feeling of terror that swept through her.

'Time we had a drink, courtesy of the gaffer,' Conrad laughed from somewhere behind her. He left the room and she decided to make a break for it. Grabbing her coat, she had reached the door when the telephone started to ring. Foolishly, she turned back. It was Molly. Joan, desperate to get away, tried to keep the call brief.

Replacing the handset, she felt Conrad's presence before turning to see him standing in the doorway.

'Going somewhere?'

'No, no. Just looking for something,' she replied lamely, making a pretence of searching the pockets of her coat.

'Who was that on the phone?'

'The gaffer.'

'What did she want?'

'Nothing. Asked if everything was all right, that's all.'

'Hope you told her what a nice time we're having together. How've they got on?'

'Don't know. She didn't sound very pleased.'

His eyes narrowed. 'She'd have bragged about it if she'd got them. I reckon she's cocked it up and lost all that bread.'

With a whoop of joy, Conrad grabbed Joan and twirled her around in a clumsy dance, spinning her slender, bird-like body, then holding her tight so that she could hardly get her breath. Pulling away, he beamed at her. 'Let's have a drink on Detective Inspector Molly Watson. She won't be needing it any more.'

Joan, hot and totally bewildered, stared at him in disbelief. 'What do you mean?'

He laughed. 'Never mind, you'll always have me to look after you.'

More confused than ever, Joan watched him pour the whisky. 'Thank you,' she said uncertainly, drinking more than she had intended and watching helplessly as he quickly refilled the glass.

'That'll do you good, Joan, you're all uptight. You've forgotten how to enjoy yourself; how to let yourself go.' He squeezed her knee and left his hand there.

She knew that she had to play along with him if she was to have another chance to escape. 'And I suppose I need someone like you to teach me,' she said, realising for the first time that he had taken off his jacket and tie.

'I've always thought you were something special.'

'I've told you, I'm a married woman.'

'No you're not. You won't see him for another six months.' He moved his hand up her leg. 'What d'you think your old man's doing now?'

She shook her head.

'I'll tell you what he's doing. He's having a chinky meal with his mates. D'you know what they have for extras? Not mint sauce, or cranberry. Oh, no. they have little girls under the table. No one says anything. It isn't polite, you see. But you can always tell whose turn it is because rigor mortis sets in. They gulp air, and their eyes sort of pop out of their heads.'

'He wouldn't do anything like that.'

'Don't be daft, they all do. How can you expect him to go without a woman for eighteen months? It's not natural. Like you, everybody's got to have it now and again. If you don't you go mad.'

'Never give up do you?'

'You're too good to be wasted. You're missing out on life, Joan. Before you know it, it'll be too late. No one will want you any more, and you'll only have regrets. A lovely woman like you should live and enjoy herself. That's what it's all about. Don't wash it all down the plug hole.'

'What about your wife?'

'What wife?' he said angrily. 'I said, didn't I? We just live in the same house, that's all; separate beds. It's been like that for months.'

He gently caressed Joan's thigh. She tensed, then forced herself to relax. 'Persistent Peter, that's what they should call you,' she said, feeling the heat of his hand. She had another drink of whisky, coughing as it burned her throat. 'This is too strong for me,' she complained.

'Run out of water.'

'I know you, Tom Conrad. You're just trying to soften me up.' Her words were slurred and she blinked to stop the room going round. 'D'you think Molly will mind us finishing off her whisky?'

He refilled the glass again. She knew what was going to happen but felt powerless to stop it; not even sure that she wanted to any more. She took a long drink then pushed the rest away, feeling that she was about to be sick.

Conrad moved closer. 'It's been so long, you can't remember what it feels like,' he whispered, busy fingers moving further up the inside of her leg.

'Yes I can.' She felt him exploring inside her pants, and she moaned, a piteous sound, from deep within her. Reaching forward, she grabbed his ears, holding them firmly so that he screwed up his face. 'Look,' she said. 'Before we start. I want you to understand one thing.'

Nonplussed, he stared back at her, unable to move his head.

'I love my husband,' she continued earnestly. 'You're just convenient, that's all.'

'Suits me,' he grinned, feeling her hot, whisky-laden breath on his face.

'And don't look so bloody pleased with yourself, I'm no conquest you can brag to your mates about. It could've been any man. You just happen to be available.'

She let him go and he started to laugh. 'It's not funny,' she spat. 'I'm a bitch on heat, that's all. Get your trousers off before I burst.'

She stood up and started to undress, jamming her zip and pulling off a button. Clutching at the edge of a desk, she tried to focus on the fire, which seemed to swing like a pendulum. The walls buckled and straightened and the carpet rose to meet her. Crying out, she fell onto her back, shielding her eyes from the hot glow of fire.

Conrad stood rampant over her, smirking at the soft white pants wrapped around one ankle, and the still-fastened bra twisted across her waist. Dropping his head back and throwing a handful of blue tablets into his gaping mouth, he swilled them down with the remains of Joan's whisky.

Her raised knees were spread and her small breasts rose and fell, the unsuckled nipples bright red in the glow of the fire. His whole body trembled with anticipation but he forced himself to hold back and savour the moment — the feeling of absolute power he had over her.

'Now it's my turn to have some fun, you stupid, stuck-up cow,' he said in a thick, gutteral voice that only another Glaswegian would have understood.

32

Early the next morning Molly opened the door of Joan's maisonette to be met by a bundle of brown and white, which hurtled down the stairs and launched itself into her arms.

'Stop it, you little perisher,' she yelled, dodging his tongue as she held him close.

She found Joan in the kitchen, standing perfectly still and looking out of the window. When she turned Molly cried out in alarm. Joan looked terrible. Her eyes were like pieces of liver in the snow. One cheek was a web of angry abrasions, and the other was badly bruised.

Molly gripped her shoulders. 'What's happened to you?'

Joan sniffed, pushed past her, and fled into the lounge. Molly followed in time to see her sit gingerly on the edge of the low settee.

'What's happened to you?' she repeated.

'Nothing,' Joan said, head bowed, voice breaking.

Molly sat down next to her. 'Don't give me that. Who's done this to you?'

'I fell over,' Joan whispered. The pain seemed to be everywhere and her stomach felt as if it was full of broken bottles.

'Rubbish,' Molly said angrily. 'Was it Conrad? . . . It was him, wasn't it?'

Joan collapsed sideways, curling up into a tight ball. 'Go away. Leave me alone,' she sobbed.

Finding the bedroom, Molly collected a duvet then returned to spread it over the distraught woman. Joan whimpered like a puppy, calling out in pain as she clutched at her back. 'I'm sorry,' she murmured.

'Are you going to tell me what's been going on?' Molly tried again, gently.

Joan tried to blank out the nightmare. Conrad probing, pushing, thrusting; hurting her. Laughing when she begged him to stop. Bending her arm up her back and forcing her over the desk, holding her head down in the hard wire paper-tray as he drove himself into her. Punching and kicking her when she tried to get away. In desperation she had wrapped her arms around his legs and pleaded with him to stop, but he had kept on in a never-ending frenzy of lust; wanting more, never satisfied, no matter what she did.

'Shall I send for a doctor?' Molly asked.

'You don't send for doctors around here. You crawl to the surgery and hope they speak English.'

'Is there anything I can do?'

Fresh spasms of pain wracked Joan's body, but she struggled to sit up. 'You've done enough,' she said, tears streaming down her cheeks.

Molly sat down on the settee and held her, rocking her gently as if she were a child until she eventually fell asleep. Straightening Joan's clothing, she then tucked the duvet around her.

Some time later Molly poked her head round the lounge door. Joan was awake.

'Your sister will be here shortly and the doctor's on his way.'

'Who covered me up?' Joan asked feebly.

Molly walked over to her. 'I did, and I've seen the bruises on your back. You're probably suffering from internal injuries and you need urgent medical attention.'

Joan cried out in anguish and buried her face in a cushion.

As Molly turned to leave the room, Joan called her back. 'There's an envelope on the sideboard. Take it with you and open it at the office.' She closed her eyes as if to cut off Molly's questions. 'Do what you have to,' she whispered. 'But, please, please, keep me out of it.'

It was ten o'clock when Molly arrived at Dinsall. With the exception of Bannister, all the squad were in the general office. Conrad was at the back of the room, eyes watchful. Seeing him, Molly's hackles rose and she started to shake as she fought to control a blinding rage. Tightness gripped her chest like a vice, cold sweat pearled her brow, and she felt faint. Strong hands held her.

'Are you all right?' Sergeant Smith asked, sitting her down. She held her face in her hands and nodded weakly, playing for time. She mustn't give herself away now. Not before she had a chance to stop Conrad. She forced her head up and managed a sickly grin at the ring of faces.

'Too much Bell's, or something.'

Smith took her to her office where she collapsed into a chair.

'Thanks, Gordon. Give me a few minutes then I'll be all right.'

'It's not a few minutes, it's a few weeks that you need.'

She shook her head.

'I mean it, Molly,' he said. 'We're all behind you. We won't let you down.'

Some time later, Molly returned to the general office and gave them a brief account of the events in London. She left out those parts where Bannister had been found wanting and highlighted his good work. Not sure why, but trusting her intuition, she didn't mention Cranleigh-Smythe and

243

his Special Operations Unit.

She could deal with Conrad now; look him in the eye as if nothing had happened. She'd been treating villains like friends for years; it was second nature to her. When he enquired about Ezra, she told him that he had done an excellent job and had escaped as arranged.

As soon as she was able, Molly returned to the sanctuary of her office and opened Joan's envelope. After a few minutes, she dropped the forged statements onto her desk. She now had sufficient evidence to charge Conrad with theft, forgery and perverting the course of justice. But she'd seen too many defendants with bright barristers escape seemingly watertight cases, usually because of some nebulous administrative technicality that had nothing to do with justice. If she was going to send Conrad to prison for a long time, she would have to arrest him in the act of trafficking.

Sergeant Smith knocked on the door and walked into the office. 'Feeling any better, ma'am?'

'I'm all right, thanks Gordon. And cut out the good doctor routine, we've got work to do.'

'As long as you're up to it. I don't know what you were doing in London, but Bannister hasn't turned up this morning.'

'Yes, I know. I told him to catch up on his beauty sleep.'

'You're mothering him, ma'am. Latent maternal instincts are clouding your judgement.'

'Don't be so damned ridiculous.'

He opened the brothel file. 'I was only joking, ma'am.'

Discussing the observation reports for Monday and Tuesday, they then made the final arrangements for the evening's raid at eight o'clock.

'By the way, ma'am,' Smith said before leaving. 'Joan rang in this morning. She'll be off for a few days. Tummy trouble or something; she didn't sound too good. It's

244

unusual for her. She hasn't missed a day since she started.'

After he had gone, Turner walked into the office and immediately launched into a long, rambling saga about his troubles at home and the difficulties of bringing up small children. Nodding occasionally, Molly tried to concentrate, but her mind was elsewhere, searching for a way to trap Conrad.

'Roger,' she said stiffly, 'we've been through all this before. Do you mind telling me what you want?'

He hesitated, afraid to make his request. After a strained silence, he took a deep breath and peered big-eyed, through thick lenses. 'My wife wants me to leave the squad, ma'am. She won't unpack her bags until she gets an answer.'

Molly didn't believe Turner would ever have a happy home life. His kind always seemed to draw the short straw when it came to choosing partners.

'Roger, you've done your best and tried to be a good squad man,' she said kindly. 'Your arrest of Catweasel was the collar of the year, and I'm grateful. But if you've got no support at home then the only thing you can do is to go back into uniform. Your family's more important than this job.' Turner nervously adjusted his glasses. 'Don't worry about it,' she added. 'I'll arrange for you to return to your old division within the week.'

Thanking her, he hurried off to give his wife the good news.

No Gaming Sergeant, Molly thought. And soon I'll be losing the man in charge of my drug team. Thank goodness for Smithy, even though he has a weird sense of humour. ''Latent maternal instincts'' for goodness' sake.

After speaking to Bannister on the telephone and leaving DC Williams to look after the switchboard, she drove to the forensic science laboratory and force headquarters.

33

'Any problems?' Molly asked, as Smith drove them towards the brothel.

'Usual trouble getting a photographer, and I only managed to rustle up one policewoman. We should be all right. The girls are only youngsters.'

'Cows.'

'Pardon, ma'am?'

'Cows. You rustle cows, not policewomen.'

'Sorry. Complaints have been after you. Didn't say what it was about. Oh, yes, and your favourite superintendent called. He's upset because you'd been to headquarters but hadn't popped in to see him.'

Molly smiled to herself. There was a certain satisfaction in getting under Davids' skin. 'The last time I paid him a visit he went all official. Told me to make an appointment if I wanted to see him again. I suppose he's straining a gut to tell the ACC about the London arrests.'

They entered an inner-city area of back-to-back terraces that had somehow escaped the bulldozers of the sixties and seventies.

'Did you hear about Roger?' she asked.

'Best thing that could happen to him. He's never been right for this job. He'll be far happier in something like Public Liaison, visiting mosques and sitting cross-legged on the floor, hoping no one will notice the hole in his sock.'

'Don't forget the knotted handkerchief. Wouldn't fancy Gaming, would you, Gordon?'

'Like a slap in the mouth, ma'am. I've been on the squad too long already. I need time for my son's soccer training.'

'He's only a week old.'

'What's age got to do with it?'

Parking the car in a side street, Smith led Molly through an open gate in a high brick wall. They walked along a narrow footpath towards a terraced house. The garden was overgrown with knee-high weeds and a row of bean canes sagged under the weight of mile-a-minute Russian vine.

Barging into the back of the house as if he were the lodger, Smith introduced Molly to an old woman who wore a once-white shawl around her frail shoulders.

'Have you lived here long?' Molly asked politely.

'All me days, m'dear. Used to be fields behind that wall at the bottom of the garden. Me and Josh did our courting down there,' she cackled, showing three brown teeth.

Molly held her bony hand, not wanting to shake it in case it fell off.

'Those young wenches would've been working down the lock factory in my younger days.' She poured stewed tea into cracked King George V Coronation mugs. 'If my Josh had've been here, he'd 'ave gone across there and given 'em what for.'

Molly and Smith finished their drinks, then, taking their leave, climbed a narrow staircase up to the front bedroom. Feeling their way in the dark, they joined Macdonald and Gilbert who were watching an identical house across the street.

'Anything doing, Mac?' she enquired.

'On a pair at the moment, ma'am. If they're sharing them out, that is. It's been quiet for the last hour though. Unusual for a Wednesday.'

Molly wondered. There was always that feeling of uncertainty before a raid. Had the men keeping observation shown out? Had the job been blown for some other reason?

'Even the Little Lion Man hasn't turned up tonight,' Macdonald added.

247

'Who's he?'

'Nutter, ma'am. Brings his own lipstick and draws rings around Kylie's nipples so that her tits look like targets. Then he gets her to hold a boiled egg between her knees and empties his fountain pen into it!'

They're right, Molly thought. It's time I found myself another job.

'Are the troops ready?' Smith asked Macdonald, some time later.

'Yes, Sarge. I've put the photographer with Fletch and told him to make sure he stays right behind us to get some action shots.'

'Who's in charge of the upstairs party?' Molly asked.

'Sergeant Conrad, ma'am. He volunteered,' Smith said.

Yes, I bet he did. Molly's mind returned to Joan, wondering why she hadn't made an official complaint . . . The bottle of Bell's! The one that'd been in the back of her filing cabinet since Christmas. It was missing. That's it. He must have filled Joan with whisky. A couple of Babychams is her limit. She wouldn't have stood a chance.

Gilbert's excited voice cut into her thoughts. 'There's a car stopping outside,' he said.

She looked out of the window in time to see a short bald man jump out of a taxi, then hobble down the entry at the side of the house they were watching.

Macdonald made a small sound in the back of his throat. 'That's "Grandad with the Gammy Leg". He's a regular.'

'And another,' Gilbert announced as a hire car dropped off a rotund man who was wearing a long dark coat and a trilby. Pulling the hat down over his face, he looked about him, then dashed after the first man.

'Keen type, ma'am,' Macdonald muttered.

Smith moved away from the window. 'If we go in now, we should catch both of them at it, ma'am.'

'It's your show, Gordon.'

Smith gave his orders then led the way down the stairs and out of the back of the house. Molly paused to thank the old lady as she locked the door after them.

At a sign from Smith, the raiding party closed on the house across the road. Everyone knew the routine. It was a system they had perfected over the years.

Standing with his party in the entry at the side of the house, Smith waited until five minutes had elapsed since the last man had entered the brothel, knowing that both punters would now be hard at it. Timing was important: an explicit photograph was worth a dozen witness statements. Most of the punters were married and more afraid of their wives than the courts. They would admit anything to prevent loved ones seeing their bare bottoms between foreign knees.

Smith, shadowed by Molly, led the raiding party up the entry to the rear of the house. As everyone closed up he tried the back door and found it unlocked. Quietly, all nine of them filed into the kitchen which was half-lit by the light of a full moon streaming through the window.

Making sure that Fletcher and the photographer were close behind him, Smith put his head to the back room door and listened. Satisfied, he turned and faced his men, mouthing an order that they were to get ready for the rush into the back room.

Slowly turning the brass knob, Smith gently pushed at the door, pressing with his shoulder and thigh when it wouldn't budge. The top and bottom gave slightly but the centre held firm.

He stepped back, measured his run, then charged foot-first at the lock. On impact, the door swung open and crashed into the wall. The raiding party rushed into the room and the photographer's flashlight fired repeatedly. The girl screamed and someone switched on the overhead light, exposing a montage of flailing arms and legs as the naked pair on the settee struggled frantically to disentangle themselves, their feet touching the floor in unison as they leaned forward to cover flaccid parts. Elbows on knees, they faced in opposite directions, as if to deny their recent coupling.

Like pink book-ends, Molly thought dispassionately.

'Get your clothes on,' Smith barked.

Standing up, they started to dress. The panic-stricken man soon became entangled in his underpants; the cool, couldn't-care-less girl was slow and deliberate; a strip tease in reverse.

Aiming his camera, the photographer took a shot of two ten-pound notes and an empty Mates packet that lay on the floor beside the settee.

'Is that your money?' Smith asked the man who had put on his trilby and socks but was still fumbling with the buttons of his shirt.

'It was,' he replied miserably.

Molly surveyed the drab, featureless room. The only furniture was the old settee which stood on a square of brown threadbare carpet. The girl, having finished dressing, waited with an air of indifference to be told what to do next.

Feet sounded on the bare boards of the stairs and Conrad pushed a fat, freckled-faced girl into the room. Her shoulders shook and she sobbed through podgy red hands that covered the lower half of her face. Fletcher and Grandad with the Gammy Leg followed. Molly guessed that he must be at least seventy. His shirt tails hung out of his trousers and he carried a tie in his hand. The policewoman covered the weeping girl's shoulders with a car-coat then took her outside to a waiting van.

Climbing the stairs and going into the front bedroom, Molly saw that a double bed had been pushed against a wall. There were no bed clothes, only a stained mattress and an army blanket folded to make a pillow. A rusty bucket stood in the corner, cigarette ends and soggy sheaths floating in urine.

Molly returned to the back room downstairs. Most of the raiding party had left, taking the hapless punters with them. The downstairs girl remained, sitting on the settee.

Molly spoke to Smith. 'Leave us for a few minutes. I want to have a few words with this young lady.' He led the cameraman and DC Gilbert out of the room.

The girl eyed Molly suspiciously. 'After a backhander?' she challenged. 'That's what coppers like, isn't it? Something for nothing.'

'Who's running this place?'

'Go fuck yourself.'

Molly fought an urge to kick her in the mouth. Instead she softened her voice.

'Ever heard of Strangeways?'

'Piss off.'

'If you talk like that to the staff in there, they'll rip your tongue out.'

Seemingly less sure of herself, the girl lowered her eyes.

'Now tell me. Who's running this place.'

'Dunno.'

'Think!'

'I dunno, I tell you!'

'Yes you do.'

The girl shook her head.

'D'you want to go to prison?' Molly asked sharply. 'They'll love you in there. They'll have you for breakfast, dinner and tea.'

'What d'you mean?'

'Sex, my girl. There's no men in those places, so they make their own arrangements. They use girls like you, the younger the better. The lifers will get you first. And when they've had their fill, they'll lock you in the showers and sell you to the others. Five fags a session.'

The girl paled and her confidence seemed to crumble.

'And there'll be no sleep at night,' Molly continued. 'They'll use you for toilet paper.'

Tears started to run down powdered cheeks. Molly said nothing for a few moments, allowing the girl's fears to multiply. She hated herself for what she was doing to the youngster, but she had to know who was running the brothel.

'Have you been in trouble with the police before?' she asked.

'No.'

'How old are you?'

'Fifteen.'

'You're still a juvenile. If you help me, I could send you home to your mum and dad.'

The girl lifted her chin defiantly. 'You're trying to trick me.'

'Don't trust your luck. You've got one minute. Tell me what I want to know or I'll call for the sergeant, and you're on the way to that hell-hole of a woman's prison.'

The trembling girl glanced up at the ceiling, fear in her eyes.

Molly kept the pressure on. 'It'll drive you insane. You'll look thirty when you get out. You're wasting a young life for nothing. All you've got to do is tell me who's running this place. Why throw your life away for someone who's been using you and your friend and taking your money? He won't care about you. You'll never see him again. So why protect him? Just give me his name.'

The girl lowered her head and spoke quietly. 'You won't tell anybody I told you?'

'No, of course not. I'll send for your parents, then you can go home with them and everything will be all right. Don't you see? No one's going to blame you for what's gone on in this place. The man who put you and your friend in here is the bad guy. He's been using you. He just wanted the money. If we don't stop him, he'll do the same thing to other young girls. He's vermin.'

Molly leaned closer. 'Just give me his name, then all this will be over: you can go home. Can't you understand that?'

'Yes, miss,' she replied, glancing upwards again.

'No one will know you've told me,' Molly promised. 'It'll be a secret between ourselves.'

The girl mumbled so that Molly had difficulty hearing what she said. 'We don't know his name. He's a black guy. Fat man. My dad's age. Always laughing, he is, so his belly shakes. Said he would take us to America. Had everything we got off the men to buy the air tickets. Gave us ten pounds a week pocket money.'

'Each?'

'No, to share.'

'When?'

'When what?'

'When was he going to take you to America?'

'Soon. He had a big drug job in London. Yesterday, it was. Said he would make loads of money and get us a place on Fifth Avenue.'

'What did he wear?'

'Suits.'

'Anything else?'

'He always had a hat on. Never took it off.'

'What was it like?'

'What?'

'The hat.'

'Round. Like they have in London, only brown.'

'A bowler?'

'Yes.'

'What's his name?'

'I don't know, I tell you.'

'Where did he come from?'

'Don't know.'

'How did you meet him?'

'Out of school. He took us to the cafe. Bought us cakes and cigarettes and things. Anything we wanted.'

'What's his name?' Again the scared look at the ceiling. 'No one up there's going to help you. Tell me his name, or you'll go to prison.'

The girl started to cry.

'I want the truth!' Molly said harshly.

'. . . Ezra,' the girl sobbed.

The door opened and Smith walked into the room. 'Duty Inspector's on the way, ma'am. Police College type, a real stickler for the rules, they tell me. If we get a move on we can be away before he arrives.' Smith looked closely at the distraught girl and frowned at his boss. 'Is she all right?' he asked with more than a trace of accusation in his voice.

Molly sighed and ushered him out of the girl's hearing. 'She's all right. There's just something I had to know, that's all. You can take her to the station. The ponce is Ezra and he's on his way to America. She'll deny it on tape, of course, but don't press her, she's a gutsy kid. I'll disappear before the academic two-pipper arrives and starts lecturing me about how to interview juveniles. Tell him if he's got any problems to speak to me.'

Bannister had been at Dinsall for an hour when Molly returned to the station.

'Put the kettle on, Bill,' she ordered, going through to her office to make a couple of phone calls.

'Everything OK, ma'am?' he asked a few minutes later, putting two mugs of coffee on the desk then settling himself into an easy chair opposite her.

254

Molly looked at her detective. Ten days ago he would have remained standing until invited to take a seat. A lot had happened since their visit to the Green Parrot Club. They were closer now. It wasn't friendship in the normal sense, the difference in rank prevented that. It was a feeling of trust; a mutual dependency.

'The brothel keeper's flown,' she told him. 'To the States. Who d'you think he is?'

Bannister shook his head, then suddenly he gasped, eyes lighting up. 'No!' he cried. 'It can't be. It's not Ezra — is it?'

'That's our man. Your very own super-snout. Told them he was going to make a few grand on a drug job in London — yesterday.'

'Ezra . . .' he breathed. 'The rotten slimy bastard! First he tried to set us up in London, and now this.'

Molly nodded. She should have guessed long ago that it was Ezra's brothel. Spence and Ezra had been at each other's throats for years. They had simply used the police to fight their battles. Ezra had helped them to raid Spence's shebeen; Spence had told them about Ezra's brothel. Two registered informants setting each other up. It happened, she supposed. There were no rules, only deceit and treachery.

'Learn from it, Bill. You nearly sank us all because you don't understand the ground rules for running informants. I've got Spence out there doing what informants are paid to do — working. He has no choice because my foot's on his neck. If he doesn't give me something good soon, he'll lose his thirty thousand pounds, and if I turn real nasty, he'll end up inside.'

She paused. Bannister's face was ashen.

'Ezra's made a monkey out of you, Bill, because you're too nice; too trusting; too soft. There's no room for sentiment in our business. Informants are terrified someone might find out that they're grassing, so you're always in the driving seat. But you've got to be harder than they are, ruthless even. It's the only language they understand. You let Ezra call the shots. Informants may drink with you and share a few laughs, but deep down they hate the sight of you. You spoil their cosy little lives. You make them sweat, put pressure on them, and cause complications.'

Bannister, still pale, put down his empty cup and stared at his boss for a moment.

'We become bastards like them in the end, don't we, ma'am?'

Molly sighed. 'Yes, I suppose so. But what else can we do? How else can we stop them taking over and ruining people's lives?'

'I don't know, ma'am . . . I don't know.'

Looking through the window at a solitary light beyond the park, Molly frowned. 'I've missed something.'

'What?' he asked, perplexed.

'That's the trouble, I can't work it out. The girl, she frightened too easily . . . almost before I'd got going. As if there was something else; something in the room. It was more than me shouting at her. She kept looking at the ceiling . . . The ceiling!' Molly yelled. 'That's it, by God!'

Bannister looked up.

'Not that flaming ceiling! Quick, get the car round the front. If we hurry we might just make it.'

34

'Pull up,' Molly ordered as they approached the brothel. 'Behind that car.' Bannister braked hard and swerved into the kerb, almost colliding with the back of a Volkswagen.

'Down,' Molly snapped, ducking to avoid the headlights of a passing police car. 'That was Inspector Ramsden. Smithy was right. He's one of those who think we should do this job by numbers.'

'Too true, ma'am. He once reported me for being late into the station for refreshments. It was the night shift and I'd chased a burglar half-way across the city. I can hear him now: "Your refreshment time is from one a.m. to one forty-five a.m., PC Bannister. Prisoner's don't matter, only the rules are important in a disciplined organisation." '

'Sounds like someone else I know,' Molly said, hoping she could avoid Davids for another two days.

Bannister studied the terraced houses on both sides of the road. Brothels were anonymous in Westhampton. No secret signs or red lights advertised their services. But word soon got around when a new one had opened. Like any city, the taxi drivers knew the addresses of all the brothels, and the owners paid them a small fee for introducing new clients.

'Most of the street will have gone to bed by now, ma'am.'

'Box-watching, you mean.'

'What are we watching?'

'Across the street. Keep an eye on the third house from the end of the row.'

An hour later, Bannister opened a window, hoping the

cold air would keep him awake. He glanced sideways at his boss. She'd been brilliant in London. She played the tough guy but she wasn't the hard woman she was cracked up to be. Deep down, she was kind and she cared about people. He thought she must be lonely, but it was impossible to tell because she only ever talked about work. Never anything about herself, her friends, or the things that the lads usually went on about when they were together on jobs like this.

That Scotland Yard gaffer hadn't been able to keep his eyes off her, and they'd all seen them slip out of The Tank together, and speculated as to their probable destination.

If I'd been the gaffer, we'd have stayed another night. There's no way I'd have rushed back to deal with a poxy brothel, or Conrad for that matter. It isn't decent to rush away from someone you'd just met, he decided, thinking of Pat and feeling a stirring in his trousers.

A fat man wearing a hat hurried across the road then walked along the pavement towards them. As he drew level with the car, Molly flung open the front passenger door, knocking him to the ground.

'Bloody hell, it's Ezra!' Bannister exclaimed.

'Who did you expect, Martin Luther King?'

Ezra's head rested on the kerb where he had fallen, blood running from his nose. 'Pick him up and stick him in the back of the car,' Molly ordered, recovering Ezra's Derby from the gutter.

'Where to?' Bannister asked, having second opinions about his boss.

'Dinsall.'

'Dinsall?'

Unmanned at night, the old police station was in total darkness. Bannister drove through the car-park to the rear of the building and stopped next to the observation van.

Getting out of the vehicle first, Molly entered the kitchen ahead of him. Closing the door, she switched on the lights. 'Get Ezra in here and clean him up. I'm going down to the cellar. Don't use the front offices or show any lights a passing patrol car might spot. We're not here, understand?'

Bannister didn't understand, but he wasn't about to argue. Helping Ezra out of the car, he led him into the kitchen and wiped his face. The nose-bleed had stopped but he had a nasty graze on his forehead and a swelling on his cheek was already closing one eye.

'You shouldn't mix it with her, Ezra. She's deadly when someone crosses her.'

They sat down and Bannister pushed his cigarettes across the table, wondering why he felt sorry for a man who put teenagers into a brothel. Watson's right, I'm too kind-hearted.

'She needn't have knocked me down and nearly killed me for nothing.'

'What were you doing in the brothel. Getting a cheap thrill?'

'No, I was hiding. Everybody's after me. Your lot, and Duke's friends. They'll kill me if they catch me.'

'Where were you hiding?'

'In the loft. I thought she'd found me when she went into the bedroom. She was right below me.'

'You must be as thick as pig-shit. What made you think you could set up a woman like her?'

Ezra held a hand over his sore face and groaned. Teaming up with Conrad had been the biggest mistake he had ever made in his life.

Molly returned and stood in front of Ezra. 'Right, ponce! Who set up the London job? I need answers now. Don't interrupt!' she shouted as he opened his mouth to speak.

259

'Tell me who organised the sting, or you're going to spend the night in a cell, and the next night, and the night after that. And if I still haven't got what I want, I'll make a telephone call. I'll ask Duke's friends to come down here to collect you.'

Ezra's good eye bulged.

'Now, tell me. Who set up the sting?'

'The Manchester guys and Isha. I was a go-between, just trying to help you.'

'You're a flaming liar,' she shouted. 'Tell me! Tell me who fixed it up.'

Ezra sighed like a man without hope. 'I just did,' he cried.

Molly turned to Bannister. 'Bounce this pathetic creature down the cellar steps and lock him up.'

Escorting Ezra to the cell, the detective allowed him to walk.

'What are you gawping at?' Molly asked when Bannister returned to the kitchen.

He had never seen her so mad, but he stood his ground. 'You can't do it, ma'am. I know you're upset but that cell hasn't been used for years. It's a store-room.'

'I've just recommissioned it.'

'It's against the law.'

'So's spitting in the street.'

He felt hot. First Conrad had got him into trouble down those same steps; now Watson was turning the cellar into an illegal prison.

'Come on, Bill,' she said quietly. 'Let's go and get a few hours' shut-eye.'

'What about Ezra.'

'Leave him. A night down there will loosen his tongue.'

'He should see a doctor. He took a right knock on the head. That eye doesn't look too good either.'

'I've told you before, Bill, you're too soft. I'll lock up. Just make sure you're back here at six.'

35

Liz cursed, got out of bed, then made her way stiffly down the stairs to answer the telephone. Moaning her way back to the bedroom, she shook her husband. 'It's five o'clock in the sodding morning. That slave-driver you call the gaffer isn't satisfied with day and night working any more. She's started a bloody early shift.'

Bannister got up and took the call.

An hour later he let himself into Dinsall Police Station. Surprised to find the cellar in complete darkness, he switched on the lights and ran down the stone steps.

There were three old cells. The Drug Store, the Confidential Waste Store, and the junk room. Outside the junk room was a pile of broken furniture and some old cricket equipment. The door was shut and there was a key in the lock.

Bannister turned the key and pushed open the door. Inside it was cold and damp. Ezra was hunched up at the far end of the wooden bed. In the corner was a bucket. Bannister gagged at the smell.

'Come on, China,' he said quietly, shaking the fat man's shoulder. It was stiff, and for a dreadful moment Bannister thought it was a corpse. Much to his relief, the head moved and the good eye opened.

Rousing himself and massaging aching thighs, Ezra shuddered violently, rasping breaths sawing through a dry throat. 'Get me out of here, man,' he pleaded.

Bannister was gentle with him. 'I wish I could Ezra, but you know Watson. She'll leave you here for a week if she has to.'

'I'll die down here, man. You've got to get me out of this stink-hole. Let me see an inspector. I've got my rights.'

'Not with Watson you haven't. Why don't you tell her what she wants to know? Then I can help you. She's not interested in the brothel. She just needs to know who set up the London job.'

'Why?'

'I don't know. But she won't give up until she finds out. Something's got to her. She's not herself any more. It's become a raging obsession, as if her life depended on it.'

Ezra put his feet to the floor, rocking himself backwards and forwards. 'Will she let me go if I tell you?'

'If I can give her the name she wants, then I can start helping you.'

'You've got no say in it, man. Watson makes the decisions. She wants to kill me.'

'Don't be daft.'

'D'you think she'll deal?'

'She needs that guy so badly, she might even let you go to America.'

Ezra narrowed his good eye so that both eyes were hardly visible. 'Who said anything about America?'

'Watson. Don't you see? The woman's got you taped. Before she's finished, she'll know what you have wet dreams about. She'll never let up. If you don't co-operate she'll send for Duke's minders.'

'That'd be murder.'

'Exactly.'

'She wouldn't dare.'

'Don't chance your luck, mate. She always gets her way in the end, believe me.'

Ezra stared at the cell floor and there was a prolonged silence.

Without warning, he flung his hat against the cell wall, gripped the top of his head with both hands, and groaned

as if his brain was about to explode. 'Conrad,' he croaked.
'Who?'

'Conrad . . . your sergeant, man. He set it up. That's why he handed me over to you. It was all part of his plan to get rid of Watson.'

Bannister's legs went weak. Feeling ill, he sat down on the hard bed. She must have suspected it. That's why she'd gone to such lengths to get a cough out of Ezra. She'd known it was someone on the squad but she'd needed to prove it. Why didn't she tell me? Surely she couldn't have believed that I would have betrayed the lads — could she?

It was seven when Molly arrived. Bannister told her what Ezra had said, watching her closely to see if she already knew. If she did, she showed no sign of it. Her reply, however, confirmed his suspicions.

'Yes, I guessed it was Conrad. He had run Ezra for some time. He also had the motive: promotion and my job. I'm in his way. He knows that as long as I'm number one on the squad, he has no future.'

Bannister lit up a cigarette, past caring whether or not she objected.

'Is Ezra all right?' Molly asked.

'No, he's a mental and physical wreck. You'd switched off all the lights and he could hardly breath down that hell-hole of a place. It hasn't been used as a cell for years and there's no heating. I don't know whether the poor sod was shaking with cold or from sheer terror.'

'Good.'

'He could've died. We'd have been done for kidnap and murder.'

Molly showed no emotion. 'We can't afford to play around with the Ezras of this world. Do you think he'll work for us?'

'In his present state, ma'am, he'd work for the devil.' Bannister stubbed out his half-finished cigarette on a saucer. 'What happens now?'

'Simple. We play Conrad at his own game. We use Ezra to set him up.'

Later, Ezra, subdued but recovering from his ordeal, thawed out in front of the kitchen fire as he wolfed down a huge breakfast.

While Molly was having a second round of toast and marmalade, Bannister returned to the temporary cell. He carefully removed all evidence of Ezra's incarceration, replacing the furniture and the cricket equipment.

When Ezra had finished eating Molly thanked Vera and swore her to secrecy. 'Don't forget, you never saw him.'

Molly followed Ezra and her detective out of the kitchen. They climbed into her Fiesta and she drove out of the station yard before the first uniformed man arrived.

'Where are you taking me?' Ezra asked, viewing the open countryside with noticeable distaste.

'My place,' Molly replied, smiling at Holmes who had made himself comfortable on Ezra's lap. He can't be all bad, she decided. Holmes was very choosy about whose lap he sat on.

As they approached the outskirts of Coovers Wood, Molly told Ezra to take his hat off and lie down on the back seat. Bannister moved forward to give him room then covered him with a blanket. Holmes, tail wagging, burrowed beneath to join his new friend.

Opening her garage doors, and pleased there was no one about, Molly drove inside. Bannister shut the garage doors then helped Ezra out of the car and through the back door into the house.

Molly drew all the curtains. 'The neighbours will think I've been on nights,' she muttered, ushering Ezra and Bannister into the study.

It was late afternoon when Molly had finalised her plans.

'Don't forget, Bill,' she said. 'Tell Monica that if she doesn't do what she's told, I'll send her back to the Liverpool young offenders' institution she absconded from. And keep her off the streets. I don't want her arrested for soliciting.'

'I'm her contact, not her ponce,' Bannister replied as he left.

Using the remote control, Molly switched off the nine o'clock news. Comfortable in her favourite chair beside the log-effect gas fire, she was too preoccupied with the arrangements for tomorrow to be interested in squabbling Eurocrats. Ezra and Holmes were asleep on the settee. What was happening to her? What was she doing, bringing a ponce into her home and keeping him for twenty-four hours? Was there nothing she would not do to stop Conrad?

Ezra snorted and woke up, disturbed by the silence.

'What did he say?' Molly asked.

'Who?'

'Conrad.'

Ezra sat up, rubbing his bleary right eye. There was nothing he could do about the other. It had closed up completely.

'I've told you a dozen times already.'

'Tell me again.'

Ezra sighed. 'He asked where I was. I told him Birmingham.'

'I know that.'

'He said something had gone smelly in London and the traffickers had been arrested. You'd been acting strange, but he didn't think you suspected him. He thought he was in the clear because otherwise you'd have reported him to

Complaints and he would've been suspended.'

'Go on,' she urged impatiently.'

'I'm the problem. He said I'd got to get out of the country before you or the Manchester crowd caught up with me.' He paused and she nodded him on. 'Like you said. I told him I had to get a flight to New York but couldn't risk going out to get the tickets. I also told him I'd got three weights of resin to get rid of before the police turned my place over.' Ezra fell against the back of the settee, seemingly too tired to carry on; shattered after his night in the old cell.

'You need some medicine,' Molly said, getting up and going over to the cocktail cabinet.

She poured the Bell's then told him to continue.

'Where was I?' he asked, downing half of his drink.

'The air ticket and the gear.'

'He said that if I gave him the gear, he could get me the tickets.'

'Tickets?'

'Yeah, me and Monica. It'll be better cover if there's two of us, and I need her for the business. . . . He's also seeing a friend of mine who'll fix her up with a passport.'

Molly frowned. Helping a seventeen-year-old abscondee to leave the country was a bit much, even for her.

A pleading tone returned to Ezra's voice. 'I need her. I've got to eat.'

'What did Conrad say?' Molly asked, accepting the situation.

'He agreed. Bound to, wasn't he. Three weights of shit for a couple of tickets to New York and a passport. It's robbery, I only bought it off him a few days ago.'

'What?'

'Bought it off him. Said he needed the money to pay off what he owed on the Saab. Claimed the repayments were crippling him.'

266

'How much did you give him?'

'He asked for five. We settled for three.'

'Three what?'

'Three grand.'

'Have you bought drugs from him before?'

He hesitated. '. . . No, I make enough out of the girls.'

She knew he was lying but decided to let it go — for the moment. Refilling the tumblers, hers mostly Canada Dry, she mulled over the new information. 'Go on,' she said after a long silence.

Ezra took off his hat and loosened his tie. 'I told him that Monica would deliver the gear and have the tickets and passport off him at the same time. You know the rest. We've been through it enough. I've been dreamin' about it.'

'It's necessary. We'll only get one poke at him.'

Ezra downed the remains of his scotch.

Later, satisfied she would learn nothing further that would improve her plans for tomorrow, Molly produced another bottle of whisky and found some stale bread and cheese.

'Nice place,' Ezra mumbled, eyeing the cut-glass chandelier and the rosewood display cabinet crammed with Molly's collection of crested china.

'Used to think so myself, now I hardly notice. I'm rarely here.'

'No husband or boy-friend around the place?'

'I wouldn't let a man stay here. He could go to court and claim half the flaming house. This place is mine and it's staying that way.'

'Don't you get lonely?'

Of course she was lonely. She'd been lonely all her life: it was her natural state. To him she said: 'Living alone is great. I do my own thing. I eat what I like, when I like. Play my CDs or watch the telly when I like. Laze about in bed until Coronation Street, then stay up all night if I want to. I can go to London for the day and wander around antique shops. Or I can go to Madeira on a bridge holiday. I can do nothing for days on end if the mood takes me, just doss around, reading, drinking, eating boxes of expensive chocolates, or whatever else takes my fancy. Then, in a sudden burst of energy, I might spring-clean until the whole place shines. I can stroll around country lanes and have two hour lunches at interesting pubs. Or, if the spirit of adventure stirs, I can take time off, pack my bags and walk the Pennine Way. Don't knock the single independent woman, there's a lot going for it.'

She stopped; it was overkill. Was she trying to convince Ezra, or herself? As he worked his way through a chunk of cheese, his expression seemed to mock her.

'What about you?' she asked. 'Have you got someone — apart from your string of girls?'

He finished off the food and swilled it down with half a tumbler of whisky. 'Woman here, woman in Jamaica. There's always women.'

'Will you go back?'

'Where?'

'Wavy palm trees, sandy white beaches.'

'Sure. When I've got my stake.'

'One place I've never been to, the Caribbean. Must be great. The people next door paid a fortune just for two weeks of it. I could visit you and we could drink rum, real rum like the matelots used to have.'

'Sure thing,' Ezra murmured.

'What d'you think of your friend, Mr Conrad, now?' she asked, forcing her mind back to work, still determined not to leave any loose ends.

'He's a right bastard. He nearly got me sent down for ever. I hope you string him up by the balls.'

'He's been selling to you regularly, hasn't he?'

Ezra lifted his glass and took a big gulp of whisky. 'About once a month. Mostly after those shit-burning parties you're supposed to have.'

'How much did you pay him?'

'Hundreds at first; thousands later. He always wanted more. Gimme, gimme, gimme.'

Ezra sprawled out across the settee, disturbing Holmes, who stretched his neck then curled up beside the hard hat. The second empty bottle dropped off the cushions and rolled up to the fireplace surround. A last drop of spirit settled on the shiny hardwood surface, a translucent yellow bubble shimmering on beeswax.

'How will tomorrow end?' Ezra yawned.

Molly stood up. 'You and Monica will fly to the States. Me and Conrad . . .?'

Ezra started to snore and she stopped talking. But her thoughts didn't stop.

— Tomorrow, me and Conrad will settle it.

36

It was ten o'clock on Friday morning when Molly arrived at the factory they had used for the shebeen raid five days earlier. She struggled to open the heavy double doors, then drove into the cold, barn-like building. Parked up, and facing the Westhampton Road, she waited.

Had it only been five days since the shebeen? She thought of London and James, reading the back of his photograph then looking longingly at the Cotswold cottage. It had been twelve months since her last affair had broken up and at the time she had sworn to herself that she was finished with men. She liked James, liked him a lot, but she couldn't stand the thought of being let down again. Even so, he had been very charming during their few hours together. He had made her feel warm and womanly and wanted.

Her thoughts were interrupted by the approach of a line of vehicles. Walter in his green leathers on the Suzuki, Killer in his Hell's Angels' colours on the Harley-Davidson, Bert's London taxi, a Santana Supplies van, two motorcycle outriders, and a motorcycle tail-end-Charlie.

Molly climbed out of her Fiesta and waved them into the factory, quickly finding volunteers to shut the doors.

There was a flurry of activity as motorcycles were rested on stands and equipment was taken out of the van. Chris Collins scampered to a corner of the factory and faced the wall. Motorcyclists, taking longer to unzip their leathers, joined them, adding to the rising cloud of steam.

Sergeant Stockley climbed out of the van.

'Dave! It's great to see you,' Molly exclaimed with genuine pleasure, as the last engine was switched off. 'Any problems on the way?'

'None at all. We did a steady ninety and didn't get stopped by the cops once.'

'How did you find this place?'

'A man in a blue turban and a Westhampton City football scarf said half his family used to work here; wanted to show us around.'

'Thanks for coming, Dave.'

'Cranny's idea. Sends his regards. He thought a party of hooligans like this needed someone in charge, if only to carry the can at the discipline hearing. He wanted to come up himself but couldn't get away. Said it wasn't right that you should have to fight this thing on your own. I think he worries about you.'

'I could've managed if I'd had to, and there's Bill. He'll be bringing along one of his admirers shortly.'

'Good job we didn't let Pat come with us. She was busting a bra to get here.'

'He's got enough to contend with,' Molly commented sourly.

Stockley smiled. 'Come and share our picnic, courtesy of the Metropolitan Police Catering Department.'

When they had finished eating, Molly spoke to the Special Operations men. 'Welcome to Westhampton and thank you for making the trip. I know you've handled most things, but I can promise you that none of your jobs have been more important than this one. At the moment the only people who know anything about it are you, me, and your governor. Certainly no one around here is aware that a top Scotland Yard undercover team is active in the city.'

She was stroking their egos because she needed everything they could give her. If there were any cock-ups today, all of them might be looking for new jobs.

'At two this afternoon we are going after a Detective Sergeant Thomas Conrad who has several years' CID experience. He's clever and he's cunning, but he has no reason to suspect that it's a set-up.' She handed Stockley a photograph she had obtained from Conrad's personal file during her last trip to headquarters.

'There's a picture of him being passed around, and it's a good likeness,' she continued. 'Be careful, he's got everything to lose and he'll stop at nothing to escape.' She then went on to outline the plan of action.

'What's he driving?' Killer asked when she had finished.

'A red Saab with all the trimmings, XAB 873.'

Sergeant Stockley rose to his feet. 'Well lads, you know what we have to do. Let's make a move.'

He unfolded a large-scale map of the area and spread it out on the table. His men crowded around and they started to memorise the streets of Westhampton.

A short time later the side door opened and those at the table looked up to see Bannister ambling towards them. Dressed in washed denims and cowboy boots, he was accompanied by Monica who, half his size, held onto his arm as if for protection.

'Why does he get all the birds?' Walter grumbled as the SOU men gathered around them, pumping Bannister's hand and admiring Monica. Two motorcyclists collided as they pushed forward to offer her a camping stool. She smiled and sat down with her hands in her lap, putting on her innocent, little-girl-lost face. Killer handed her a cup of coffee and stood guard.

'Gee fellas, ta very much. This is mega.' Her Liverpool accent was as strong as ever and they loved it.

Molly beckoned Collins over. 'Thanks for coming along, Monica,' she said, 'This is Chris who's going to fix you up with some kit. There's nothing to worry about. It's just a precaution, OK?'

The blonde hair bobbed and men edged closer.

'Don't you worry, I'll look after you,' Killer assured her,

keeping the others at bay. She lifted her face to him, eyes sparkling as she mouthed a quiet thank you which ended like a kiss.

'Come on, duckie. Let's go and do the business,' the TSU man fussed.

'Don't bother about him, luv, he's harmless,' laughed one of the motorcyclists as they watched her climb into the back of the van. Collins slapped the air with his hand, shutting the door behind them.

'Is she really on the game?' Stockley asked.

'Afraid so,' Molly answered. 'A product of Birmingham's white slave trade.'

'She's a beaut,' Killer said in a soft dreamy voice they hadn't heard before.

Molly and Bannister exchanged looks and went out through the side door.

'What's going on?' he asked. 'You never said the Met would be involved.'

'Officially, they're not. I've just borrowed a few of them.'

'I'm surprised Davids gave permission.'

'He didn't. Only the people here and Cranny know anything about it.'

'Bloody hell. The chief'll crucify you when he finds out!'

'It can't be helped. We couldn't do it ourselves and if I'd gone to headquarters it would have leaked back to Conrad before I'd left the building. I had no choice.'

'What about Complaints? They're supposed to deal with things like this.'

'They couldn't detect mail in a letter-box. I've got to do something now, before it's too late. In addition to everything else, I've got evidence to prove Conrad stole at least half the gear we found at Delroy Jackman's place. He also forged Jackman's statement and planted some of the gear on a guy at Cliff Spence's shebeen.'

'How did you know it was Jackman's gear?'

'When we first found it, I noticed faint traces of blue paint on one side of each block.'

'Paint?'

'Yes. You see it sometimes. The man at the lab said it's marine blue. Probably off the hold of a ship, a newly painted deck or a bulkhead.'

'The man must be mental. How the hell did he expect to get away with it?'

'After you left my place yesterday I worked on Ezra. He told me that Conrad has been selling him gear regularly in pound weights. He's been making thousands.'

'It's all crazy. I don't want any part of it,' Bannister gasped.

'That's down to you. If you want to walk away, do so. You're in the clear because you've been acting under my orders. I've asked a superintendent from Complaints to be at South Road nick later this afternoon. Go and see him if you wish. Just give me time to sort out Conrad.'

It was some time before Bannister replied. 'I've already promised Liz that I'll pack the job in. I may as well go out with a bang.'

37

Bannister stopped his car outside a city-centre cafe. Monica, sitting next to him, looked up and down the street, hoping that none of the girls were out.

'Have you got the gear?' Bannister asked.

'Of course I've got the gear. It's our bleeding air tickets, ain't it?'

'You need a brain transplant, going to Tom and Jerry land with a guy like Ezra.'

'It's better than being thrown in the jug with a bunch of kinky women.'

'Let's have a look at it.'

Monica laughed. 'Cost you a hundred quid, fella.'

'The gear!'

'What d'you want it for?'

'Just checking.'

'You bleeding coppers are all the same. You don't believe anybody's straight.'

True, he thought, not after the London job.

'Stop yapping. Let me have a shufti.'

Checking the street again, Monica opened her shoulder-bag and produced three blocks of cannabis resin. Each one was sealed in clear plastic.

After he had examined them, Bannister returned the resin to her.

She gave him an impish grin. 'Satisfied, are we, Whacker?'

'I reckon you're not bad for a young'un,' he replied, looking across the road at a group of men who tumbled out of a betting shop and wheeled into the boozer next door.

'Ha! Listen to Mr Universe himself. You're getting a right big 'ead you are. Ever since you started running around with that Watson woman.'

He laughed. 'You're jealous.'

'Screw you, mate. I should avoid you lot like the cowin' plague.'

'It's your duty: assisting the upholders of law and order.'

'Naff off,' she laughed. 'You're all as bent as arseholes.'

'No we're not,' he said seriously. 'Just a few bastards like Conrad.'

After a long silence, she poked Bannister in the ribs. 'You should wear a black 'at, you should. You look like a bleedin' undertaker.'

He nodded absent-mindedly. So many things could go wrong. 'You be careful. We'll hear everything that's said by you and Conrad, and there'll always be one of the lads a few metres away. Don't try to do anything clever. Just give him the gear and take the tickets and passport.'

Monica linked her arm through his and gave him a squeeze. 'You're worse than my old lady, you are. She was always going on. " 'Ave you got your sarnies? 'Ave you got your bus pass? 'Ave you got your 'omework?" I can 'andle a prick like Conrad in my sleep.'

Giving the area a final check, Bannister let Monica out of the car, waiting until she had entered the cafe before he drove off. Killer, straddled across his Harley-Davidson, kept watch from the end of the street.

The red-brick library, standing on the corner at a city-centre road junction, dwarfed a modern mishmash of flat-roofed shops and offices.

Parked in a nearby side street was the SOU Santana Supplies van. Inside, Chris Collins could still smell Monica's talc. He had enjoyed the scouse banter as she had bent over his work bench while he fitted a small transmitter into the hollow of her back. She was slender, like a young boy, and his breathing had quickened as he smoothed the tape along the firm white flesh.

Opening switches and turning dials, Collins checked his radio equipment, calling Kremlin Control for a test transmission. Why change a good name? he thought.

Control was Bert's snub-nose taxi. It faced the library and was stationary on the opposite side of the junction. Hearing the transmission, Sergeant Stockley, sitting next to Bert, carried out the test.

A few minutes later Collins came back on the air and reported that he had checked communications with the five SOU motorcyclists. Reception was good.

The sky was overcast, and pedestrians hurried along to keep warm in a raw east wind.

Bannister joined Molly in the back of Bert's taxi.

'Everything's fixed up, ma'am. I think she'll cope.'

'She'd better,' said Molly softly.

The four detectives watched the library and waited.

'D'you think he'll use his own car, ma'am?' Bannister asked.

'He might not even show. He could send her all over the place, wait until he's satisfied that she's not being followed, then pick her up. He could also use a courier.'

Collins informed them that Monica had left the cafe and was heading in their direction.

'There she is!' Bannister declared, a short time later.

Monica stopped beside the telephone kiosk next to the main entrance of the library. Her black shoulder-bag was clutched under her arm where it looked less bulky.

'Inform all mobiles, Dave,' Molly said, trying to fathom out Conrad's next move. Ezra had been told that Monica was to wait for Conrad's telephone call, then follow his instructions, but Molly knew that he was likely to alter the arrangements, and she must be prepared for the unexpected.

Killer, arms outstretched, left knee almost touching the road, leaned his American machine around the corner in front of the library.

Stockley chuckled. 'I don't think he's taken his eyes off that girl since she arrived at the factory.'

'She must be freezing!' Bannister said.

Molly checked her watch. 'Don't worry about it. That's what she does — stands on street corners waiting for men. More importantly, where's our Sergeant Conrad?'

'Perhaps the phone's on the blink,' Bert chipped in. Because he had been servicing his taxi, not normally used for hundred-mile dashes up the motorway, he had missed most of the briefing.

'It was tested by engineers at midday, and again at one o'clock,' Molly informed him.

There was a tense silence in the taxi as they watched Monica tighten the belt of the coat she had stolen at the January sales. Her purple high-heeled shoes had been paid for by Ezra, not out of kindness, but to give her extra height and make her look more like someone on the game: too many cars had driven past her without slowing down.

Molly spoke to Stockley. 'What happened to the Manchester crew and their Arab friend?'

'I thought you'd never ask, ma'am. They all coughed it and have been charged with conspiracy to steal seventy-five thousand pounds. Crown Prosecutor's Office has OK'd it. According to them, they should draw at least three years apiece.'

'Hum!' she said. 'With remission and parole they'll be free in a few months, conning old ladies out of their pension money. What about the Minder?'

'Soft in the head. They'd promised him fifty quid and a day in the big city without bothering to mention what he was supposed to do. He's made a statement and apologised for his rude remarks about Pat. I should think they'll let him go on the grounds that he's mentally incompetent.'

The afternoon traffic was building up. A motorcycle stopped outside the fish and chip shop opposite the library. Killer reluctantly moved on to another location further down the road.

Bert wiped his windscreen. 'He's half an hour late, ma'am. What happens now?'

'She's supposed to leave at about this time and go to her flat up the road, behind the District Hospital.'

What's Conrad up to? Molly thought. He's about somewhere, I can sense it. She felt hot but knew it had nothing to do with the temperature. This was it — her opportunity to stop the rot that would have ruined her squad. She had set the bait. Where was he?

A black cat entwined itself around Monica's legs, tail brushing the bottom of her coat.

'Supposed to be lucky,' Stockley opinioned.

Molly scanned the street. 'Only if you treat them right.'

Monica bent down to stroke the mangy animal but it arched away and scooted up the library steps.

'Good job I'm not into superstition,' Bannister murmured.

Drifting towards the edge of the pavement, Monica looked briefly along each of the four roads, making it obvious that she was waiting for someone. A gold coloured Rover pulled into the kerb, the driver leaning over his passenger seat to talk to her.

'Is that Conrad?' Bannister asked, straining to see across the wide junction.

'No,' Molly replied, 'but he's not asking the way to the town hall either.'

The car pulled away and Bert laughed. 'That must've

hurt. She'll be putting in for loss of earnings.'

Monica returned to the telephone kiosk, then went inside.

'It's rung!' Bannister shouted.

'No it hasn't. She's just lifted the receiver to see if the flaming thing works,' Molly said as Monica returned to her former position.

A sudden rush of people spilled out of the library as if there had been a fire alarm. The pavements were filling up. Women mostly, weighed down by bulging bags, and besieged by fractious kids.

'What's going on, ma'am?' Bannister asked.

'How the hell should I know?' she snapped, her mind racing as she tried to anticipate Conrad's next move.

'I don't care what you say about that young gal,' Bert said stoically, 'she's got plenty of spunk.'

'She should be doing what she was flaming-well told to do,' Molly said sharply. 'Making her way home.'

Bert raised an eyebrow at Stockley.

A few minutes later they watched Monica go to the edge of the pavement again. With a shrug of her shoulders, and an enquiring glance at the taxi, she walked off in the direction of the hospital.

'She's moving away,' Bannister exclaimed unnecessarily.

'Let the others know what's happening, Dave,' Molly said quietly, looking all around her for any sign of Conrad.

She tapped the driver on the shoulder. 'Follow her, but keep well back.'

Bert switched on the ignition, drove across the junction, then slowed to walking pace. Monica stopped opposite the hospital, waiting to cross the road. A red saloon pulled up in front of her, then drove off at speed. Monica had gone.

'Conrad!' Molly yelled, 'After him. Warn all units.'

They were thrown back against the seats as Bert slammed his foot down and the taxi surged forward in pursuit. 'That

Saab'll do a ton in third gear. I'm never gonna catch him in this old tub.'

Molly gripped the door handle and said a silent prayer. Conrad must not escape now. Not after all the hard work, the risks and the planning. Too many people were involved and there was too much to lose.

After half a mile they screeched around a traffic island and stopped. The Saab had disappeared.

'Where to now, ma'am?' Bert asked, looking helplessly down five empty roads.

Stockley, who had been talking on the radio to the motorcyclists, turned to Molly. 'They've lost him, ma'am. Must have gone to ground. He can't be far away.'

'Far enough,' she said angrily.

The radio clicked several times, as if it was being tested.

'Guv! Guv!' Collins screeched. 'I'm picking up conversations from the Saab!'

'Put it on talk-through,' she ordered.

Sounds crackled over the airwaves. '. . .*waiting for, aren't I,*' said a familiar voice.

'Conrad!' Molly hissed. Reception faded and they strained to hear.

'*Now what have you got for me?*' the voice continued a few seconds later.

'*Well, well, you have been a good girl. I think you deserve a big reward.*'

'*What the fuck's your game, Whacker? Get your filthy paws off me and gimme the tickets and my passport.*'

'*Ezra told me you needed a few lessons.*'

'*Not from you, you bastard. Let me out of here.*'

'*That's no way to talk to a friend of Ezra's. He's told me I can have you any time I feel like it.*'

'*Stop it! You're hurting me.*'

'*Now, now. If your man wants to get away from Watson, you'd better start being nice to me.*'

In the taxi they stared helplessly at the speaker, listening to the sounds of Monica's struggles.

'*No! don't!*' she screamed.

Bannister groaned and beat out his frustration on the back of Bert's seat. 'I'll throttle the bastard!'

'Killer calling Kremlin Control. We've spotted him. South Park, I think you call it.'

'How many of you?' Stockley asked.

'Me and Walter.'

Bannister snatched the radio out of Stockley's hand and pressed the transmit button. 'Take the bastard! Now!' he shrieked.

'No! No!' We're not ready you fool,' Molly shouted, desperately grabbing at the radio as it fell uselessly between them.

'Round the island,' she yelled into Bert's ear, realising she was too late to stop the SOU motorcyclists. 'Move!'

Conrad's panic-stricken voice sounded over the air-waves.

'*Who's set me up?*'

Monica screamed, then started to sob.

'*It's Watson, isn't it?*' The detectives listened to blows being struck and the sounds of another struggle inside Conrad's car.

'*Get out, you bastard cunt! Out, out!*'

Bert spun the taxi around the island, impervious to the honking drivers as he cut through a line of traffic.

Following Molly's shouted directions, he drove through a series of back streets and into South Park, an island of green surrounded by grey council houses and a small industrial estate. A canal ran through a deep cutting on one side of the park.

Foot jammed down hard, Bert raced along the narrow perimeter road, passing football pitches, swings, slides and a boating lake as he aimed for a small humpback bridge.

The black taxi bounced over the brow of the bridge and Molly, hanging onto the back of Bert's seat as she was thrown into the air, gasped as she saw the red Saab speeding towards them. Trees lined the road on their right, and on the left there was a steep embankment down to the canal.

Killer was riding alongside the Saab, and Walter on his Suzuki was close behind. Monica, in the distance, was picking herself up off the road.

As the taxi and the Saab hurtled towards one another, Killer stood on the foot-rest of his bike like a stunt rider, and struck the windscreen of the car with his truncheon, smashing a hole in the laminated glass and causing Conrad to swerve across the road.

Killer went with him and managed to regain his seat, but saw the approaching taxi too late. Making a desperate attempt to save himself, he aimed for a gap between the two cars, but there was not enough room and his Harley-Davidson hit the front bumper of the taxi, sending man and machine catapulting over the bonnet and down the embankament into a clump of rhododendron bushes.

The taxi, meanwhile, veered onto the grass verge at the top of the embankment. Bert, fighting to stop the vehicle rolling over, had no option but to yank the wheel to the left and drive straight down the steep slope. Bumping and sliding across the rough grass, the vehicle hit the towpath and bounced into the canal, sinking fifteen metres to the bottom and coming to rest in an upright position.

Thrown about like dice in a shaker, and bumping into Bannister several times, Molly had hung on grimly and yelled 'Open the windows!' as they had hit the water, knowing from her navy days that once the taxi had sunk, the pressure would have to be equalised before they could open the doors.

Taking a deep breath, she ducked under the rush of water, but was kicked on the head as Bannister and then

Stockley struggled frantically to get out of the taxi.

Wanting to panic but forcing herself to keep calm in the muddy water, Molly struggled out of her heavy sheepskin coat and felt her way forward to release Bert who was trapped by his seat belt. Thinking her lungs would burst, she then opened his door and pushed him out of the car, so that they rose through the water together.

Breaking the surface, Bert thrashed about and called for help. Molly, on the verge of collapse and feeling as though she had swallowed gallons of dirty canal water, somehow found the strength to tow him to the bank where Bannister and Stockley hauled them both on to the towpath.

Anger and frustration driving her on, Molly, thinking only of Conrad, staggered to her feet and clawed her way up the slope. Reaching the top with a last gasp of energy, and seeing a Traffic Patrol car, she sank into the arms of the driver and observer who carried her to the car and put her in the back. Bannister, dripping wet and fighting for breath, fell onto the seat beside her.

'Hospital, foot down,' Molly heard.

'No!' she managed to call out, 'city centre.'

'You need treatment, ma'am,' said the observer, staring in disbelief at the distraught woman in the back of the car.

'City centre. Look for a red Saab.'

'A doctor's what you want.'

'Do what you're fucking well told!' she screamed back at him, wiping the blood from her eyes and holding a tissue to the gash on her forehead. She hadn't known that her head was cut until she saw the blood and guessed it had happened in the taxi.

Sirens on and blue lights flashing, the powerful police car left the park, crossing the inner ring road and speeding past the District Hospital.

'What's going on, ma'am?' the driver asked. 'Old man Davids at HQ is going spare. He wants to know why a

Drug Squad sergeant is tear-arsing around town with a pack of weirdo bikers stuck up his tail-pipe.'

'Where's the Saab now?' Molly demanded. Davids could think what he liked. She was going to get Conrad and Jesus Christ himself wouldn't stop her.

The observer glanced over his shoulder. 'After three trips around the city, and shooting through every red light on the way, nobody seems to have a clue.'

Vibrations rocked the patrol car an instant before they heard the explosion.

'Oh shit!' exclaimed the driver as black smoke mushroomed into the sky ahead of them.

'Conrad!' Bannister managed through badly cut lips.

The police car skidded to a halt as the driver struggled to avoid the build-up of traffic.

Molly, fighting nausea and tiredness, but determined to stop Conrad escaping again, fell out of the car, her legs almost giving way as she led Bannister past stationary vehicles and on towards the wreckage ahead of her. She forced a way through the crowd of onlookers who watched in amazement as the bloodied pair in torn and muddy clothes weaved their way towards the scene of the accident.

Above them there was a railway bridge, supported by blue brick walls on each side of the road, and three iron stanchions on the central reservation. The stanchions were scored with red paint, and the Saab, looking as if it had narrowly escaped from a car crusher, had slewed around some distance farther on so that it was facing the detectives. Closer to them, embedded into a recess in the wall, was a Royal Mail van, a plume of black smoke rising into the air from where the engine had been. Another van, lay on its roof.

Molly guessed that Conrad had tried to overtake at speed as he had approached the bridge, but had been trapped between the stanchions and the vans when he had attempted to cut in. Several people from the damaged vehicles had been dragged to the side of the road, but Conrad was not amongst them.

Suddenly an engine revved, the noise reverberating under the bridge so that it sounded like a car preparing to streak out of the pits at Silverstone.

Molly, stranded in the centre of the road, stared in horror as the Saab screeched towards her, the crazed and bloodied face of Conrad behind the wheel. The jagged mass of metal seemed to expand like the jaws of a ferocious, steel-toothed monster and Molly, unable to move, waited to be crushed to death. Mercifully, she fainted and collapsed onto the road. At the last moment the Saab swerved away from her unconscious body and smashed into the iron bridge supports, sending up clouds of dust and showering the road with shards of broken glass and plastic moulding.

Opening her eyes, Molly blinked at the underside of the bridge and the sky beyond that she hadn't expected to see again.

'Molly! Molly! Are you all right?' Bannister cried out in alarm.

Drifting in and out of consciousness, she felt the warmth of his strong arms as he lifted her like a baby, and she heard his voice, soft and gentle, as if she was something very special to him. 'Christ, woman, you gave me a fright. I thought you were a gonner, truly I did.'

Slowly coming round, she let her head rest on his shoulder for a minute, then looked up at him, noticing for the first time his cut lips.

'I think you'd better put me down, Bill.'

'Yes ma'am,' he said quickly, glancing over his shoulder at the watching crowd.

He carefully lowered her to her feet, but kept hold of her arm as they stumbled towards the remains of Conrad's car.

As Molly looked inside, hot, acrid smoke from the engine scorched her lungs. Conrad, head bent back, was slumped against the steering wheel. A diagonal chain-saw trench had been ripped out of his face, and blood dripped off a chewed-up eyeball that dangled alongside the gold locket around his neck.

Killer's smashed windscreen, Molly thought, noticing the jagged, red-tipped glass. Feeling giddy, and wanting to vomit, she held on to the side of the car. Whatever he'd done, he didn't deserve this. Her shoulders dropped and she tasted tears, not sure whether they were for Conrad or herself.

'You all right, ma'am?' Bannister asked.

'Yes thanks, Bill,' she said, brushing a grubby hand across her face. 'It's all this damn smoke.'

She lifted a white envelope out of Conrad's pocket, briefly checking the contents before handing it to Bannister. 'Give these tickets and the passport to Monica, will you. She's meeting Ezra at the central railway station.'

'What about him?' Bannister asked, staring like someone in a trance at the blood-splattered body of his former sergeant.

'He's dead, I'm afraid. We can't help him now.'

'He couldn't do it, ma'am.'

'Couldn't do what?'

'Kill you.'

'We'll never know, Bill. He might have lost control. He looked gone out to me.'

Bannister turned away from the gory mess. 'Perhaps he decided to finish it. He'd pulled some diabolical strokes, and he'd got terrible problems at home.'

Molly shook her head. 'It's down to me. He was one of my men, and because of me he's dead.'

'You're in shock, ma'am. It wasn't your fault — none of it was.'

Her green eyes softened as she looked at Bannister. 'Thank's anyway, Bill. You're a good detective.' She had wanted to say friend, but even now, her natural reserve got in the way of her emotions and she cursed herself for not being able to say what she really felt.

She turned her attention back to the dead man, his gold locket now dark red with crooked lines of congealed blood. 'His wife will have to be told before the press start knocking on the door. Mary, I think she's called . . . He never talked about her.'

Reaching into the car, Molly searched Conrad's pockets and removed three blocks of cannabis resin. She peered through plastic and saw the faint traces of blue paint. They were part of the drugs she had found at Delroy Jackman's house eleven days earlier. A world away, she thought tiredly. So much had happened since. It had been like a ride on a roller-coaster that could only stop when the carriages crashed off the end.

'Shall I take them as exhibits, ma'am?'

'No,' she replied, putting the cannabis back into the dead man's pockets. 'Let "Armchair" Davids work it out.'

Bannister nodded towards the floor of the car, next to the front passenger seat. 'Maybe *that* was the trouble.'

Molly followed his gaze and saw an empty green mineral water bottle surrounded by blue tablets. 'Yes, you could be right.'

She moved away from the smouldering wreck, seeing for the first time the circle of SOU motorcyclists holding back the crowds, pleased that Killer was apparently none the worse for his accident.

'Come on, Bill. It's all over.'

The big detective shook his head. 'It might be over for Sergeant Conrad, ma'am, but our problems are only just beginning.'

Bannister looked dead on his feet, Molly thought. His

face was drawn and tense, dark shadows under his eyes, but he still held himself erect and she was proud of him. They had been through so much together and in many ways, she felt he was stronger than she was.

She didn't care that Davids thought she was too close to her men. If they were all like Bannister, then it was right. The chief can stick his rotten promotion, and if after this lot he decides to sack me, so what. There are more important things in life.

She tried to smile but stopped, her eyes dim with moisture. She didn't want to make a fool of herself.

'Don't worry about it, Bill. Go and tell Liz that you're all right.'

'What about you?'

'Me?' Fearful that she would break down completely, she turned and walked away, through the motorcycles and the silent crowd, beyond the crouching police cars and into City Road. She was cold, wet and tired, and her back hurt.

Pulling herself together, she willed her legs to move and weaved along the pavement towards a telephone kiosk. Reaching the door, she managed to open it at the third attempt. She staggered inside, leaning against the glass walls for support. The notices in front of her seemed to dance as a fresh wave of nausea dulled her senses. Having no money with her, she found the "nine" button and steadied her shaking hand sufficiently to press it three times, asking for police.

Her voice breaking, she fought a hostile emergency operator. Pulling rank, she demanded to be put in touch with New Scotland Yard. She had to speak to Detective Superintendent James Cranleigh-Smythe. She needed him now more than she had ever needed any man; his tenderness, his strong, comforting arms. She needed him to take care of her. . . . She needed to be loved.

THE END

289